HAPPILY AFTER ALL

LAURA C. STEVENSON lives in Vermont, on the farm where HAPPILY AFTER ALL is set. She has two daughters: Kate, who lives in California, and Meg, who lives in Vermont. Dr. Stevenson teaches writing and humanities at Marlboro College and has written a book and several articles about Elizabethan literature. This is her first book for young readers.

HAPPILY AFTER ALL

LAURA C. STEVENSON

AVON BOOKS
A division of
The Hearst Corporation
1350 Avenue of the Americas
New York, New York 10019

Published by arrangement with Houghton Mifflin Company
Library of Congress Catalog Card Number: 89-24709
ISBN: 0-380-71549-X
RL: 4.5

First Avon Camelot Printing: March 1993

CAMELOT TRADEMARK REG. U.S. PAT. OFF. AND IN OTHER COUNTRIES, MARCA REGISTRADA, HECHO EN U.S.A.

Printed in the U.S.A.

OPM 10 9 8 7 6 5 4 3 2

This is Kate's book

Chapter 1

Rebecca leaned back in her plaid armchair and looked at Mr. Jarvis and Molly. Mr. Jarvis smiled at her as he dialed the phone; Molly was absorbed in her fashion magazine. At least, she seemed absorbed. She didn't look up, but she wasn't turning any pages, either. The traffic outside hummed up and down the sunny street, but inside the office it was cool and absolutely quiet until the call went through.

''Hello! Bob Jarvis here, from Jarvis and Dixon Attorneys,'' said Mr. Jarvis, looking down at his notes. Rebecca knew it wasn't polite to listen in on other people's phone calls, so she watched Molly twist her ring around and around. As it turned out, there wasn't much to pretend not to hear, anyway. All Mr. Jarvis was saying was ''Yeah,'' or ''Fine.'' A lot of good *that* was.

She edged a tattered nail to her mouth and started chewing on it. Why was she here, anyway? Mr. Jarvis only turned up when important things happened. Like last September, when Dad had gotten very sick. Mr. Jarvis had taken her for a walk on the beach and explained that Dad's cancer was more serious than the doctors had thought, and he'd have to have several operations. Then after the third operation, a week before Halloween, Mr. Jarvis had come to her house and explained that Dad wouldn't know who she was if she went to visit him. And a couple of days after that, he'd fetched her out of school and told her that Dad had died. Today, here she was at his office, with Molly, like a regular client. Something bad was going to happen, you could tell.

"Becky!" Molly hissed from behind her magazine. "Don't bite your nails!"

Rebecca dropped her hands into her lap and sighed. Even Dad hadn't been able to get Molly to stop calling her Becky. He'd tried. He'd explained that the Davidsons were an old Puritan family, and ever since the *Mayflower* they'd all had Old Testament names, and Becky wasn't an Old Testament name. But Molly just hadn't understood what the *Mayflower* had to do with what you called your kid. Dad had stopped arguing after a while. That was how Rebecca had known he was really, really sick. She'd never seen him give up on something important before.

Mr. Jarvis hung up the phone, and Molly leaned forward in her chair, her blond curls hiding her face from Rebecca. "Can she . . . ?"

But Mr. Jarvis held up his hand. "Rebecca!" he said. "Could you do an old man a favor?"

He wasn't all that old, but Rebecca nodded.

"Great! Now, if you look carefully out this window, you'll see a sign that says 'Cafe and Bakery.' It translates, 'High Cholesterol Junk Food for the Masses.' See it there?"

Molly giggled; Rebecca almost smiled. Mr. Jarvis talked a lot like Dad; probably it had something to do with being a lawyer.

"Okay," said Mr. Jarvis. "Now, cross that street. Get me a raised doughnut, a cup of coffee regular, and a napkin. And while you're there, you might see some doughnuts you and Molly would like . . ."

"Oh, no thanks, not for me," said Molly quickly. Models had to be very careful about what they ate. "But go ahead, Becky."

"Get two, in case she weakens," smiled Mr. Jarvis. He handed her three dollar bills. "All set? Now don't get run over. I hate flattened doughnuts."

Rebecca stuffed the bills into her back pocket and slipped through the door into the secretary's office. It was nice to get up after all that sitting.

She'd gotten all the way into the Cafe and Bakery and placed the order before she realized Mr. Jarvis was smarter than she was. Well, there wasn't much she could have done, even if she had realized he just wanted to talk something over with Molly. She took the bag and dropped the change into it. Before, when she'd come here with Dad, they'd always walked up and down in front of the case after they'd paid, just to make sure there wasn't something else they really couldn't do without. Rebecca thought of doing that, but she decided to skip it. She hadn't been much interested in food lately.

Outside, the air smelled like bakery and eucalyptus. Across the street, behind Mr. Jarvis's office building, the gold and gray mountains were cut by deep late-afternoon shadows. As Rebecca waited for the lights to change, a few clouds that had blown in from the ocean hung themselves on the highest peaks. She could see more clouds coming to join them, which meant it was probably going to rain tonight. She would have liked to watch the clouds gather, but she hurried back instead. Maybe if she got there fast and stood very quietly in the secretary's office, she could hear what they were talking about.

She was in luck. The secretary was on the phone, so she couldn't call Mr. Jarvis in his office. And the door wasn't shut all the way.

There was Molly's voice. "... think I'm leaving her. Really. I mean, talk about guilt!" Her voice began to sound sort of funny. "You know, I shouldn't have let any of it happen. I mean, after a few times, I knew he didn't give a—well, anyway. But such a gentleman, and ... well, you know. Handsome. Great dancer. Prince Charming, and all that. With one of those Secret Sorrows, like in books."

"I suppose you could put it that way," said Mr. Jarvis's voice dryly.

"And this smart, grownup's kid, you know? They were so ... well, nuts about each other. It was really cute. And then, when he found out, it was, you know, so *sad.* Like, what was going to *happen* to them? Everybody told me to get out, but I couldn't make myself. ..." There was a little pause. "I just wish I'd known earlier, so I wouldn't have, you know, told her and all. ..."

"Listen," said Mr. Jarvis's voice. "You've done more than your share. And now you'll just have to tell yourself that declaring neutrality is the only sensible course in the face of dynastic wars that don't concern you. You've been a great buffer state. But you're young, and you're free now to negotiate a new alliance. I hope it works out, Molly. You deserve the best treaty you can get."

Rebecca frowned. It would sure make life easier if Molly made sense and Mr. Jarvis talked like other people. She was almost glad when the phone rang in Mr. Jarvis's office and she heard the secretary telling him she was back.

Mr. Jarvis opened the door. "So." He smiled. "Survive the crossing?"

She nodded, though she didn't quite understand what he meant. He took the bag, put his hand on her shoulder, and steered her back to the plaid chair. As he walked around his desk and sat down, Rebecca stole a glance at Molly. Her eyeliner was a little smeared, and she was holding a Kleenex.

Mr. Jarvis dove his hand into the bag, pulled out the coffee, flipped back its lid, and took a sip. He didn't even look at the doughnuts. "Well," he said, "we have things all worked out for you, Rebecca."

He looked at Molly, and Molly opened and shut her thin, perfectly manicured hands. Boy, whatever it was must be more awful than you could possibly imagine.

"Well, you know," she said finally, "I was going to be your stepmom, but your dad . . ."

Rebecca nodded patiently. Dad said you had to be patient with Molly.

"And since I'm not really your stepmother, it doesn't make much sense for us to live together in that big, beautiful house of your dad's. . . ."

They were going to move, then? Move out of the house she and Dad had fixed up just the way they wanted it? Rebecca looked down at her chair.

"So Mr. Jarvis and I decided—" Molly's voice started sounding funny again—"decided it would make lots more sense for you to live with your . . . your mother. You know . . . in Vermont."

Her mother? Rebecca's ears began to sing. Rachel, who'd run away from Dad and ruined his whole life? Her *mother?*

"I mean, it might be nice." Molly's voice filtered through the roaring in her ears. "There's snow in Vermont. You've always wanted to see snow. . . ."

Rebecca felt a hand drop on her shoulder. Looking up, she saw Mr. Jarvis had come to sit on the plaid arm of her chair. "You okay?" he asked.

Rebecca turned her face away, wishing her ears would

stop. She felt dizzy, and all of a sudden she thought of all those cakes and cookies in the bakery. She gulped. Everybody was quiet. Mr. Jarvis patted Rebecca's shoulder. Molly touched the corners of her eyes with her Kleenex.

"I mean, she *is* related to you . . ." Molly said finally. "And I've been dating Ben and all . . ."

Rebecca stared out the window—not the one facing the Cafe and Bakery, the one on the other side of the office. There was a hibiscus bush just outside it; she began to count the red blossoms.

Mr. Jarvis cleared his throat. "Tell you what, Molly. Why don't Rebecca and I have a chat here, while you do errands? I'll drive her home."

Rebecca could feel Molly looking at her, but she kept her eyes on the hibiscus blossoms. After a minute, Molly said, "Fine." She got up slowly. "Becky . . ."

Rebecca stared so hard at the blossoms they went blurry.

"I'm going to the store. I'll get ice cream for dessert, if you want. What flavor would you like? Isn't Heath Bar Crunch your favorite?"

The thought of ice cream made Rebecca gulp. She shrugged.

Mr. Jarvis got off the arm of her chair and opened the door. Molly didn't move for a moment; then she picked up her purse and walked into the secretary's office, the usual tapping of her high heels muffled by the carpet. Outside the door, Rebecca could hear her sobbing.

"If she'd just *talk!* I've done everything I can think of, but she just won't . . ."

Rebecca couldn't hear what Mr. Jarvis answered; he was opening the outside door. But in a moment he was back. She could feel him standing behind her.

"A quarter for your thoughts, Rebecca."

Rebecca shrugged.

Mr. Jarvis walked to his desk and sat down. "No, I want you to talk to me." He said it nicely, but she knew that tone of voice. When Dad had used it, she'd quit messing around and done what he told her to.

"Okay," she muttered.

"That's better." He smiled at her. "Now, I need to hear your point of view about this case. Do you understand what's going on?"

"Sort of. . . . Well, not really."

"Well, tell me what you *do* know, and we'll start from there."

"Okay. . . . Dad was going to marry Molly, because she seemed to sort of, well, like me better than the others had. At least I thought she did, until—"

"Hold on. What others?"

"The . . . those ladies he went out with." There had been quite a few of them, all slim and suntanned, like Molly. She hadn't paid much attention to them. They hadn't been interested in her, and they'd never stuck around long, anyway.

Mr. Jarvis tapped his fingers on his desk. "I see."

"Well, Molly was the one he was taking out when he got sick, see. And before he went into the hospital, he told me she was going to live with us, and then when he got out of the hospital he was going to marry her, because if he . . ." She swallowed hard and tried to concentrate on what she was saying instead of remembering how nice Dad had been about it, sitting in his big chair with her curled up in his lap, like he'd done when she was little. "What he meant was, he wanted to be sure there was somebody to take care of me." She looked up at Mr. Jarvis. "But he said I mustn't ever tell Molly that, because she'd feel bad if she knew he was just marrying her because of me."

Mr. Jarvis nodded. "I hope you didn't tell her."

"Of course not! That'd be like telling the lady he was going with that he'd gone with others before her. Or mixing up their names. I mean, they made him sort of happy, sometimes. So you wouldn't want to hurt their feelings."

Mr. Jarvis rubbed the side of his nose, looking a little sad.

"But then, he went into a . . . what you told me that day . . ."

"A coma."

"Right. So they couldn't get married. And I guess . . . I guess Molly got tired of looking after me, or maybe I was too much trouble. . . . Anyway, she must've talked my mother into taking care of me, or something." She stopped because her voice sounded sort of chokey.

"And what do you know about your mother?"

"Not much."

"Then it won't take you long to tell me what you know, will it?"

Dad had given orders that way. "Well, I know she lives on a run-down farm somewhere in Vermont. She's a journalist . . . a free-lancer or something. She has lots of degrees. And she ran away from Dad and me when I was two."

"Who told you that?"

"Well, nobody, I guess. I just . . ."

"Picked it up? Put it together?"

"I guess so."

Mr. Jarvis got up and walked around his desk. He half sat on it, right in front of Rebecca. "Did it ever occur to you that hearsay is a poor source of information?"

She shook her head. It was the best source she had.

"Maybe you should ask somebody what you want to know," he said.

"That only worked with Dad."

"Nobody else?"

"Other people say you're not old enough to understand. Or else they, well, parade around the truth."

"That's so," admitted Mr. Jarvis. "But then, if the truth were easy to tell, we wouldn't make people testify under oath. It's pretty ugly stuff, the truth. But try me, Rebecca. Ask anything you want to know."

She looked up at his friendly glasses and brown beard. Maybe she could. He *was* sort of like Dad.

"Did Dad get cancer because he was unhappy?"

"Did anybody say he did?"

"Well, Molly's dating this guy called Ben. And my bedroom's off the living room, and . . . anyway, one night she told him Dad had gotten cancer because he was so unhappy." She looked out the window. "It was all my mother's fault he was unhappy."

"Hey, waaaiiit a minute! Are you saying he got cancer because Rachel made him unhappy eight years ago?"

It didn't make much sense, when you put it like that. "Well, no."

"Glad to hear it. There are lots of people who are unhappy and who don't get cancer. So no fair blaming that on Rachel."

Rebecca started to nibble at her fingernails again, then stopped herself. "I didn't know Dad was unhappy—at least before he got so sick."

"Nobody's unhappy all the time," said Mr. Jarvis. "And your dad was happier with you than he was with anybody else."

"Think so?"

"I know so. He loved you better than anybody else he knew, and when you're with somebody you really love, you're happy. I promise you. Anything else you want to know?"

Rebecca looked out the window. "Why . . . ?"

"Go on. Why . . . ?"

"Why do I have to go live in Vermont? I mean, she never even *wanted* me."

Mr. Jarvis picked up his pipe and looked around for his tobacco. "What makes you say that?"

"Well, she *did* run away from Dad and me, after all. And then, she never called, or wrote, or visited, or sent presents, or any of the things most divorced kids' parents do." She drew a shuddery breath. "I mean, I don't even *know* her!"

Mr. Jarvis lit his pipe, and the room began to smell of sweet smoke. The smell made Rebecca think of Dad, smoking his pipe on the deck after they'd gone for a walk along the beach at sunset. She wiped her hand across her eyes.

"It's more complicated than you think," said Mr. Jarvis finally. "Sure you're old enough to hear the answer?"

"Sure I am." Rebecca snuffled, then sat up as straight as the plaid chair would let her.

"Okay, then," said Mr. Jarvis. "Here we go. Let's start at the very beginning. Your mother did *not* run away from you and your dad."

"But Dad *said* . . . !"

"I thought you said you were old enough to hear me out," he said.

She shut her mouth and listened.

"Okay. Your dad and mother weren't ever very happy together. She's very difficult; he was never a one-woman man . . . and, what with one thing and another, she asked him for a separation when you were about two. Her plan was to take you to Vermont, where she'd inherited her father's farm, and negotiate a divorce from there."

Mr. Jarvis puffed on his pipe a minute. "The day she was supposed to leave for Vermont with you, she went out to do some last-minute errands, leaving you with a sitter. When she came back, you were gone. Your dad had come to the house, paid the sitter, and . . . well, taken you for a little trip of his own."

Rebecca's eyes opened wide, but she held her tongue.

"When he came back, a week or so later, he had a court order. It said Rachel had abandoned you and was an unfit mother, so she couldn't see you, or write to you, or send you presents, or anything." Mr. Jarvis drew hard on his pipe. "Now, why do you suppose your dad did that?"

"Because he wanted me to live with him, not her."

"Sure. But don't you think he might also have hoped Rachel would come back to him if she realized she'd lose you if she left?"

"Sure. I see." Dad was pretty smart, all right.

"But that kind of tactic just didn't work with Rachel. Instead of coming back, she got flaming mad. She went to court and appealed the order. She lost, though. The judge was a really good friend of your dad's."

Mr. Jarvis sighed. "So then she appealed to a higher court, and it went on and on. But she had to move to Vermont because she couldn't afford to live here. You were doing well with your dad. And, most important, your dad was well known all over the state. Your mother never got an unbiased hearing."

Rebecca looked down at her hands.

"Now, from your dad's point of view," said Mr. Jarvis, "she *did* run away. He said she couldn't have you if she wouldn't have him, and she left. That's the way he felt about it, and I'm sure that's what has come through to you. But believe me, she *did* want you. She tried and tried to get permission to see you. When your dad died, she called right away, asking to take you. Molly was agreeable, but it took a couple of months to work things out legally." He looked at her closely. "I'm afraid it's not a pretty story, Rebecca. But all you really need to know is that your mother wants you very much."

"But Dad said Molly had *promised* . . . !"

"Rebecca, suppose you were barely twenty-one years old and were taking care of a kid you'd only known a couple of months before her dad died. If you found out the kid had a mother who had tried to get custody of her for years, wouldn't you arrange to send the kid to her mother?"

Rebecca wrinkled up her nose. "Not if I were Molly," she said. "I'd let somebody else handle the whole thing because I couldn't figure out what to do on my own." She felt bad right after she'd said it. Like Dad said, Molly wasn't a towering intellect, but she was goodhearted and pretty. "How come you know all this?" she asked, changing the subject.

"Me? I'm your mom's lawyer."

Rachel's lawyer! Well, no *wonder* he'd told her all those horrible stories about Dad!

"You okay?" he asked, frowning a little.

She shrugged. She sure didn't have to answer him. In fact, if he'd handled Rachel's case against Dad all these years, then talked Molly into going back on her promise after Dad was . . . after Dad couldn't do anything about it anymore, she wouldn't talk to him ever again. She stared out the window at the stupid red hibiscus blossoms, suddenly hating them.

"Rebecca," he said gently, "I may be your mother's lawyer, but before you were born, I was your dad's partner. I knew him very well, and I thought he was one of the smartest, wittiest men I'd ever met. I still think so, even though we disagreed about . . . certain things.'' He stepped between her and the hibiscus window, so she'd have to look at him. ''My dear, do you think I'd have taken on the case if I hadn't cared for your dad, your mother, and you?''

''I don't know.'' Rebecca's throat choked up and her eyes began to tingle. Ten-year-olds don't cry, she told herself fiercely. Not in front of their mothers' lawyers, anyway.

Mr. Jarvis moved to the arm of her chair again and put his hand on her shoulder. ''Rebecca, no amount of wishing is going to bring back your dad to make your life what it used to be, is it?''

That's what the doctor Molly had taken her to had said! And the school counselor! Why did people think they had to tell her that? Did they think she was dumb or something? ''Of course not!''

He sighed. ''I'm sorry. It *was* a silly question. But what I was leading up to is the simple fact that you have to work out a new life for yourself. Your mother wants to help you do that. She's a remarkable person, Rebecca—very different from the ladies your dad dated after the divorce. Trust me; I know her well.''

Trust him? When he was just trying to win a case he'd lost before? She shrugged his hand off her shoulder. He got up, fetched his pipe from his ashtray, lit it, then sat down on the arm again. After a minute, he stroked her hair a couple of times, the way Dad did after they had words. It felt sort of good, so she let him do it.

''Have you ever seen a picture of your mom?'' he asked finally.

She shook her head.

He stood up and rummaged around on his desk. "I have one here," he said. "Take a look." He shoved it right under her nose. There was no way she could refuse to see it unless she closed her eyes, so she looked.

The first thing she saw was the horse—tall, with an arched neck, standing like a statue. Beside it . . . the face that looked back at her was so much like her own that she jumped. Red hair pulled back in a switch, big green eyes . . . : an older, taller, completely unbeautiful edition of herself. So that's why she was so homely, even though Dad was so good-looking! She took after her mom! Great.

"She isn't very pretty," she said, handing back the snapshot.

"Think so?" Mr. Jarvis inspected it. "Well, reserve judgment until you see her."

"How many does she have?"

He looked at her blankly. "How many what? Eyes? Teeth?"

Rebecca willed herself not to smile. "No, horses."

"Oh," he said absently, as if horses weren't really important. "At least four, I think. Some to ride, some to work. I've lost count."

"Work?"

"Plow with. Pull logs with. That sort of thing."

"That doesn't sound very ladylike."

"No?" He grinned. "Well, there are all sorts of ladies. And this lady, in this office, had better get home soon. It's getting pretty late."

Rebecca slid out of the chair and stretched her stiff legs. "When do I have to go to Vermont? Next summer?"

He stared at her. "Oh, no, Rebecca. Next week."

Next week! She put her hand on the chair, feeling a bit dizzy.

"Well, the school semester stops for you this week, and

it starts in Vermont next week. With the rest of your life all topsy-turvy, we thought it would be best to keep your schooling regular, at least. I'm sorry I didn't tell you that sooner. I got a little involved in explanations, and I forgot."

He held the door open, and she went through it into the dim, empty secretary's office. "Get addresses from your friends, so you can write to them," he said as they walked down the stairs together.

Rebecca followed him out to the car, wondering if there were any kids she really wanted to write to. There were some girls she ate lunch with and played horses or tetherball with, of course, but she wasn't really one of them. It was kind of hard to be good friends with kids when Dad was your best buddy. For one thing, Dad was smarter than kids (smarter than teachers, too, for that matter), and you got used to joking about things most kids didn't understand. And for another, when you had private riding lessons three days a week, and walks on the beach or kite-flying afternoons the other days, and spins in the MG and dinner parties with Dad on weekends, you didn't have much time left over for hanging around with kids. Since October, of course, that hadn't been true. But since then she really hadn't felt like talking or playing, and she'd started spending lunchtime and recess in her special corner in the library.

Mr. Jarvis unlocked the car door and opened it for her, the way Dad had always done. "Oh!" he said suddenly. "Do you want to take the picture of your mom with you?"

"No, thank you." She didn't want to look at Rachel any more than she had to, right now. It wasn't until he'd started the car that she remembered she could have looked more carefully at the horse if she'd taken the picture with her. And then it was too late.

Chapter 2

They were quiet in the car as it sped along the palm-lined avenue by the beach. Rebecca looked out toward the sunset; it was very red over the gray winter ocean. A few surfers, glistening in their black wet suits, were taking a last run before quitting for the evening; between them and the avenue, roller skaters slid silently along the bike paths on plastic wheels.

"Nice evening," said Mr. Jarvis.

Rebecca nodded.

They turned off the avenue onto a winding road. Dully, Rebecca watched the familiar landmarks slip by: Mr. Abenworth's stucco mansion with the two ancient live oaks in the front yard; the little gatehouse where the dog who chased cars lived; Mr. Judd's big house, with orange, purple, and red bougainvilleas spilling over white walls. It was funny to think this wasn't going to be the road home after next week. She slouched down in the seat and stared at the glove compartment.

"Oh my gosh! I *told* them to wait . . ." muttered Mr. Jarvis as he turned into the pillared gateway.

"What?" Rebecca sat up straight and stared. There was a sign by the gate: "Heritage Associates Real Estate, Inc. FOR SALE. (805) 687-7447." Rebecca swallowed and swallowed as the house came closer. It was so beautiful: white stucco walls, red tile roof, cyanothus shrubs in front of the atrium, and in back, the acanthus-lined path you couldn't see from here that led to the cliff and the stairs down to the beach.

"I didn't know the house was for sale," she said in a trembly voice.

"It just went on the market. I called the agency while you were getting doughnuts. But I asked them to wait a week before they listed it, so I could talk to you about it first." He shook his head. "This is the last way I wanted you to find out about it."

So Mr. Jarvis paraded around the truth, too, just like everybody else, except Dad. Rebecca undid her seatbelt while they were still moving, and when the car stopped, she jumped out. "Thank you for the ride," she said.

He looked around. "Where's Molly? I don't see her car."

"Oh, she probably stopped off at Ben's place."

Mr. Jarvis switched off the engine. "Want me to stick around until she gets here?"

"No, thank you. Molly gave me a key, so I can get in. And she'll be home real soon. She promised Dad not to leave me on my own much."

He shook his head and looked as if he was going to say something, so to show him she really didn't want him around, she hurried through the atrium and unlocked the front door. As she stepped inside, she heard him start the car and drive away.

There were no lights on in the living room, but the skylight and the big west windows let in enough gray light for her to see by. Rebecca slipped off her sandals and wiggled her toes in the deep pile of the carpet, looking through the gloom as if she'd never seen the room before. Everything was exactly where it had been when she and

Molly had gone to see Mr. Jarvis. But somehow the house looked like it belonged to somebody else already. If you stood still, you could almost *see* other people living here, with other furniture, not knowing Dad had designed the house, not even knowing Dad had lived in it.

She'd been going to think about what Mr. Jarvis had told her, but you couldn't think very well in the living room, with all those ghosts of people who hadn't bought the house yet walking around in it. She looked toward her room but decided against going there; you couldn't think there unless it was cleaned up, which it wasn't. She ran the toes of her left foot back and forth, watching the pattern they made in the carpet. Then, all of a sudden, she knew where she'd go.

She slipped past the velveteen couch and low-backed chairs, through the dining room, across the kitchen to the breezeway. The breezeway door stuck; it always had. She wrestled it open and tiptoed along the passageway, feeling the cold cement prickle her feet. When she reached the door at the end of the breezeway, she stopped. She hadn't been here since Dad had . . . gone. She'd told herself that was because the door would be locked. But really it was because she'd been afraid she'd get the awful feeling she'd gotten that day after Mr. Jarvis had fetched her out of school, and she'd gone into Dad's bedroom—just to get something—and seen his keys and other pocket stuff sitting on his dresser, all waiting for him to come home. . . . She stretched out her hand toward the doorknob, half hoping it *would* be locked. But it turned easily.

The room smelled just the way it always had. There was something about the smell of pipesmoke; it just didn't go away. She looked out the windows at the shadows of the eucalyptus grove, the dark expanse she knew was the ocean, and, far away, the winking lights of the oil derricks, five miles out to sea. Dad's study had the best view in the house.

She took a deep breath and turned on his desk light, waiting for that creepy feeling. But nothing happened. Dad's stuff wasn't waiting for him here. Somebody had cleaned up the rubble on his desk and vacuumed the tobacco flakes off the oriental rug. It was sort of nice to see it neat. In fact, it was sort of nice to be there, with Dad's books sitting in the bookcases they'd built together when she was too little to be really helpful, and his pipes lined up in the rack she'd given him for his birthday. She sat down, not in his special chair but in the leather recliner, where she always sat and read while he worked in the evenings. When he got done, if she hadn't read herself to sleep, they'd read something together—real books, the kind Dad said were companions, not just books—like *David Copperfield* and *Oliver Twist.* You could understand those books if somebody read them to you, especially since Dad read all the conversations in different voices and explained things when the sentences got too long.

Rebecca leaned back in the recliner and shut her eyes. If you didn't see the emptiness in Dad's chair, you could believe he was just opening one of the leatherbound Dickens books, pushing his glasses up on his forehead so he could read the print. Just as if Mr. Jarvis hadn't told her all those lies about him. Just as if the house were still his. Just as if she didn't have to go to Vermont. . . .

"Why, Becky! What're you doing out here?"

Rebecca woke up with a jounce and scrambled out of the recliner. "Just fell asleep, I guess," she muttered.

Molly tried to give her a hug, but she pulled away. Like Dad said, Molly hugged people too much.

"I'm sorry it's so late," said Molly, closing the study

door behind them. "Ben and I got talking. Come help me put away the groceries before the ice cream melts."

Rebecca followed Molly's tapping heels into the kitchen and looked into the bags. The ice cream hadn't melted; Molly must've put it in Ben's freezer. Sometimes she thought of things you wouldn't expect. Rebecca stuck the ice cream tub in their freezer without even checking the flavor. It was hard to get enthusiastic about ice cream when your house was being sold and you had to live with your mother next week.

Molly tapped back into the kitchen, carrying two more bags. "How was your chat with Bob Jarvis?" she asked.

Rebecca shrugged and started unloading the second bag.

"I hope he, you know, explained everything . . ."

Rebecca nodded.

Molly took a little steak out of one of the bags and rummaged around in the cupboard for the broiling pan. "I guess you saw the house is for sale," she said, looking over her shoulder. "That means your room has to be, you know, really clean. All the time. Could you . . . ?"

"Okay." She'd meant to clean it up anyway. You could hardly walk across it.

"You're a good kid, know that? I'll help you. Maybe we could, you know, put some things in boxes. I mean, it'd be nice to have your stuff in Vermont already when you get there."

Boy. Molly could hardly *wait* to get rid of her.

Molly sighed. "Please, Becky! I know this is hard for you. But listen! When Bob told me about the custody case, well . . . I realized your dad wanted me to take you so your mother couldn't. And I really didn't think it was fair. Not to me, I mean—to your mom."

Rebecca decided not to listen, since Molly was just going to bad-mouth Dad the way Mr. Jarvis had. Besides, when you didn't listen to Molly and just watched her, you could see she was really beautiful. Her clothes were always the Latest Thing—you always felt homely and shabby in your jeans, next to Molly. Dad said modeling was what you did when you weren't smart enough to do anything else, but you could tell he'd really liked watching her, even so. She moved like those expensive horses that grazed in the neighbor's paddock. Each step was absolutely perfect.

"Well, do *you* think it's fair?" Molly stopped in front of her.

"I don't know. I guess so. I mean, I'm just hungry."

That worked; Molly quit talking and made a salad double quick. She was always ready to see you eat—especially if you hadn't been eating much lately, and your clothes just hung on you. The catch was, though, that since you'd said you were hungry, you had to eat, and even steak tasted just like sawdust.

When they'd finished, Molly poured herself a second cup of coffee, while Rebecca stirred the Heath Bar Crunch in her bowl until it was just a puddle with little bits of chocolate in it. These days, during dessert Molly usually read one of those romances Dad had laughed at, but tonight she seemed to feel like talking.

"I think you'll like Rachel," she said.

"*You* know Rachel?" The second she'd opened her mouth, Rebecca was sorry she'd asked. It made her sound interested in Rachel, which she really wasn't.

"No, but Bob told me about her." Molly flipped her curls over her shoulder and smiled. "You know, she sounds like the kind of girl I was always scared of in high school. Really, really smart. And serious about books and ideas that make you think. But that's the sort of thing you like, isn't it?"

Rebecca stirred the ice cream faster. It was funny to

think of Molly's being scared of somebody. Though, when you thought of it, hadn't she been sort of scared of Dad? "Yes, Caleb," "Sure, Caleb"—as though she was always afraid he was going to scold her. He didn't, though. He just laughed at her, or asked her questions you knew she couldn't answer.

"Yeah, Bob says she and Caleb are the two smartest people he's ever met—in really different ways," said Molly. "Say, did you know Bob was your dad's partner and best friend?"

Rebecca nodded. "How come he stopped being those things?"

Molly shifted in her chair. "Well, I guess there were lots of people who were shocked at the way Caleb treated Rachel after she . . ."

Rebecca got up and poured her ice cream into the sink. "I'll go clean up my room now," she said. There really wasn't any use listening to people lie about Dad.

But Molly wouldn't leave her alone. She tapped right into the bedroom with some boxes, and the moment they started picking up stuff, she started in again. "You see, Caleb was really upset because Rachel wanted to leave him . . ."

Well, he should have been. Who would leave Dad?

". . . so he took you away, and she couldn't find you, even though she called the police and . . ."

"Don't pack that!" interrupted Rebecca, pointing to the Slinky in Molly's hands. "I never play with it anymore."

Molly's blue eyes opened wide; then she sighed and put the Slinky down. "I guess you're just not old enough to . . ."

There it was again. Why didn't anybody realize she was *plenty* old enough to understand that Rachel had ruined Dad's life, broken up his partnership with Mr. Jarvis, and . . . ? Rebecca brushed her wrist across her eyes and put some books into a box very, very carefully.

Molly stopped packing and tried to put an arm around her. "Look, Becky," she said. "I know you were crazy about your dad. And he was nuts about you, too. But since you're going to live with your mom now, you know, you just *have* to understand . . ."

Rebecca pulled away from Molly's arm and stood up. "Did you remember to tell Ben he could come to your show tomorrow?"

"Gee, no! I forgot all about it!"

"Well, you'd better give him a call. It's getting pretty late."

Molly looked at her watch. "Boy, it sure is. Okay. But I'll call really fast. I mean, this room just *has* to be neat tomorrow."

She hurried out, and Rebecca listened to her heels tap-tap on the hardwood floor until she reached the livingroom carpet. Mr. Jarvis would be proud of her, she thought. It was just like sending a little girl across the street for doughnuts.

And when Molly tapped back into the bedroom half an hour later, she'd apparently learned her lesson. She didn't try to tell any more stories about Dad, and she didn't say one more word about Rachel. Not that night, and not for the rest of the week.

Chapter 3

Mr. Jarvis drove Rebecca to the airport. It was a long drive, and they had to start at six A.M. because of the traffic. Molly just didn't feel up to it. That was probably just as well. Dad always said you had to watch Molly when she got sentimental; it was like those grade D movies they laughed at on the VCR. She even cried at the *house* when they said good-bye. Think what she would have done at the airport!

You could trust Mr. Jarvis not to make a scene, though. He just drove out the gate as if they were going on a spin, lit his pipe, and fiddled with the radio. He got nothing but static, so he shut it off.

"Molly's very sad to see you go," he said after a while.

Rebecca shrugged. "She could've kept me if she'd wanted."

"She *would* have kept you if she'd had to. Even though that was hard for her to do when she was working so much. Not many twenty-one-year-olds would be as kind to an unhappy kid as she has been."

Rebecca looked out at the miles of yellow and white daisies that grew in three wide gardens down the median and along both sides of the freeway. If they were in a bakery, she thought, they'd be driving along the cake, and the daisies would be the icing. Or would it be the other way around?

''You listening, Rebecca?''

She nodded, but she kept her eyes on the daisies. He stopped talking about Molly; Mr. Jarvis knew how to take a hint.

They drove along quietly for a while, and she thought of going to sleep. But just as she was drifting off, he asked, ''What do you know about fairy stories?''

She looked at him suspiciously. He was leading up to something. ''Lots,'' she said.

''What happens in a fairy story?''

''Well, a prince finds a lovely princess who's guarded by a dragon. He kills the dragon, rescues the princess, and carries her away. Then they go back to his castle and live happily after all.''

He laughed. ''Happily *what?*''

She almost smiled. ''Oh, that was a joke Dad and I made up. When I was three or four, I got mixed up on 'happily ever after,' and I said 'happily after all' instead. Dad said that was a smart mix-up, because 'happily after all' was all most people got, and lucky to get it, too. So we always said it that way, even when I grew up.''

''Sounds like your dad,'' Mr. Jarvis said with a chuckle.

The beach was gone now; there were neatly clipped office buildings instead, mixed in with lemon groves.

''What I was driving at,'' said Mr. Jarvis, ''is that fairy stories have a way of coming out all right at the end, no matter how awful the middle part is. Right?''

She nodded.

Mr. Jarvis put his hand on her knee. ''Well, then, think of everything that's happened to you in the last four months—your dad's dying, your leaving the house you grew up in, moving—think of those as the scary parts. That way, you may just see that you have a chance to live happily after all, in spite of everything.''

Rebecca moved her knee away. "Fairy tales aren't real, you know," she said. "Nobody'd believe all that prince-and-princess stuff after they were five." That's what Dad had said, anyway.

Mr. Jarvis looked at her. "You mean people have been wrong all these centuries, making up stories that come out all right at the end?"

They were passing another lemon grove; the gentle smell of blossoms filtered through the window, and Rebecca sniffed it. She hated it when grownups asked questions like that.

Mr. Jarvis sighed, looked at his watch, and sped up.

By the time they got to the airport, Mr. Jarvis was looking at his watch every five seconds. He was out of the car before the engine had even died, and the way he threw the suitcases out of the trunk told Rebecca they were late. But she couldn't move. All of a sudden she'd realized she was really leaving. She'd known that all week, of course. But it had seemed . . . well, like a dream or a movie. Not something you'd really have to *do*.

A man with a handtruck came to pick up the suitcases; he looked at his watch, too. "They're boarding," he said. "Last call."

"I know," said Mr. Jarvis, handing the man some money. "Just make sure this luggage gets on the plane."

The man looked at the money, grinned, and scurried away with the suitcases. Mr. Jarvis opened the car door. "We're really late!" he said. "If you don't run, you'll miss the plane!"

Rebecca stared at him. He was out of focus. Maybe he *was* just a movie. He sure didn't seem his usual self, with all those cars zipping around him, honking, and other people hurrying by. . .

"Rebecca! Please!" He tugged at her hand. "Will I have to carry you?"

She shook her head dizzily, and in a minute they were running the way she ran in nightmares, pushing past people down a huge conveyor belt in a sort of tunnel. Pretty soon she'd wake up, and all her stuffed animals would be lined up on the end of her bed, next to her clothes. Dad would come in and say "Hi there, Princess! Sleep well?"

They were in a huge round room now, and Mr. Jarvis was arguing with a lady in a blue suit. He put something in Rebecca's hand.

"Rebecca!" He shook her a little, and she finally focused on him. "This is your boarding pass. Hold on to it. These are your claim checks. Hold on to them, too. And here's Rachel's number and my number in case something goes wrong. Got all that?"

In case something goes wrong. Maybe the plane would crash. They did, you know. She'd seen bits of plane wreckage on TV, with all sorts of policemen and reporters wandering around, looking interested. . .

"Please, sir," said the lady in the blue suit. "The plane is waiting for your little girl!"

"I'll take her up the ramp," he said, pushing past her.

The ramp was long and red. When they got to the end of it, another lady in a blue suit was waiting for them. "You can't come any further, sir," she said politely. "I'll take care of your daughter just fine."

She reached for Rebecca's hand. Rebecca looked at Mr. Jarvis.

"Good-bye, champ," he said in the voice grownups use when they're trying to keep your spirits up. He gave her a big hug. "Just remember the 'happily after all' comes after the scary dragons."

She should say good-bye. Dad said you should always

be polite, even when you aren't happy. But her voice didn't work, and she felt awfully sick. Mr. Jarvis gave her another hug, then turned around. She would have liked to watch him go, but the lady in the blue suit took her hand and led her to an empty seat. Behind her, the big door slammed shut, and another blue-suited lady began talking over a microphone about what to do if the plane crashed.

All of a sudden, Rebecca hoped it *would* crash. Well, not really. . . . But being in a plane crash sounded lots easier than going to wherever this plane was supposed to be going, then getting off and meeting . . .

Chapter 4

"Ladies and gentlemen, we have just landed at Bradley International Airport," crooned one of the blue-suited ladies over the microphone. "The captain requests that you remain seated, with your seatbelts fastened, until he has brought the aircraft to a complete halt."

All around Rebecca, people got up and started looking for their coats. By the time the aircraft *had* come to a complete halt, everybody was standing in the aisles, not talking to each other. Rebecca stayed where she was; the blue-suited lady had told her to stay put until everybody had gotten off, so she could help her look for Rachel. Only, she hadn't said "Rachel," she'd said "your mom," as though your mom was somebody you wanted to meet.

Slowly the people filtered down the aisle and out the big door. The flight attendant came last, smiling at Rebecca. "What does your mom look like?"

It seemed funny to admit you didn't know. Rebecca thought. "She has red hair," she said. Her voice sounded kind of funny after not saying anything for hours and hours.

"Well," said the flight attendant, "she should be easy to find, then."

Rebecca nodded and got up, but as they started down the ramp, she felt her heart beat where her stomach was supposed to be. Maybe her heart and stomach had switched places and she would die. That would make things easy, unless it hurt.

"See your mom anywhere?" asked the flight attendant.

Rebecca looked around the big gray-carpeted room. A man kissing his girlfriend . . . a grandmother hugging an embarrassed little boy . . . a man in a hat and coat kissing a pretty woman on the cheek . . . : how could you even find somebody you *knew* among all these people?

"Is this Rebecca Davidson?" asked a quiet voice next to the flight attendant.

Rebecca couldn't look up. The flight attendant handed something to the woman who had spoken. "Sign here, please." Rebecca heard the rustle of paper and pen. Then the flight attendant patted her on the head and left.

"Let's get out of this crowd," said the quiet voice. A hand fell on Rebecca's shoulder and guided her to a hall where there weren't many people. Rebecca still couldn't look up. All she saw was a pair of jeans and boots. Not riding boots—hiking boots. They took one step to every two of hers, until they reached a row of chairs.

"So," said the voice. Rebecca knew she was supposed to look up and be polite, now. But her eyes wouldn't quit staring at the floor.

"Well," said the voice gently, "if I sit down, will you look at me?"

The boots backed up a few steps and the knees of the jeans bent. One of the hands reached out and took hers. It was rough and chapped, and the nails were grubby. Rebecca thought of Molly's hands, with their perfectly painted nails and pretty rings. Gradually, she looked up. A dirty down parka, unzipped. A wool shirt underneath. A sharp chin, a mouth without lipstick, a slightly arched nose. And finally, green eyes that looked at her critically.

Scary green eyes. Rebecca quickly looked at the hair, instead—red hair, a bit messy, pulled back in a clasp.

"Have you finished studying me?"

Rebecca jumped and looked down. She hadn't meant to stare. Neither of them said anything for a minute.

"Well," said Rachel, "we'd better go get your suitcases."

Rebecca nodded, then looked back at the floor. Rachel stood up and strode down the long hall. Rebecca almost had to run to keep up. She was out of breath by the time they got to the baggage claim—or was she only puffing so she wouldn't cry? Rachel *wasn't* glad to see her! Just as she'd thought.

"Claim checks?" asked Rachel, holding out her hand. Rebecca fished in her back pocket and pulled them out. Rachel stared at them. "Five suitcases? You brought *five* suitcases?"

Rebecca nodded miserably. What was wrong with having five suitcases, anyway? It wasn't like she was going on a vacation. She pointed to the suitcases silently as they swung around the bend on their conveyor belt, and Rachel lifted them off.

"Okay, that's it," said Rachel, when the fifth one turned up. "You take this one—I'll take the rest. Zip your jacket."

Rebecca's hands shook as she fumbled with the zipper. She'd never zipped the jacket before. It was down, like Rachel's, but new and clean. Molly had gotten it for her the day before she left . . . yesterday? She picked up the fifth suitcase and dragged it toward the door. Turning, she saw Rachel behind her, with one suitcase under each arm and one in each hand. Gee . . .

The cold air outside made Rebecca gasp as the door opened. She could see a little cloud where her breath was, and her hands felt like they were freezing to the suitcase handle.

''Left!'' shouted Rachel against the wind. Rebecca turned left, shivering. It was like this all the time? And people lived here? They slithered through a parking lot, where mounds of dirty snow were heaped around lamp-posts. All the cars were filthy. Especially that awful pickup truck. . .

''Hold it!'' said Rachel. She threw the suitcases into the back of the awful pickup truck, then took Rebecca's suit-case and threw it in, too. ''Inside!''

Rebecca scooted under the wheel, catching her jeans on the torn seat cover. Rachel jumped in next to her. ''Better wrap yourself in those quilts,'' she said. ''The heater doesn't work very well.''

Rebecca did what she was told, but she wondered what good it'd do; the quilts were ice-cold. The truck shivered, shook, and sputtered out of the parking lot and onto the freeway. There was snow on both sides of the road instead of daisies, and the snow wasn't like the snow in pictures. It was dirty brown. Rebecca wrinkled up her nose.

Except for the snow, everything looked disappointingly like California. Housing tracts, office buildings, freeways, traffic—it was more or less the same. Only there was a big river instead of a beach, and (here was a big difference) everything looked dirty and poor. Rebecca suddenly re-membered driving along the freeway with Dad, asking why they lived in Santa Barbara. ''Because the rest of the world is ugly,'' he'd said. So he'd been right. Dad had just about always been right.

''Bob told me you didn't talk much.'' Rachel's voice made Rebecca jump. She looked across the cab; Rachel was staring straight ahead at the gray, grim road, looking a bit gray and grim herself. What were you supposed to say when somebody said that to you? Rebecca couldn't think of anything. Anything at all.

"Well, what do you like?" said Rachel. "Books? Horses? Chocolate cake? Peanut butter and ketchup sundaes? There must be *something* you like enough to talk about."

"Horses." Rebecca's voice sounded really squeaky. Rachel was going to think she was some sort of nut.

"Yeah?" Rachel looked at her quickly. "Can you ride?"

"A little."

"Do you like it?"

"It's okay."

Rachel looked back at the road. Rebecca looked out the window at the tall buildings of some dreary city they seemed to be passing. Why had she said those things? She rode pretty well, actually. Dad had said she just couldn't have a pony of her own, but he'd taken her to the stable three times a week until he'd gotten sick. And this winter, Mr. Jarvis had taken her out there on Saturdays. Amity, the teenager who taught kids at the stable, had even let her take lessons on Fanfare. Fanfare was a real horse, not just a school horse. Most ten-year-olds weren't even allowed to ride him. He was old, but he'd been a dressage horse once. Amity could make him do all sorts of fancy things.

"I have five horses," said Rachel, glancing across the cab.

Five! Mr. Jarvis had said four.

"We ride in the spring, but not now," said Rachel. "It's pretty cold on a horse in January. Your toes freeze."

That figured. Why on earth would you want to live in a place where you could only ride a few months a year?

There were fewer buildings now. The pickup wheezed

up a hill, with lots of cars passing it. At the top, Rebecca looked out at a gray valley. A few lights began to go on here and there between the white church spires that seemed to grow out of every little town. The mounds of snow by the road were much higher, and not quite so dirty. A few feathery things started to float around in the air.

"Is that snow?" Rebecca asked.

"Afraid so. We're supposed to get a winter storm."

"Oh." What was a winter storm? A hurricane? A blizzard?

It got dark very fast, and the snow seemed to be coming down much more thickly than it had been. It was beautiful, especially after Rachel turned on the headlights and all the flakes danced in the beams.

They drove off an exit ramp onto a smaller road that had lots of gas stations and hamburger places along it—"a strip," Dad had called roads like this. "Are you hungry?" asked Rachel.

"No," said Rebecca. "I mean, no thank you."

"All right, then," said Rachel. "We'll push on. It's only twenty miles more but it'll be skiddy."

They started up a steep hill. Lots of cars were sliding around, going sideways, but the pickup chugged past them. Rebecca began to wonder if Rachel was a magic driver. How come they could make it when everybody else couldn't? You couldn't see anything out the side window now, and out the front window, it looked like you were driving through a white wall. Rebecca looked at the snowflakes and wondered sleepily where they'd come from and where they were going.

After quite a while, she sat up straighter and peered out at the road. There wasn't one. "How can you see where we're going?"

"Native cunning," said Rachel. "You develop it up here."

"Is native cunning why we passed those cars on the hill?"

"No, that's four-wheel drive," said Rachel.

Rebecca wasn't sure what four-wheel drive was, but she didn't feel like asking. They were going awfully slowly now, and there seemed to be nothing except the white, flying snowflakes and the headlights.

Finally Rachel said, "Well, we're almost there."

Outside, a streetlight slipped closer, looking like a lantern suspended in a cloud of snowflakes.

"It looks like Narnia!" said Rebecca.

Rachel turned left. "So you've read the Narnia books?" She sounded almost pleased.

"Yeah. Every once in a while, I get some books from somebody Dad used to call the Book Fairy. Last year, the Book Fairy gave me the Narnia books for my birthday. I read them all in a week, and then I read them over again." Suddenly she saw Dad's study, and herself, curled up on the recliner and reading. It seemed awfully far away.

"You don't know who sent the books?"

"Nope, I used to think it was Dad, because he was Santa Claus and the Tooth Fairy. But the books kept coming even after . . . last September. So then I thought it might be Mr. Jarvis. . . . Was that a skid?"

The rear of the truck shot to the right, and the suitcases smashed against the side. Then it swung left, and Rachel, cursing softly, swung the wheel to the left. Just before they hit a drift, the wheels started going around again. Rebecca hid her head in the quilts. If only this *were* Narnia, Aslan could walk in front of the truck and keep her safe.

The truck turned sharply, spinning its wheels, then

lurched a couple of times and died. Rebecca poked her head out of the quilts like an Eskimo peering out of an igloo.

"We stuck?"

"In a manner of speaking," said Rachel dryly. "We're home."

Rebecca looked around. "You sure?"

"Think I'd drive up a road like that in the snow for entertainment? Sit tight a moment—I'll turn on some lights."

When Rachel jumped out of the truck, you could see the snow was higher than her knees. She slogged through it and disappeared; in a few minutes, lights blazed on all over the place. White barn, white house, white snow: Vermont seemed to be all one color.

"Planning on coming in?" Rachel was back, looking into the cab. "Take a suitcase as you come."

Walk through all this snow with a suitcase? But Rachel trudged by her with two suitcases, so there was nothing she could do but stumble along with another one. She fell twice, but Rachel didn't seem to notice. When she finally staggered through the door, she found she was in a kitchen, not a hall or an atrium. But it wasn't a kitchen like the one at home. That had been all tiled, with a dishwasher, two ovens, a microwave—everything. This kitchen didn't even have linoleum on the floor, just wide boards and braided rugs. There didn't seem to be a dishwasher. All the dishes were piled up around the sink.

Rachel stomped in with the two remaining suitcases. " 'Fraid the fire's nearly out," she said. "Can you get it going while I take these to your room?"

"Couldn't I just turn up the heat?"

"This *is* the heat," said Rachel. She pointed to a big furnacelike monster set back against a brick wall. "Didn't your Book Fairy give you the Little House books and *The Open Gate?*''

How would Rachel know that? Funny. But maybe not so funny as actually living with an old-fashioned stove. Rebecca watched Rachel open the lid, stick some wood in, and close it again.

''That's how it's done,'' said Rachel. ''Don't forget. It'll need more wood soon. After you put it in, push the damper up.''

Damper? Something you poured on the fire?

Rachel looked at Rebecca's puzzled face. ''The silver thing—there. That's the damper. It controls the airflow in the stove. If you don't shove it up soon enough, the house catches on fire. So don't forget.''

She clomped up the stairs with two suitcases. Rebecca tiptoed closer to the stove. How hot did it have to be before you had to push the damper up? Who on earth would heat their house with something that would burn it up, anyway? Well, it sure wasn't going to burn up anything right now. It wasn't even warm when she stood beside it.

''How's it doing?'' Rachel clomped into the kitchen and lifted a stove lid. ''Okay, I'll put some more wood in, and you sit here and wait until it's hot. Should take about ten minutes. I've got to see to the horses.''

Rebecca thought of asking if she could see the horses, but then she remembered she wanted Rachel to think she wasn't too interested in horses. ''Okay,'' she said. She was tired, anyway, and the rocking chair in front of the stove was probably the only warm place in the house. She sat down, not looking at Rachel. Rachel went out.

Rebecca rocked a few times, then looked around. It wasn't a very cheerful kitchen. Dirty, for one thing. There were cobwebs hanging from the ceiling, and the walls were a sort of sooty gray. All the cabinets had fingerprints on them, and the refrigerator door was almost black around the handle. Boy, Molly would just *die.* She liked things the way they should be—clean and neat and new. Rachel's house was old and dirty, and cold and . . . The stove crackled and Rebecca pushed the chair back a bit. Oh! The damper. Cautiously, she gave it a little shove, and it flicked up without offering any argument. There.

It got warmer and warmer. Rebecca took off her jacket. There was a horse magazine on the table next to her chair, and she flipped through the pages. She stopped when she came to a picture of a big gray jumping a fence that was higher than it was. The gray's rider was a woman, and she looked as if she were as excited as the horse. It would be fun to jump like that. Did Rachel's horses jump? Just imagine, pointing a horse like that at a jump—up, up, then over the top, floating down . . . She stirred a little in her chair, and her head drooped against the back.

All of a sudden, it was dark and freezing, and Rebecca needed to go to the bathroom. It took her a moment to figure out that she was lying down under something light and warm without any shoes on. Well, since she didn't know where she was, she'd better go back to sleep. . . . Nope. If she waited, she'd wake up in a frozen puddle.

She groped around and felt what might be a light. Yeah. When she stopped squinting, she saw she was in a room with walls that turned into a ceiling and met in an upside-down V. Her suitcases were piled in one corner, next to a pretty white desk and a chair large enough for three of her. It would be a nice room, if it weren't so cold. Shivering, she pulled her jacket off the chair back and put it on.

There were several doors in the hall. Probably one of them was the bathroom door. She gave the first one a push. A bedroom. So was the second. The third was half shut, the way bathroom doors often are. She shoved it open and slid her hand along the wall for the light. Something big and black leaped off the floor and started toward her, its teeth gleaming. A bear? A wolf? She tried frantically to close the door, but whatever it was had already shoved its shoulder through. She tried to run, but she tripped over an irregular board. . . . A gigantic wet tongue sloshed across her face, and she opened her eyes. A dog! She pushed it away, and it obligingly backed up and let her stand. It was nearly as tall as she was. She patted its huge head, and it slapped its tail against the wall.

"Quiet, Xeno!" called a sleepy voice. Peering in the door, Rebecca saw a lump in the bed with two cats curled up beside it. Oh—that must be Rachel's room.

"Shh!" she whispered to the big dog. He sat down and cocked his head. She scratched him under the collar, in the place where Mr. Jarvis's dog liked to be rubbed. This dog liked that spot, too; it leaned its head to one side and thumped its left leg softly on the floor. It was going to be great, having this dog around.

But she still hadn't found the bathroom. Maybe downstairs. Wow! Talk about steep! She grabbed the railing and went down very carefully. Behind her, Xeno slid down much faster and landed with a bump at the bottom. It was lots warmer down here. She turned right and saw another iron stove. The room was deliciously hot; even the oriental rug under her feet was warm. But where was the bathroom? She pushed a door behind the stove: at last, at last!

Back in the living room, she curled up next to Xeno in front of the stove. Two cats (the same ones as upstairs? no, these must be different ones) snoozed on a chair on her left, their paws curled around each other. This was nice—much warmer than her room. Maybe she'd just sack out here. She closed her eyes. . . .

What was that? The wind? Rebecca sat up, but the cats and Xeno snoozed on. Something was sure making a noise—a whimpering sort of noise. Then there was some scratching.

"Hey, you stupid kitties," she whispered. "Go get yourselves a meal!" The larger of the two cats blinked at her with its yellow eyes. She heard the noise again. It came from the kitchen. She got up and looked. The door was wiggling a little. What could it be? In this house, she wouldn't be surprised if it were a tame llama or something—but llamas probably didn't scratch at doors. She opened the door.

"Ooooh—how cute!" A black puppy rolled over on its back, then stood up and wagged its whole self in excitement. She picked it up and kissed it.

"Hey!" she yelped, holding it away from her suddenly. A tiny fountain squirted yellow liquid on the floor. She found some paper towels and cleaned it up. "Are you done?" she asked the pup, but it had disappeared. Oh, no! What would it do to the rugs? She rushed into the hall and looked in the living room, then in the bathroom. Maybe it had curled up under the stove. Would it get burned? She knelt down to look, but nothing was there.

"Xeno, where's the pup?"

The big dog looked up at her and thumped his tail. Curled up next to him, the puppy looked up and thumped his tail, too.

"Aw . . ." It was an awfully cute puppy. It'd be nice to be a puppy and curl up next to somebody like that. . . . Well, why not? She picked it up and tucked it under her arm. "Want to come sleep with me?" she asked it. It licked her face. That settled it. "Okay, but if you start to leak, wake me up, huh?"

In her freezing room, she pulled the covers way up on her bed and on top of them spread two extra blankets that had been folded up near the chair. Then she slipped in, holding the puppy. It sighed, burped, and snuggled against her. She kissed it. She'd been wanting a puppy for years, but Dad didn't like animals, and Molly said dog hair messed up the rugs. Well, it did; that rug in front of the stove downstairs was just gross. But, still . . .

She heard toenails clicking on the stairs, and soon Xeno licked her face. Seeing the puppy's nose, he heaved himself up on the bed, turned around three times, and sank down. Rebecca eased her legs out from under him and shoved them into the only empty corner. This was kind of fun. Dad certainly wouldn't approve of sleeping with dogs—but, then, your bedroom wasn't this cold in California.

As she drifted off to sleep, she thought of Molly's blond curls, and then of Rachel's scary green eyes and long strides. No wonder Dad and Rachel hadn't gotten along. Rachel was so . . . unfriendly. The puppy wiggled in its sleep, and she hugged it a bit tighter.

Chapter 5

The dogs were gone when Rebecca woke up, and her room was filled with sunlight. It must be warm outside, then—good. What time was it? Her watch said eight o'clock, but that was California time. While she shivered into her clothes, Rebecca tried to remember whether it was earlier or later here. They'd studied it in school, but she hadn't been listening.

Rachel wasn't anyplace downstairs, but the kitchen was warm, and it smelled like a bakery. There were two loaves of bread sitting on the counter, and a few slices were gone from one of them. Rebecca inspected it suspiciously. Warm, dark brown, heavy—but it might be okay to eat. She hacked off a slice that was thicker at the top than at the bottom, put butter on it, and took a bite. It was okay, actually. All it needed was a little chocolate milk to wash it down. She opened the grimy refrigerator door; the only milk there was just plain white. She hunted around, but she couldn't find any chocolate mix. Rachel sure didn't know much about food.

She took the bread and milk to the window and looked out. The barn didn't seem nearly as big this morning as it had last night. It needed a coat of paint, too, and it leaned so far to the right it looked as if it were held up by the huge snowdrifts around it. Rebecca thought of the house in Santa Barbara, with its pure white stucco walls and gracious, perfectly clean rooms. What would Dad say if he knew she'd been sent off to a dirty, shabby house with all this snow around?

A little distance from the barn, Xeno barked and galumphed through the snow. After him plodded two big, heavy horses, pulling something that looked like a giant rolling pin. Rachel was sitting on whatever it was, her face muffled in scarves. Maybe she'd let you sit up there too, if you asked politely. Rebecca gulped down the rest of the bread and milk, then headed for the door.

A knife of cold air and three cats zipped in as she went outside, and she decided she'd better put on her jacket, even though the sun was shining. She grabbed it and stepped out into the path between two drifts. It certainly was cold! Her face tingled all over, and she coughed when she breathed.

"Becca!" Rachel's voice shot across the yard. "Get back inside!"

Rebecca stopped and stared.

"I said, inside!" Rachel was standing up on the rolling pin thing, pointing to the house.

Rebecca turned around and trudged back in. Whatever was wrong with going outside? She sat down in front of the stove, rubbing her frozen hands and face. Tears floated in front of the stove as she stared at it, and she thought about Santa Barbara, where you could go outside anytime you wanted and Dad never yelled at you . . .

The phone rang. She let it go for six rings, but whoever it was really wanted to get through, so she finally answered it.

"Rachel?" It was a man's voice.

"I'm sorry, she's outside. This is her . . ."

"Rebecca! This is Bob Jarvis! How're you doing?"

Mr. Jarvis! The tears overflowed and poured down her face, feeling very hot after the cold air outside. "Oh, okay, I guess."

"Glad to know you got in okay. The weather report here said Vermont got an arctic storm—first a foot of snow, then below-zero cold."

"Oh, we got in okay."

"Rachel must be quite a driver! How're you two getting along?"

"Not very well."

"Not very well, huh? What's wrong?"

"Well, she sure isn't very glad to see me. Like I just got up and she isn't even here . . ."

"Well, it *is* eleven-thirty there, you know. She may have had things to do besides sit around and wait for you to wake up."

"And last night in the truck, she didn't talk much."

"Did you?"

Rebecca decided not to answer. "Supposing she never gets to like me?"

"Hey, look. Give the thing some time," said Mr. Jarvis. "It's a big change for both of you. And think of it this way: it's probably hard for her to talk to you, because she knows how you feel about her."

Why did he always stick up for Rachel? Couldn't he see Rachel just wasn't going to like her, and that was that? "But supposing I stay here and stay here and she *never* gets to like me?"

"Well, if you stay there and stay there and are really and truly miserable, and nothing works out . . . why, then I'll come and find you someplace else to live. But be patient. It'll work out. Give it six months."

"Y'mean, you'll really take me back?"

"Hey, waaaiiit a moment! I said I would take you back

after a good, long time. Only if things are really miserable for months and months. You can while away the time by meeting the animals. There must be animals—Rachel always has too many.''

''There aren't too many. Just a dog and a puppy and some cats. I haven't met the horses yet.''

''So make friends with them. That's a start.''

''Okay. Where'll I live when you take me back?''

''That's *if* I take you back. I don't know. I'd have to arrange something.''

''Oh.'' She'd hoped he'd say she could move in with his family. She'd met them once—two huge boys and a dog in a big, barny house.

''Well, I have a client waiting, Rebecca. I just called to make sure you'd gotten in. Chin up, now. Give the thing some time.''

He'd already said that. ''Sure.'' She listened to him hang up, then put the phone down slowly. Six whole months! Why, Dad has only been . . . gone . . . for four months, and that seemed ages ago. Well, at least she wasn't stuck here forever.

The door banged open, and Xeno bounced in, followed by the puppy. Both dogs shook, sending icicles shimmering all over the kitchen. No wonder the floor was so dirty. Rachel strode in behind them, unwinding three scarves from around her face and stomping snow off her boots.

''It's twenty below zero,'' she said, shoving the scarves into a drawer and kicking the boots into a large boot pile in the corner. ''That's why I didn't want you to come out and watch. You'd get frostbite.''

Rebecca nodded. Why didn't Rachel hang up her jacket? Didn't she *care* about messing things up?

The puppy had been investigating his dish; now he saw Rebecca and threw himself into her arms, yapping. A smile forced its way across Rachel's sharp face. "He seems to approve of you," she said.

"He was lonely last night," said Rebecca, leaning way back to avoid a series of frantic puppy kisses, "so I took him upstairs with me."

"That's where I found him. Luckily, I found him early, or you'd have been drowned in your bed."

Rebecca looked up, surprised, but Rachel's face was as grim as ever. Weren't *you* supposed to smile when you said something funny? "Well, tonight I won't be so tired," she said. "I'll let him out early."

"He's going to sleep with you tonight, too, huh?"

"If that's okay . . ."

"It's fine with me, but *you* may be sorry after a while. He's part shepherd, part Lab, and part Great Pyrenees, so he'll be at least as big as Xeno when he grows up. He'll take up a lot of room."

"Oh, I won't . . ." She'd been going to say she wouldn't be here when he grew up, but then she remembered Rachel didn't know that yet. So she just said, "I won't mind."

"Okay then." Rachel put some wood in the stove. "Want some cocoa?"

"No, thanks." Why had she said that? She'd looked all over for chocolate just a few minutes ago. She fluffed the puppy's ears, waiting for Rachel to go away.

But Rachel didn't go away. She made herself a cup of tea and sat down at the table. Uh-oh. That probably meant she felt like having a little talk.

"I think I'll go unpack now," said Rebecca, getting up off the floor and dusting off her jeans. Why couldn't Rachel keep the house clean?

"Need help?"

"No, thanks." She hurried out the door, but when she

saw the telephone, she remembered something and turned around. "Mr. Jarvis called."

Rachel looked up; her face looked frozen. "Something wrong?"

"Nope. He just wanted to be sure I got in okay."

Rachel nodded. Rebecca scurried up the steep stairs, so Rachel couldn't ask her any questions about what else Mr. Jarvis had said. But that left the puppy at the bottom of the stairs, yelping. She hurried down the steps, grabbed him, and scurried up again. You sure got lots of exercise in a house that wasn't all on one floor.

It took a long time to unpack, because she kept dreaming off every time she took something out of the suitcase. Here was the sweater Dad had given her for her birthday, just before he found out how sick he was. Here was the special jewelry box he'd gotten her in San Francisco when he'd taken her on that business trip. Here was the calendar he'd given her last fall. It was a funny one—an academic calendar, he'd said. That meant it went from September to September, like school. Rebecca flipped through it, looking at stuff she'd marked down. Dad's funeral. Christmas vacation, which had been simply awful without Dad. Appointment with Mr. Jarvis. She hunted around and found her pen. Next to January 21, she wrote "flew to Vt.," then crossed it off. That meant—how many days was it until June 22? She started to count, but she lost track halfway through. Besides, he hadn't said *exactly* six months. She could probably call Mr. Jarvis June first. Until then, she could just cross off one day at a time.

She put the calendar under her pillow, then started unpacking her stuffed animals. She could remember just when Dad had given her each one of them, and the fun they'd had naming them. All the names were out of the books they'd read together. But he'd never given her books; the Book Fairy had done that.

"Well," Rebecca said conversationally to the Book Fairy, "all those books are on their way here. And there's lots of room for them, too. Look at all those shelves! There'll be room for all of them to stand up." She smiled at the Book Fairy, . . . then she remembered Rachel was downstairs. Supposing Rachel heard her talking to the air? She'd think she was a weirdo.

But who could she talk to if she didn't talk to the Book Fairy? She'd *always* thought of herself as "we" when she was alone—Rebecca and the Book Fairy. She told the Book Fairy stories she made up on her own, and sometimes she even told the Book Fairy stuff you weren't supposed to say. Like the fact that she didn't want to come to Vermont, or that she was worried when Dad was sick. And when Dad had died, she hadn't cried until she'd tried to explain to the Book Fairy that he wasn't coming home anymore, ever.

The puppy sat up sleepily on her bed and yawned. Well, maybe she could talk to him. Rachel wouldn't think that was too weird, would she? I mean, it wasn't quite so nutty to talk to a puppy as it was to talk to air.

"What do you think, pup?" she asked. "Can I talk to you?"

The puppy wagged himself all over, then slid clumsily off the bed and started running in little circles, sniffing. Uh-oh. Rebecca scooped him up, carried him carefully down the stairs, and put him out. He squatted instantly, then came back in.

"Hey, you're a great puppy!" She tousled his ears and started down the hall. The puppy followed her to the bottom of the stairs, but then he trotted into a room across from the living room. Rebecca ran after him, then screeched to a stop. The room was piled high with books—books in bookcases, on the floor, in piles under lamps, and on a huge desk where Rachel was hunched over a typewriter. Xeno lay in the middle of the floor on a pile of old magazines. He seemed to have spent a fair amount of time in there: the whole room was covered with black hair, except the high parts of the walls; they were filled with cobwebs.

Rachel looked up, and she didn't look terribly friendly. "Something wrong?"

"Nope. The puppy just ran in here. I'll get him." She grabbed for him, but he bumbled away, knocking over a stack of books and a pile of paper. Typed pages flew everywhere, and Rachel jumped up.

"Get him out of here, will you? I just finished that!"

Rebecca grabbed the puppy and ran upstairs. Safe in her room, she hugged him and cried a little bit. Dad would never drive her out of *his* study like that. Some people were *happy* when you came into their study to visit them.

They had lunch at three. Rebecca was almost starving to death, but she hadn't dared ask for anything. Not if Rachel was going to yell at her for coming into her study. Rachel tried to talk, but Rebecca managed to be busy with her sandwich and those really good cookies that seemed not to have come out of a box. When they'd finished, Rachel said she had to give a riding lesson—how about a visit to the barn? Rebecca jumped up, but then she remembered she wasn't supposed to like horses much. So she just said "Sure," and hoped she didn't sound too eager.

It had "warmed up" outside. That meant it was 20 degrees and you didn't have to wear scarves over your face. The snow in the yard was packed down (that's what the rolling-pin thing did, Rachel said), so Rebecca didn't get any snow in her sneakers. But her toes were frozen before they got halfway across the yard. Like Dad said, there were places in the world that just weren't fit to live in.

It was surprisingly warm in the barn, and five heads stuck out over stall doors. It looked just like a picture from a horse magazine, only the floor slanted and there were cobwebs all over the ceiling.

"The two at the end of the row are the team—Mutt and Jeff," said Rachel, handing Rebecca a bag of carrots. Rebecca followed her to their stalls, trying not to look excited. The two huge heads rubbed themselves on Rachel's parka. Rebecca pulled out a carrot. Jeff leaned forward and took it. "Good boy," breathed Rebecca. "Hey! Ow!" Mutt's nose sent her three strides backward into the wall.

"Better give the devil his due," said Rachel, smiling a bit.

Rebecca held out the carrot, and the big gelding took it daintily. She reached up and stroked the shaggy brown face. "He's nice."

"He's the poet," said Rachel. "Jeff's the football star. Mutt stands around all day, thinking sensitive thoughts; Jeff kicks up his heels and trots around the pasture, looking for adventure."

Rachel's voice sounded different when she talked about the horses. You could see she liked them, the way she scratched them behind the ears. Rebecca began to wish she hadn't tried so hard not to seem interested in horses.

They walked down to the next stall. This horse was smaller than the big Belgians, but it too had a kind, solemn face. "Dimwit," said Rachel. "She's my teacher."

"Teacher?" Rebecca held out a carrot.

"To give lessons, you need a horse that teaches," said Rachel. "She could teach you, if you wanted."

Just in time Rebecca remembered not to say she was already too good to ride school horses. By the time she'd thought up something else to say, Rachel had stepped down to the next stall.

"Let me introduce you to my baby," said Rachel. "Killiger's Sundance. Better known as Dancer."

The chestnut head that poked over the door was thin and refined, with delicate ears that rose to two perfect points. He was less shaggy than the other horses, and his coat gleamed red-gold even in the dim light.

"Ooooh! He's *gorgeous!*"

"He is, isn't he?" said Rachel, stroking his white star. "I bought him when he was a weanling, and now he's four. This spring, I'll break him—to saddle, that is. I've been driving him for two years."

"Can I watch you break him?"

"Sure, but it won't be too exciting, I hope. I don't break horses the way cowboys do on TV. I get on very gently, and we walk around the ring. That's all."

"Sounds like *Black Beauty,*" said Rebecca.

"*Black Beauty* is a very sensible book," said Rachel.

Rebecca moved down to the last stall. A bay pony looked up at her, a few wisps of hay dangling from his mouth. Except for his color, he looked like a smaller edition of Dancer: tiny hooves, delicate legs, pointed ears, and a white star on his aristocratic face. Rebecca stared at him. Why would Rachel have a pony? Was this, maybe, just maybe, a pony for . . . ?

A car stopped next to the barn, and in a minute the big door slid open. In slipped a girl a bit older than Rebecca, dressed in riding breeches and boots. "Hi, Rachel!" she said. "Get the ring packed down . . . ? She saw Rebecca, and stopped.

"Oh, hi!" she said. "You must be Becca! I've been really looking forward to meeting you! Rachel *said* you might like horses. You going to get one?"

"All in good time," said Rachel, coming up behind Rebecca. "Becca, this is Patty Ellrow. She owns the pony you've been admiring."

Patty looked like the girls you smiled at in school—the ones who made you secretly wish you were more outgoing and popular yourself, even though you wouldn't really want to be like them. And *she* owned that lovely pony. It wasn't a present, or anything. Somehow it was very hard to be friendly with this girl.

"Hi," said Rebecca, hoping that would do.

"Want to help me brush Goner?" asked Patty. She got a lead rope off the hook and slipped into his stall. "His name is Gone With the Wind, but I call him Goner. He's a Welsh-thoroughbred cross, and boy, can he jump! I was just starting him this fall, and he'd just gotten the hang of it when it started to snow." Patty made a face as she led the pony out to the crossties. "But we'll start up again in the spring." She hitched the crossties to Goner's halter and began to curry him. "You jump?"

"Nope. My dad didn't want me to. Said it was dangerous." Then she remembered she wasn't supposed to be able to ride well enough to be interested in jumping, anyway. She watched Patty's hands as they groomed the shining coat, then put on the saddle and tightened the girth. Maybe it was just as well she'd pretended she didn't know much about horses. At home Amity had never let her tack up a horse herself, or brush it.

"There!" said Patty, buckling the cavesson of Goner's fancy black and white bridle. "You set, Rachel?"

Rachel had been diddling around in the grain room, but now she came into the barn. "All set. Come and watch, Becca, if your toes aren't too cold."

It was cold outside the barn, but Patty and Goner didn't seem to notice. Patty swung on easily (not like the kids who took lessons from Amity in Santa Barbara), and Goner pranced down to the ring. Rachel stood in the center of the ring, smiling, as Goner took a few little bucks that didn't even seem to shake Patty in the saddle.

"Trot him around until he stops that snorting," Rachel said.

Rebecca waited for Patty's legs to thump the pony's sides, but Goner trotted as if she'd just pushed a button. He whisked his tail harder and harder, but he didn't buck, and Patty posted fluidly, gracefully, as if she weren't even thinking about it.

All of a sudden, Rebecca was really, really glad she hadn't said she was a good rider. So, she could ride Fanfare at a walk, trot, and a canter in Santa Barbara—if Amity was there to watch. But Patty was obviously way beyond that stage. She looked professional—boy, she probably knew as much as Amity did! And if Rachel was teaching her, that meant Rachel knew even more . . . !

The puppy cantered up behind her and started fighting with her sneaker laces. Rebecca picked him up. "C'mon, pup," she said miserably. "Let's go in."

It was almost dark when Rachel and Patty stomped into the kitchen, though it was only a bit after four-thirty. Rebecca had been dozing by the stove, feeling bad about being a lousy rider whenever she woke up. But she'd kept the fire going nicely between snoozes. Rachel and Patty crowded around it, holding out their red fingers over the top.

"It's my toes that are really cold," said Patty cheerfully.

She pulled off her boots and watched her toes wiggle inside her socks. The puppy woke up from his nap and saw she was sitting on the floor; in a second, he was bouncing all over her, washing her face and ears with his tongue.

"What a *cute* puppy!" laughed Patty. "What's his name, Rachel?"

Rebecca had been meaning to ask that herself. How come Patty made asking sound so easy?

"You'll have to ask Becca," said Rachel. "He belongs to her."

Rebecca stopped rocking the chair. Hers? Her very own puppy?

"Oh, you lucky . . . !" said Patty. "I've *always* wanted a puppy! What'd you name him?"

Rebecca thought fast, so she wouldn't look dumb. "Tumnus," she said after just a second. She'd been saving it for a stuffed animal, but it went much better with a puppy.

"Hey, that's a great name—right out of Narnia!" said Patty. "I really liked those books, didn't you? Rachel gave me the whole set right after she sent them to—"

"Here—have some cocoa," said Rachel. She handed each girl a steaming mug, then went into the living room to stoke the stove in there.

"Mmmmm," said Patty happily. "Rachel makes the best cocoa in the world." She took another sip. "What grade are you in?"

"Fifth."

"Really? You look older than that. I'm in sixth. I should be in seventh, but I got put back. My parents were in a car accident three years ago and . . . well, I just couldn't keep my *mind* on anything."

"Gee—were they in the hospital long?"

Patty shook her head. "They were both . . . killed. I live with my grandparents now. I guess Rachel didn't explain—"

"Oh! I'm sor—"

"It's okay. Really. It was a long time ago, and Grandpa and Grandma are really great. I was lucky they were around—otherwise I'd have had to go live in a foster home."

"A what?"

"*You* know, those places social workers send homeless kids to. And boy, they don't give you any choices, either. 'You're going to the Smiths'!' they say, and off you go. And probably the old Smiths just take you for the money."

"Yuk!" Rebecca stared. She'd never heard of anything like that—though, when you thought of it, there had to be somewhere for kids without parents to go. There were places like that even when Dickens was writing, after all.

"Yeah, I'm lucky, all right," said Patty. "There's a boy in school whose mom ran off or died or something, and his dad went on the skids—I'm not sure how. Anyway, he's lived in seven foster homes in the last two years. You can tell by the way he acts, too."

Rebecca thought about it. "Well, I suppose he'd *have* to act up—"

A car beeped outside. "Hey! There's Grandpa!" Patty jumped up and shoved her feet into her boots. "Bye, Rachel!" she called. As she started out the door, she turned around. "You going to school tomorrow, Becca?"

"Tomorrow!"

"Yep. Today's semester break, but tomorrow everything starts all over again. Well, if you come, I'll introduce you to everybody. Seeya." She waved and slipped out the door. Rebecca watched her run to the car outside.

Rachel strode into the kitchen and put on her boots

again. "I've got to feed the horses," she said. "I just came in to get warm." Tumnus dove for her boot laces, and she patted him. "Tumnus, huh? That's a good name."

"Yeah." Rebecca suddenly giggled. "Only we'll probably call him Tummy."

"Entirely appropriate," said Rachel, smiling a little.

Then Rebecca remembered there was something important she wanted to tell Rachel. "Er . . . about nicknames . . ."

"What about them?"

"My name isn't Becca; it's *Re*Becca. It's an Old Testament name, like all the names in Dad's family since the *Mayflower,* and you don't make nicknames out of Old Testament names."

"What is this about the *Mayflower?*"

"Well, Dad said—"

"That his family came over on the *Mayflower,* and that's why you had an Old Testament, Puritan name?" Rachel laughed. "Well, I hate to disappoint you, Becca, but until a couple of generations ago, none of your ancestors on either side had ever heard of the *Mayflower.* Most of his family came from Poland—his mother married a fine hard-working factory worker named Davidson. Most of my family came over on an Irish boat during the potato famine—that's where the red hair comes from. My mother married a Vermont dairy farmer named Herrick. And as for our Old Testament names, that was entirely a coincidence. Yours wasn't. When you came along, our friend laughed and said that with names like Caleb and Rachel, we'd better name you something off the *Mayflower.* And we did—partly because my mother's name was Rebecca. But we always called you Becca. Isn't that what your father called you?"

"Nope. He called me Princess."

"That figures," muttered Rachel. Her green eyes looked awfully scary for just a minute.

Rebecca's ears began to sing, and she wished she hadn't drunk that cocoa. "But Dad said *nobody* in the Old Testament used nicknames. . . ."

Rachel's eyes stopped looking scary. "Now that," she said, "is an interesting point. Of course, today, people named Judith get called Judy, and so on—but back then? I don't know. Maybe we should check it out." She smiled the way Dad did when he was going to ask you a question you weren't supposed to know the answer to. "You *do* know what the Old Testament is, don't you?"

"It's . . . the first half of the Bible . . . isn't it?" Boy, she'd better be right.

"It is indeed. Well, there's a big Bible next to the desk in my study. Go in and start looking for nicknames. You might run into Caleb and Rachel and Rebecca as you read along—that would be instructive. Anyway, if you can prove to me that nobody in the Old Testament ever used a nickname, I'll admit your dad was right and call you Rebecca. Is that a deal?"

"Sure!" Rebecca scurried into Rachel's study before Rachel even finished lacing her boots. The Bible was right where Rachel had said; she hauled it off the shelf and flipped through the pages. The Old Testament, the Old Testament . . . it was a lot more than the first half of the Bible. More like the first three quarters. There sure was a lot of it.

She opened it to the beginning and found she knew the story. It was kind of pretty, when you read it in those old-fashioned words. But as she read, her ears began to sing louder and louder; finally, right after Adam and Eve got driven out of the garden, she looked out the dirty window. Had Dad really read all this? Was he *sure* about those nicknames? And that stuff Rachel had told her about their families having nothing to do with the *Mayflower*—could it be true? Dad wouldn't kid about names, would he? He said they were very important; they told people who you were. Like she was his princess. What was wrong with that?

Tumnus trotted in gaily from the kitchen and climbed into her lap. She stroked him as she looked over his head at the double columns. They blurred, and she began to feel sort of sick again. Of *course* Dad was right, but it would take her an awfully long time to prove that. Maybe . . . she tried reading some more, but she felt sicker and sicker. Yeah, maybe it would be easier just to let Rachel and Patty and everybody else in Vermont call her Becca. It would only be for six months, anyway.

She rocked Tumnus back and forth, thinking about names, about a new school full of faces she didn't know, then about foster homes. Foster homes! Maybe *that* was what Mr. Jarvis had meant when he'd said he'd have to find her a place to live. You'd like to think Mr. Jarvis wouldn't do something awful like that, but then, he'd sent her here. So he might.

Well, one thing was for sure. She wasn't going to stay here in this cold, dirty house with a mother who wouldn't even call her by the right name, or be friendly to a girl who rode a whole lot better than she did—not for any longer than she had to, anyway. And if Mr. Jarvis came out on June first and said it was either Rachel or a foster home, she'd . . . run away. Sure. Like Oliver Twist. It wouldn't be hard in summer.

Tumnus sighed in his sleep on her lap, and she bent over and kissed him. She'd take him with her when she left, of course.

Chapter 6

Gee. It was only ten-thirty. Rebecca sighed and looked around the classroom. You could never believe how slowly the time went by in school if you didn't have a good book. Sure, this was a different school, with different kids, but it felt just like school always felt—boring. She was finished first, and there was nothing else to do. She turned her dittoed arithmetic paper over and started drawing on the back. She did a barn first, then some trees and the front half of a horse. Just the front half; she couldn't do back legs, so she always hid half her horses behind barns or trees.

When she'd finished, she sighed again. Dad was right: you learned more at home than at school. If she'd stayed in Santa Barbara, he'd have sent her to a private school next year . . . but there wasn't any point thinking about that. She put her chin on her hand. They *still* weren't done—except for that strange-looking boy on the other side of the room, the one with the patched jeans and the thick, dark forelock that fell over his eyes. He'd finished when she had, but he was still bending over his paper. From the way his pencil was working, she thought he was probably drawing, too.

She watched him, not really thinking about him. Suddenly, he finished and pushed his chair back so hard that it hit the desk behind him. The girl at that desk looked up, but she didn't say anything. Everybody seemed a bit afraid of that boy; when he slouched to the teacher's desk with his paper, nobody tried to whisper to him or hand him notes.

The teacher (what was her name?) looked up from the papers she was correcting and took the boy's arithmetic. She looked it over carefully, nodded, and set it down. ''All correct. Would you like to go use the computers now, Bill?''

Bill shrugged, but Rebecca noticed he looked pleased when he turned around. He swaggered toward the door to the computer room as if he owned the class. King of the mountain. Oboy.

''Becca, are you done too? Well, bring your paper here, then.''

Rebecca walked slowly to the front desk, trying not to feel all the kids' eyes looking at her. The teacher took her paper, and while she looked at it, Rebecca's eyes drifted to the desk. Bill's paper—it must be Bill's paper, since it was the only one not in the teacher's stack—lay upside down, and it had a drawing on it. She bent over, staring at it. It was a horse, but not a horse like her horses. This was a real horse, prancing, with its neck arched. It had muscles right where real horses had muscles. In one more moment, it would prance right off the page.

''Have you done this math at your other school, Becca?'' The teacher's voice made her jump, but she nodded.

''What else have you done?''

''Fractions. Factoring. Decimals.'' She'd been doing seventh-grade math out of a special book; it had been nice, because it meant she didn't have to sit with the other kids much.

"I see," said the teacher. "Well, fortunately, there's another student in this class who has done those things too. You can work with him, starting tomorrow. For right now, would you like to work with the computers?"

Rebecca took one last look at the horse and started toward the computer room. It seemed to be some sort of privilege to go there, but she'd never worked a computer in her life. They were just putting them in her school in Santa Barbara. Dad had complained for years about there being no computers, but for a long time the principal had just said all the extra money in the district went to the bilingual program. Finally, a lot of parents had gotten together, and the school had agreed to set up a computer program, but it wasn't going to start until this semester.

Bill's back was turned to her as she slipped in the door, and he didn't turn around. Rebecca sat down at a computer as far away from his as she could and stared at the blank screen. What did you do? She shot a glance at Bill. Unless she was just going to sit there like an idiot, she'd have to ask him what to do. Rachel had told her that asking other kids what to do was a good way of making friends; it made them feel helpful. It had sounded like a good idea—but then, Rachel hadn't had to face the meanest kid in the class all alone in a room full of computers. Rebecca looked at Bill's back again. On second thought, maybe she'd just sit there like an idiot.

Bill's computer flashed green with red letters, then with numbers. He grinned and pushed another key, and the whole display disappeared.

"How did you do that?" asked Rebecca, in spite of herself.

Bill whirled around. "What're you doing here?"

Rebecca pulled back a little, telling herself that somebody who could draw beautiful horses couldn't be *all* bad. "I'm trying to figure out how to turn this thing on."

Bill stared at her as though she was a creep from outer space. "See the buttons marked 'on' and 'off'?" he said patiently—too patiently. "Try pushing the one that says 'on.' "

She did. The screen lit up and said HI!

"Now what?" she asked. But Bill's back was turned, and he was pushing keys like crazy. Maybe that's what you did. She pushed an A; nothing happened. The computer seemed as friendly as ever, but absolutely nothing. . .

The teacher opened the door and looked into the room. "It's time for reading now," she began. Then she caught sight of Rebecca's screen. "Is that as far as you got?"

"I . . . I've never worked a computer before," admitted Rebecca.

"Jeee-SUS!" said Bill, staring at her.

"Bill!" said the teacher. She smiled a teacher's smile. "Bill, this is Becca Davidson. She's doing the same level math you are, so after today, you'll be working together."

She was going to be working with Bill? Oh, great! She didn't dare look at him to find out what he thought about that cute idea. She already knew what she'd see. She dawdled behind them, hoping nobody would notice they'd come out of the computer room together. When she got back to her desk, she saw two reading books sitting on it. She'd read one of them in second grade and the other in third. She sighed.

The teacher stopped next to her. "Have you read either of these books?"

Rebecca nodded. "Both of them. And the three after that."

"How about this one?" The teacher held out the book in her hand.

"That one, too—I did it this fall. I was in the next one after that—the blue one with horses and a chariot on it."

"Oh! That's the one Bill's working in. Well, you can read with him too. That'll be nice. He'll be glad to have company." The teacher smiled and fetched the book. "Read the fourth story," she said.

The fourth story turned out to be the one about the horses and the chariot. A boy named Phaeton wanted proof that he was the son of the sun god, Apollo, so he asked if he could drive Apollo's horses. Apollo didn't want him to: the horses were perfectly wild for everybody but him, and the chariot towed the sun around the world. Phaeton finally talked Apollo into it, though, and off they went. Just as you'd expect, the horses ran away with him; they went too high and messed up the ozone layer, then too low and scorched the crops. Finally Zeus got fed up with all the damage, and he knocked Phaeton out of the chariot into the ocean.

Rebecca glanced around the room when she'd finished the story. Bill's pencil was going like mad. Boy, if she could draw the way he did, she'd do a picture of those wonderful, flaming horses. She picked up her pencil and gave it a try, but after a few minutes she scribbled over it. She just couldn't draw what was in her head.

The lunch bell rang, and the kids hurried to line up, boys in one line and girls in another, just like in California. Bill was still drawing as Rebecca wandered to the back of the girls' line, where there was no pushing and shoving.

"Bill!" said the teacher.

Bill stood up, still looking at his picture. He added one final touch, then slouched toward the line. Rebecca's jaw dropped: he walked right past the end and went to stand in front of all the boys! And nobody so much as gave him a push; the boys just moved back a little so he'd have a place to stand. What had he *done* to make them let him get away with stuff like that?

Patty was in the lunchroom, and Rebecca decided to sit with her. "What do I do with my money?" she asked, looking around.

"You give it to your teacher," said Patty. "But you can't sit here—we have to sit by classes. See you at lunch recess. That's the only one we have together."

Rebecca looked for her teacher and finally found her down at the end of the lunchroom, eating with the other teachers. She gave her the money and hurried back to the fifth-grade table. She wasn't hungry, of course, but she'd better eat something or she'd . . . she stopped. All the seats at the girls' end of the table were taken—and all but two seats at the boys' end too. The only free chairs were on either side of Bill; he had the whole end of the table to himself. She was going to have to sit *there?*

She looked across the lunchroom at Patty, but Patty was talking and giggling with a bunch of sixth-grade girls. Well . . . Rebecca picked up a plate, scooped some Spaghettios and gray beans onto it, gritted her teeth, and sat down on Bill's right. The girls at the other end of the table stared at her and whispered to each other. The boy on her right moved over, brushing imaginary cooties off his arm. Very funny. Rebecca tucked her head down as far as it would go and managed to swallow a few bites, even though she knew she was redder than the Spaghettio sauce. Bill didn't even look up.

Rachel and the pickup truck were waiting for her after school; the bus didn't go up their road because the first hill was so steep and slippery, and Rachel said if she had to drive Becca to the bus, she might as well go the whole hog. Which meant, take her to school and back.

“How did it go?” Rachel said, pushing the pickup door open.

That’s what grownups always asked about school; they didn’t really want to know.

“Okay,” muttered Rebecca.

Across the parking lot, Patty was waiting to get on her bus. Rachel beeped and beckoned; Patty said something to the teacher on duty, then ran carefully across the icy pavement to the pickup.

“We’re going to the post office,” said Rachel. “Hop in!”

“What a treat!” said Patty, bouncing onto the torn seat next to Rebecca. “I can introduce you to Grandma, Becca. She works there.”

It was funny to think of a grandmother working. Things were sure different in Vermont.

“Did Becca tell you yet?” said Patty to Rachel. “She has reading and math with the toughest kid in the school!” Rebecca had told Patty all about it at lunch recess, and Patty had been very sympathetic.

Rachel frowned at Rebecca. “You at the bottom of the class?”

“Of course not!”

Patty jumped in to keep the peace. “No, no, it’s not like that. You see, Bill is supposed to be in sixth grade, but Ms. Thompson can’t handle him. He was always in trouble in our class, and one day all the sixth-grade guys ganged up on him and said he was a fag . . . I mean, said he was weird because he draws pictures all the time. But he beat up a lot of them. It took three teachers to stop him. After that, they put him in Mrs. Standish’s class even though she has fifth grade this year, because she’s been teaching a long time and doesn’t put up with any guff.”

"I see," said Rachel. "So this rough artist is bright, is he?"

Rebecca nodded, and Patty added, "Really! In sixth grade he was way ahead of the rest of us. Which is funny—most foster kids are way behind."

"Oh!" said Rebecca. "Is he the one . . . ?"

"Right," said Patty.

"Enlighten me," said Rachel.

"Oh! I was telling Becca about him yesterday, because he's a foster kid and we aren't. Poor Bill—lucky us."

"So all foster homes are terrible?" said Rachel.

If you'd lived with Dad all your life, you knew a trap when you saw one. Rebecca nudged Patty to save her, but Patty kept right on going.

"Sure. They're run by people who need money, so they take JDs."

"And if you were a foster kid, you'd be a JD?" said Rachel. "And your grandparents took foster kids when your dad was a teenager because they wanted to make money on kids' misfortunes?"

Patty stared so hard Rebecca almost laughed. Traps were funny—unless you were the one who walked into them.

"But tell me," Rachel went on. "Whose foster kid is Bill?"

"The Amidens'," said Patty. Her voice was a bit smaller than usual.

"Sounds like a good deal to me," said Rachel. "I don't know the Amidens very well, but they have a nice little place. And Ed's Clydesdales are the best horses in the state."

Patty was perking up again. "Grandpa says you can tell where Mr. Amiden's heart is. He has a little house for his wife and a big barn for his Clydesdales."

"Shows he has his priorities in order," said Rachel solemnly, turning into the post office parking lot.

Patty slid out of the cab as soon as the truck stopped. "Want to get the mail, Becca? I'll show you the combination to your box."

Rebecca looked at Rachel. Rachel probably wouldn't want her to. After all, Dad was a lot less touchy than Rachel, and even he had said she must never, never open the mailbox downtown.

"What's the matter?" said Rachel. "You'd better hurry, or Patty will have the box open by the time you get there."

That was strange, Rebecca thought as she slid across the parking lot. Inside, it took her three tries to get the box open, but Patty said that was about average for the first time. "You'll get on to it," she said comfortingly. "Now reach in and—hey! A pink slip! That means there's a package and you have to come see Grandma."

Rebecca followed Patty into the side room. There was a strong-looking woman with curly gray hair and glasses leaning on the counter. She smiled as Patty came in, and Rebecca decided that must be Grandma.

"This is Becca!" said Patty. "She has a pink slip."

Mrs. Ellrow had a nice smile, and her beautiful sweater made her post office shirt look a lot more cheerful. "You sure look like your mother," she said kindly. "It's real good having you here. We've been looking forward to meeting you."

"Thank you," said Rebecca. It was nice that *somebody* around here was really glad to see her.

"Now let's see," said Mrs. Ellrow. "Boxes. Yes, you got four." She trotted back to some shelves and returned, carrying two huge packages, then went back to get two more. "What's in them, rocks?"

Rebecca smiled. "Books, mostly. And plastic horses."

"How many horses do you have?" asked Patty. "I've got—"

"Patty, you'd better go tell Rachel to give Becca a hand with these boxes," said Mrs. Ellrow.

"Sure!" Patty dashed out, colliding with an old woman in the doorway. "Sorry!" she said over her shoulder.

Mrs. Ellrow shook her head and seemed about to say something, but the old woman needed stamps, so she had to wait on her. Rebecca wandered over to the bulletin board at the far end of the room and looked at the "Lost Child" pictures. Where were all these kids? Had they run away from their mothers? Or from foster homes? You had to wonder.

". . . Rachel Herrick's girl?" the old woman was saying in a low voice. Rebecca kept her eyes on the pictures and pretended not to listen so they'd go on.

"That's right." Mrs. Ellrow didn't seem too happy about talking.

"Well, it's about *time* that poor gal got her child," said the old woman. "I've hated to see Rachel, that used to be so cheerful all the time, just hiding away up on that hill. Her dad must be turning in his grave with grief."

"I'm sure things will be better now," said Mrs. Ellrow hurriedly, as if she didn't want the old woman to say any more.

"Must've been eight years, now, that no-good man of hers kidnapped—"

"Hello, Rachel!" said Mrs. Ellrow, a bit louder than she had to. The old woman shuffled over to the side of the counter and looked hard at Rebecca while pasting the stamps on an envelope.

"Looks like your stuff has come," Rachel said. "Mostly books, huh?" She lifted two of the boxes.

"Bet most of those books came from here," said Mrs.

Ellrow, smiling at Rachel. "Never seen anybody like Rachel for mailing books to a certain girl in California."

What was that supposed to mean? Rebecca looked at Rachel, but Rachel was frowning and shaking her head at Mrs. Ellrow.

"This must be the horses," said Patty, lifting the only light box and handing it to Rebecca. "I'll take the other box."

They trudged out into the cold, carrying the boxes. Something jangled at the back of Rebecca's mind like a phone that needed answering, but she was too mixed up to deal with it.

"Seeya tomorrow," said Patty, throwing the box in the back of the pickup. "Can I see your horse collection when you get it unpacked?"

"Sure."

Rachel started the complaining pickup, and Rebecca waved to Patty as they chugged out of the parking lot. The sun was getting ready to set already; it sure got dark early in Vermont. Rebecca leaned back in the seat and watched the small, run-down houses slide past her. *Kidnapped.* That's what the old woman had said. "That no-good man of hers kidnapped . . ."

"Something wrong?" Rachel asked, turning onto their road.

"Just tired."

"Bet you are. Long day."

Kidnapped. . . . And then there was that thing Mrs. Ellrow had said, about the books. But she must be wrong. Rachel hadn't sent her any books; if she had, Dad would have said so. Wouldn't he? *Kidnapped.* All of a sudden, she felt sick, really sick.

They jounced up the driveway, and Rachel shut off the engine.

"You *sure* nothing's wrong?" she asked.

Rebecca's ears sang louder and louder; she could hardly move her hand to the door handle. "What books . . . ?"

Rachel froze, her gloved hands gripping the wheel. "What books, what?"

Rebecca swallowed and swallowed, like you did before you threw up. There was no point in asking. If Rachel had sent her books, Dad would have said so. Of course he would have. But he hadn't. "Never mind."

Rachel gave her a long, funny look, but all she said was, "I hear Tumnus yapping inside. Maybe you should drain him before he floods the kitchen."

Rebecca slipped out of the truck and plodded to the back door through the snow. Dad *would* have told her if Rachel had sent her books, wouldn't he? Sure he would have. Dad hadn't had any secrets from his favorite princess. Mrs. Ellrow must have meant something else.

Tumnus was so excited to see her that he drained himself on the kitchen floor before she could get him outside.

Chapter 7

The next couple of weeks were sort of peculiar. On the one hand, Rebecca's room got prettier and prettier as her stuff came. The books looked wonderful all lined up in the bookcase; she and the Book Fairy even alphabetized them by author, like books in a library. The plastic horses trotted, cantered, and stood on the top shelf, looking like real horses (or at least like real horses in the summer; in Vermont, anyway, real horses were pretty shaggy in wintertime). There hadn't been enough room for the stuffed animals at first, but one day Rebecca came home from school and found a new shelf, right under the dormer window. It was the perfect size; all the animals fit on it, and you didn't even have to put the little ones in front of the big ones. That was really nice. Rebecca spent a lot of time up there, sitting in the big, comfortable chair, wrapped in the mummy quilt that had turned up the same day as the stuffed animal shelf.

On the other hand, there was school, and there was Rachel. School started out being kind of awful because Rebecca worked with Bill. That meant nobody would talk to her. But one day she told that to Patty, and the next day two really nice girls asked her to eat lunch with them. After that, all the girls would talk to her if she felt like talking. But mostly, she talked to Patty. Patty was friends with everybody—it was amazing. But then there was Rachel. She seemed to spend most of her time in the study and in the barn, but she did try to talk a little, usually at supper, when you couldn't get away. She talked about riding, which would have been okay, except you had to be careful not to let her know you knew more about horses than you let on. She talked about the Book Fairy books (it turned out she'd read them—*all* of them), but you had to pretend not to be interested. The Book Fairy was too special to share with somebody else, especially Rachel. But Rachel didn't give up easily: she tried reading aloud after supper. That was a tough one, because she chose really good books and she read almost as well as Dad. For a couple of nights, Rebecca lay in front of the livingroom stove on that filthy rug with the dogs, and listened. But when they got to the middle of the second book, she began to think how hurt Dad would be if he knew she and Rachel were sharing books the way she and he had. So the next night, when Rachel sat down to read, Rebecca said she'd finished the book on her own. Rachel didn't say anything; she just got up and went into her study.

It was pretty soon after that—a couple of days, maybe—that things stopped being peculiar and got awful instead. You wouldn't have expected it; things seemed to be just the way they usually were. Rebecca went to school, stopped by the post office on the way home, and got the mail. Rachel looked through it and handed her a letter from Molly.

"Didn't you see it?" she asked.

Rebecca shrugged. She still didn't feel comfortable about looking at the mail. It had been the only thing Dad had ever gotten really angry at her about. The letter smelled like Molly's cologne, and you could almost see her writing it, making circular dots over each i, and writing bigger than usual so any kid could read it. Didn't Molly realize if you could read Dad's handwriting, you could read anything?

"How's Molly doing?" asked Rachel, looking up from a long envelope.

Rebecca stared out the window. "The house is sold," she said. Her voice sounded a bit funny. "Molly's moving to Ben's place."

She felt a hand on her knee. "That doesn't mean she didn't care for your dad," said Rachel's voice.

Rebecca moved her knee, but she looked across the cab. Rachel must think . . . well, it was sort of nice of her, even though she didn't understand. "Oh, no, that part's fine. Ben's a nice guy. It's . . ." she gulped. "It's just the house."

Rachel's eyebrows went up a little, but she nodded after a moment. "I have a letter from Bob Jarvis here. He says to tell you he's going to send your dad's Dickens set to you, and anything else you'd like to keep. Is there anything?"

Rebecca thought of the beautiful pictures, the velveteen sofa, the antique diningroom table. No, all those lovely things would look dopey in Rachel's shabby house. The sofa would get dog hair on it, and the pictures would be all covered with cobwebs in no time. . . . "No, that's okay."

"Well, let me know if you change your mind. There's plenty of time to call."

At least the Dickens books were coming. All of a sudden, Rebecca felt as if she were sitting in Dad's study, looking at them. She blinked a couple of times and looked hard at the snowflakes that were starting to drift down out of the gray sky. Then she knew what she'd like to have. "Do you remember that oriental rug in Dad's study?"

That's when it happened.

"I've never seen the house," said Rachel shortly.

Rebecca stared at her. "You *haven't?* But I thought you lived there with Dad!"

Rachel started the pickup, roaring the motor much harder than she usually did. "Oh, no. We lived in a little cottage ten blocks down from the Mission. Your dad built the new house after we got divorced." Her voice had a nasty ring Rebecca had never heard before. "What we'd had wasn't enough—oh, no. There had to be a special castle for Prince Charming and his little princess."

Rebecca clenched her hands inside her mittens. "That's not so!"

"What's not so?"

"It isn't a castle! It's just a real nice house! And it's *clean,* too, and everything looks nice all the time. *Everybody* says how nice it is, when they come there . . . !" Rebecca felt tears burn down her face.

"Oh, I'm sure it *is* nice." Sarcasm practically dripped from Rachel's tongue. "He had to show the judge how rich he was, so he could keep you. Keep you away from everybody but dear, dear Daddy." She swung the pickup onto their road so fiercely that it skidded back and forth. Rebecca looked at Rachel's white, angry face and shrank to the other side of the cab. Maybe she'd stop now, since they were sliding around like this . . .

But Rachel didn't stop. "Good God! Can't you see what he *did* to you? He shut you up in a stucco and red-tile-roof cage, that's what! Did you have friends over to his castle?"

"Sure—he gave dinner parties almost every week!"

"But not for your friends!"

"His friends *were* my friends!"

"Sure, why share your princess with kids her own

age?'' Rachel took the big bump on the hill at killing speed. "And another thing! You don't dare look through the mail. Isn't that because he said you'd better not?''

Rebecca curled up as small as she could.

"Well, isn't it?''

Rebecca didn't like to think of the only time Dad had been this angry. Still. "Yeah. But that was because there might be important business stuff in it.''

"Since when do lawyers get business mail at home?''

She just wasn't being *fair!* "He didn't get his mail at home! He had a box in the post office, like yours!'' He'd gotten it after she'd looked through the mail and he'd been so angry, but Rachel didn't need to know that.

"Okay—a box. Were you allowed to open it?''

Rebecca looked out the window. She had just realized . . .

"Were you?''

Rebecca shook her head. If Rachel would only stop!

"And why do you think that was?''

Rebecca began to feel sick, the way she had that day at the post office, when the old woman had talked to Mrs. Ellrow. "I don't know.''

"It was just in case I'd disobeyed orders and tried to write to you! Why else would he care?''

"That's not true! You never wrote, anyway!'' Rebecca's voice choked her.

"How do you *know* I never wrote, if you never saw the mail?'' Rachel turned up the driveway. Rebecca's hand was on the door handle before the pickup had even stopped running.

"Hold it!'' snapped Rachel. "Did he let you answer the phone?''

"We . . . he had an answering service . . .''

‘‘So you never answered it when he wasn’t there—right?’’

Rebecca nodded. ‘‘Can I get out, now?’’

‘‘No, dammit!’’ exploded Rachel, smashing her hand down on the dashboard. ‘‘You stay right here in this truck until you see the *truth,* not some fairy tale Caleb Davidson made up for you to believe in!’’

Rebecca felt herself shaking all over, but her body didn’t seem to belong to her anymore. She’d felt this way when Mr. Jarvis told her Dad had died. . . .

Rachel turned and looked at her. ‘‘Take the Book Fairy, for example. Now, tell me who those books *really* came from. You must have figured it out by now. You almost told me two weeks ago.’’

Rebecca’s ears made tornadoes, thunderstorms, sirens as she looked across the cab to Rachel’s ferocious face. The Book Fairy! Her dearest, secret friend, who’d given her the stories she loved better than any others. The Book Fairy she’d talked to when Dad was in the hospital and Molly was working late. The Book Fairy . . . was . . . ‘‘You?’’ It must be true. *But Dad would have told me,* her mind insisted.

‘‘Sure, me. I never wrote in them. I never sent a letter. I would have been in all kinds of legal trouble if I had, since your dear daddy was just waiting for me to slip up. But I sent books to you, from me, and since they didn’t get sent back, I assumed you got them. It was the *only* way I could tell you I was thinking about you and trying to see you.’’ Her voice shook. ‘‘But even in my most spiteful, vindictive moments, I never even imagined he would unwrap them, search them for messages, and give them to you without telling you they were from me!’’ She turned away. ‘‘But he did.’’

‘‘He did n—!’’ Rebecca stopped. It was true. He’d

never let her unwrap the books. He'd never told her who sent them. He'd just brought them to her, and said they were from the Book Fairy. That meant. . . . The old woman in the post office suddenly said "Kidnapped!" right in her ear. She put her hand over it, but in the other ear, she heard Mr. Jarvis say, "Your dad had come home, paid the sitter, and . . . well, taken you for a little trip of his own."

"Excuse me," she said suddenly. She pushed the door open just before she threw up. There wasn't much *to* throw up, because she'd hardly eaten for weeks, but she retched and retched, leaning over in the driveway, trying to keep her hair out of the way.

When she finally finished, she stood up and leaned against the pickup, looking around dizzily. The barn was still there, leaning toward the road. The woodpile was still there, leaning toward the house. Far away, the sun hung low over blue, velvet-soft mountains, in a little break it had made in the gray sky. The only difference was that Rachel was standing right next to her.

She looked up, almost pleading. "Would it be okay if I went in and got myself a drink of water?"

Rachel looked off at the mountains. "Sure."

Rebecca moved away unsteadily, putting out her hand to balance herself on the truck.

"Becca . . ."

Oh, no! She just couldn't *take* any more of this!

"I'm very sorry, Becca. I really didn't mean to . . ."

Rebecca shook her head, then pushed herself off the truck like a swimmer at the end of a pool and walked all the way to the kitchen door without looking back. Tumnus and Xeno jumped all over her, but she shoved them away. First she walked to the bathroom and rinsed out her mouth. Then she went upstairs and looked at her bookcase.

The Book Fairy. She heard Rachel's furious voice buzz

in her ears: ''The *truth,* not some fairy tale Caleb Davidson made up for you to believe in . . .''

The Book Fairy. Kansas and Aunt Em. Narnia and Lucy. Hungary and Jansci. Dakota Territory and Laura. She pulled the books out one by one and stacked them carefully in the very very back of her closet. Then she lay on her bed and stared out the window, watching the light turn from blue to gray to black.

After a long time, the hall light went on and she heard footsteps coming up the stairs and then into her room. ''Becca . . .''

The footsteps stopped, and her light snapped on. When she got through blinking, she could see Rachel in the doorway, looking at the empty bookcase.

''What is it?'' said Rebecca

Rachel drew a deep breath. She had red rings around her eyes, and her cheeks were a bit puffy. ''Supper's ready.''

''I'm not hungry, thanks.''

''Come down, anyway. You might change your mind.''

So Rebecca followed Rachel down the steep stairway, into the kitchen, and to the table. During supper, neither of them said anything about the books. In fact, neither of them said anything at all.

Chapter 8

Things were pretty miserable for a couple of weeks after that terrible day. Rachel strode around with a gray, set face, looking as though she'd given up smiling for good. Rebecca wasn't feeling very smily herself. She tried not to think about what Rachel had said, but little things about life in Santa Barbara that hadn't made sense before kept coming back to her, and now they sort of did make sense. The mail. The answering service. Being driven to school and picked up, instead of going on the bus with the other kids. Having grownups for friends instead of kids. Some of those things had changed a little after Molly moved in, mainly because Molly hadn't thought they were important, and Dad had been so sick he'd lost track. She'd actually spent quite a lot of time at home alone when Dad was in the hospital. Had he known that? Maybe that's what the big row with Molly had been about, the day he came home from his first operation. Yeah, probably. After that, she'd had a sitter, which was so silly Molly had just left her at home alone after Dad . . . didn't come back.

There was no way around it: if Dad hadn't thought Rachel wanted to see her, he wouldn't have done all those things. Right? So maybe Mr. Jarvis *hadn't* been parading around the truth. But what didn't make sense was why Dad didn't want Rachel to see her, and why he was afraid she'd try. Rachel was pretty strange, but she was the kind of person who kept her promises. She'd never written or tried to call; she'd just sent . . . Rebecca decided not to think about it. It didn't fit in with the things she'd always thought about funny, joking Dad, with his books, his pipes, and his princess. Rebecca wished there were somebody she could talk to about it, but the Book Fairy wasn't around anymore, and Tumnus was too little to understand. Mr. Jarvis would have been the perfect person, but he was in California.

By the middle of February, things had gotten so bad that Rebecca decided she just *couldn't* stand it anymore. She'd run away—except she'd freeze in all the sleet, snow, and freezing rain that fell out of the perpetually gray sky. But then she discovered the barn. It started one dreary Saturday when Rachel got up from breakfast and put on her boots.

"Can I come?" Rebecca asked.

Rachel looked surprised, and no wonder. Rebecca hadn't gone out to the barn since the first day she'd been in Vermont. But she nodded, and Rebecca tagged along with her.

There turned out to be a lot to do. The horses needed hay and grain. They needed water in heavy buckets. Their stalls needed to be cleaned out. It took a long time. So that's why Rachel spent so much time outside! Well, it seemed sort of stupid to let her do all that work by herself.

"Could I brush Dimwit?" she asked Rachel, after they'd finished.

"Sure. She may die of shock, though. She hasn't been brushed since last fall." But Rachel put the big mare's halter on and led her to the crossties. Rebecca found a brush with stiff bristles, and took a few passes at Dimwit's flanks, where the worst dirt was.

"Start at the head," said Rachel. "That way, you don't brush dirt back on what you've already brushed."

That made sense. Rebecca got a box to stand on and went to work. Dimwit's long hair was all static, but after an hour, she looked pretty good. Rebecca looked around for Rachel, but she had gone. What was she supposed to do now? Well, she could lead Dimwit back to her stall; that wouldn't be too hard.

It wasn't. It was so easy, in fact, she decided to try brushing Mutt. She looked carefully at Dimwit's halter to see how it went, then tiptoed into Mutt's stall with the huge halter that hung outside the door. How was she going to reach way up there and put it on him? But he made it easy for her. He stuck his nose right into the loop where it went, then bent his head down so she could buckle it. He practically walked out to the crossties by himself.

"Nice monster," she said, patting him. She brushed and brushed, humming a little song, while he stretched out his neck and told her how good it felt. Why hadn't Amity let her do this at the stable in Santa Barbara? It was really fun! And suddenly she felt pretty proud to think that she could to it. Rachel must've known she could do it, too, because she'd left her on her own. Not like . . . well, other people, who hung over you every minute you tried something new, telling you what you were doing wrong.

After that, Becca spent almost every afternoon in the barn. She swept it. She cleaned the cobwebs off the rafters. She brushed all the horses but Dancer (Rachel said she'd better not try that, and she believed her). Things began to look pretty good out there; even Rachel said so.

Then, in the evenings, she curled up with Tumnus in her big chair and did her homework. That was because of Bill. Whenever she got a problem wrong in math, he gave her his creep-from-outer-space look, and she hated that.

He never got problems wrong himself, and he always knew all the vocabulary words in reading, so of course she had to get all the problems and vocabulary right, too, just to show him. That took an awful lot more work than she was used to putting into school, and it wasn't very satisfactory: he never noticed when she did stuff *right.* But anything was better than that look he gave her when she got something wrong, so she slogged away every night. It kept her out of Rachel's way, too.

Something interesting happened with Bill at the end of February. She'd left her book at home one day, and that meant she had nothing to do during recess but play relay races. Just the thought of running around with all those screaming kids made her sick, so she nipped into the library on her way to the gym. If Mrs. Standish noticed, she didn't say anything; she never got on your case if you didn't cause trouble.

''I need a book really quick,'' she told the librarian as she hurried in. ''I'm supposed to be in gym.''

The librarian smiled and pulled out a book from the middle of a stack on her desk. ''I've been saving this one for you,'' she said. Librarians were always friendly if you liked books. ''Have you read it?''

Beauty, by Robin McKinley. Becca shook her head.

''It's a fairy story, but one of the main characters is a horse,'' said the librarian, stamping the book out. ''You might show it to your mom. She likes to keep up on what's coming out, so she can send . . . though, of course, she doesn't need to do that anymore.''

''I'll be sure to show it to her.'' said Becca over her shoulder as she pushed the library door open. Did everybody in town know Rachel was the Book Fairy? It just wasn't . . . oooffff!

Somebody tore by her, knocking her against the wall.

"Bill! Come back here!" a man's voice shouted. It was Mr. Corey, the principal. Oh, no! And here she was in the hall during morning recess! But he just asked her if she was okay. Ahead of them, Bill turned around, but he didn't come back.

"You knocked this young lady over!" said Mr. Corey. "If you plan on going to gym, you'd better say you're sorry."

Becca watched Bill put his hands in his pockets and toss the hair out of his eyes. You really had to wonder about principals, sometimes. Anybody could see Bill would rather sit in the office all day than say he was sorry.

"It's okay," she heard herself say suddenly. "I was coming out of the library door, and he couldn't see me. I was right in his way."

Mr. Corey made a surprised noise. Bill looked at her for a moment, then dropped his eyes. "Sorry I ran into you," he muttered. Then he whirled around and dashed through the gym door.

Mr. Corey looked at Becca and raised his eyebrows. But all he said was, "How are things going, Becca? Settling in?"

She nodded.

"Mrs. Standish tells me you're doing seventh-grade work with Bill."

She nodded.

Mr. Corey scuffed his feet and jingled the change in his pockets. "You two get along okay?"

She shrugged. What was he getting at, anyway?

"You know," he said, tapping his fingers together, "Bill has had a real hard time. It'd sure be nice if he had somebody to talk to who was as good a student as he is."

She shrugged.

Mr. Corey pulled himself together. "Are you supposed to be in gym? Well, you'd better hurry."

No problem—she could hardly wait to get away. Inside the gym, she sat on the top row of bleachers and started in on *Beauty.* After a few pages, she could see it was going to be really good, so she resettled herself and looked around. Bill was standing in a corner, throwing a basketball against the wall as hard as he could. All by himself.

"Bill Lavoie apologized to you?" said Patty at noon recess.

"That's what I said." Becca felt sort of good about it.

"Wow! I can see those headlines now!" giggled Patty. " 'JD Falls in Love with Redhead!' "

"Shh!" Becca decided not to say any more about it. Sometimes you could tell Patty was twelve, almost thirteen. And that's what Mr. Corey didn't understand: if she and Bill even spoke to each other at school, all the kids would be putting up "Bill and Becca" hearts on the walls of the bathrooms. Which would be awful, since she didn't even like him.

But it was hard not to be interested in Bill. For one thing, he could draw. For another thing, he went places he shouldn't—or at least it looked like he did. He was on bus 4, but sometimes he didn't get on it after school. You weren't supposed to do that, but, well, nobody seemed to feel like hassling Bill about that or anything else. So when Rachel was late picking her up, sometimes Becca saw Bill hanging around, as if he were waiting for somebody. And if Rachel was really late, like more than five or ten minutes, Becca would see Bill walking across the icy playground toward the snowmobile path that led back into the woods. Nobody else seemed to notice, and Becca decided she'd keep it that way. She knew kids did drugs here as well as in California, and if you did drugs, you had to get them somewhere. But the school was really strict about it here; they had to sit through a "drugs are awful" lecture almost every week. So if Bill was getting something he shouldn't out there, he'd be in trouble if she said anything. She wasn't a squealer.

One day, though, Rachel was almost a half hour late, and when Becca stepped out the school door for the fiftieth time to look for the pickup, she heard the putt-putt-putt snowmobiles make when they slow down. She glanced in the direction of the sound just in time to see a snowmobile cut around the corner of the path and stop. Somebody in a red jacket stepped out from behind a maple and hopped on behind the driver—Bill! The snowmobile started up again, and in a second, it was gone. Becca shook her head. Maybe she should say something. But who should she say it to? Mr. Corey? No way. Mrs. Standish? Better not try.

She thought about it all the time she was cleaning stalls, then all through supper, then when she and Rachel were doing the dishes. (They did dishes every night now, instead of when they ran out of plates. She couldn't say just when that had started, but it did make the kitchen look nicer.) Rachel kept giving her funny looks, and that made her uncomfortable. It was hard to think, when somebody looked like they wanted to know what was on your mind. Molly had always been so busy and tired, she hadn't noticed when something was bugging you; Dad was so moody, you had to pay attention to what was on *his* mind if you didn't want to get snapped at. But it was awfully hard to put something past Rachel.

Becca sighed and flapped her dishtowel at Tumnus.

"Why don't you tell me what it is?" said Rachel.

Becca jumped. She couldn't remember when Rachel had said anything that wasn't a brief order or an answer to a question since that awful day she'd had to put the Book Fairy books in her closet.

"Oh, I was just thinking."

"Think away." Rachel shrugged and washed some forks.

She certainly couldn't tell Rachel about Bill, because . . . well, on the other hand, why not? She wouldn't have to tell her everything. And maybe Rachel would have an idea about how to keep Bill out of trouble. Rachel wasn't stupid, you could tell that; she was almost as smart as Dad, even though she wasn't nearly as nice.

"I was wondering what Bill's problem is," she said.

Rachel sloshed water over a plate. "Bill?"

"*You* know! Bill Lavoie, who's staying with the Amidens."

"Ah, yes. The unfortunate foster child. He has problems?"

She'd better be careful. "Well, he doesn't talk to any of the other kids, and he slouches around like he's angry at something. Kids don't act like that unless they have a problem."

A ghost of a smile flickered across Rachel's face, but it was gone before Becca could figure out why it was there. "Maybe he's just shy."

"No way! When we line up for lunch, he goes right to the front, and everybody just about bows to him. Even the teachers leave him alone, unless he's fighting. Remember how Patty said he beat up all those sixth-grade boys? But his pictures are really great. . . ." And before she knew it, she'd told Rachel all about the picture Bill had drawn of Phaeton the first day she'd been at school: how the horses seemed to be made partly of fire, and how the sun was attached to the chariot, and how Phaeton looked like a torch on his way down. "And he's done other pictures, too—he usually does them in social studies. Mrs. Stan[illegible] was going to take them away from him because he was[illegible] listening, but when she saw how good they are, she decided to let him do it. She tried to get him to show them to the class, but he wouldn't. He always says he tears them up when he's done."

"If he tears them up, how do you know they're wonderful?"

"Oh—he brings them to reading table to finish up, just in case he gets done faster than me. But I really hurry, so I can look at them."

"Maybe he brings them to the table so you can look at them," said Rachel.

"Never in the world . . . !" she began, but then she remembered that she'd seen a lot of Bill's pictures. He sort of left them around where she was. "Well, maybe," she amended.

"So you think his problem has to do with being artistic? You may be right. Guys around here are supposed to be good at logging, hunting, football, soccer—that sort of thing. Remember why Patty said those boys ganged up on him?"

"Sure. And I think he still fights with them, sometimes. Last week, he came to school with a great big bruise on his face."

Rachel wrung out the sponge with a snap. "A bruise? Has he had others?"

Becca thought about it. "Now and then." Maybe that's what he was doing in the woods. Fighting. But who would pick him up on a snowmobile, just to fight?

Rachel looked at her hard. "You promise you're telling the truth, with no additions or corrections?"

Fortunately, she hadn't said anything about omissions. "Yes."

Rachel let the water out of the sink. "Maybe I'd better have a chat with Ed Amiden."

Oh my gosh! Supposing Bill was really doing drugs or something? And supposing Rachel found out about it. Then it would be all her fault! "Maybe . . . maybe you could wait a bit. I mean . . ."

Rachel smiled with one corner of her mouth. "Don't worry. All I'll do is ask Ed if he and Bill can come over with the Clydesdales and help Mutt, Jeff, and me move some deadfalls before sugaring starts. If there's anything wrong, it'll probably come up."

Becca nodded. That sounded okay. But it was a good thing she hadn't said anything about the snowmobile.

That night, Becca heard Rachel talking on the phone after she went to bed. The next morning, the phone rang just as they were finishing breakfast. Rachel answered it, and when she came back, she looked the way Rachel looked when she'd finished something up.

"Brace yourself," she said.

Becca looked up from peanut butter and toast.

"Ed Amiden is coming up this afternoon to help me with those deadfalls. That means I won't be able to pick you up after school. So Mrs. Ellrow is going to do that. She'll bring you, Patty, and Bill up here and maybe sit a while so Patty can brush Goner."

Becca looked around the dirty kitchen. Patty didn't care about cobwebs and black refrigerator doors, but what about Mrs. Ellrow? Rachel pursed her lips as she followed Becca's glance. "Maybe I'd better clean things up a bit before she gets here," she said. "Well, jump into the truck. The faster I get going, the more I'll get done."

Becca scooted out to the pickup. They were going to have company? Rachel was going to clean? Amazing.

Chapter 9

Mrs. Ellrow was waiting for them at school, and Patty piled into the front door of the Chevy. That meant Bill and Becca had to share the back seat. Becca wasn't sure, but she thought there was a wicked grin on Patty's face when they got in.

''Hi, Becca. Hi, Bill,'' said Mrs. Ellrow. ''Good to see you.''

''It's awfully nice of you to give us a ride,'' said Becca politely.

Bill didn't say anything. Becca was *sure* Patty was grinning now; as they drove out of the parking lot, she felt herself beginning to blush. Bill slumped against the Chevy door, as far away from her as he could get.

''Still drawing, Bill?'' asked Mrs. Ellrow.

Bill pushed his forelock out of his eyes and looked out of the window. ''Some.''

''Patty says you draw very well. Ever take lessons?''

''Nope.''

That sort of capped conversation. They drove up the road in silence, and when they pulled into Rachel's driveway, Bill scooted out the door as fast as he could. ''Gotta help Ed now!'' he called over his shoulder. ''Thanks for the lift!'' In a second, he was over the wall and slogging up the steep track toward the maple grove.

Becca led the way toward the house, wondering how Mrs. Ellrow felt about dirt. But when she opened the door, she could hardly believe what she saw. Everything was *clean,* even the refrigerator door. The floor had no dog hair on it. Best of all, the whole kitchen smelled of coffee and . . .

"Doughnuts!" breathed Patty. "Oh, wow! *Look* at them!"

Mrs. Ellrow smiled at the plate of doughnuts on the clean tablecloth. "Well, it's nice to see Rachel is making doughnuts again," she said. "Her mother was famous for her doughnuts. Bake sales used to line her up months in advance. And of course she taught Rachel all her secrets, though she wouldn't give her recipe to anybody out of the family."

Becca bit into a doughnut. It was soft and puffy, with just the right amount of glaze on it. Mmmmm. "How come Rachel quit making these? Boy, if I could make something like this, I'd eat it for breakfast every single day!"

Mrs. Ellrow smiled the smile that always made you feel welcome when you got the mail. "Well, you know, I think she hasn't been terribly happy up here by herself. And when you're not happy, you let a lot go by that you'd look out for if things were going the way you'd like them to."

Becca chewed her doughnut slowly. You could get pretty lonely up here with just the animals, all right. Was that why the house looked so awful? Nope—it didn't seem likely. Rachel was just a slob, that was all.

"Bill shouldn't have run away so fast." Patty grinned at Becca. "He'd like these."

Mrs. Ellrow laughed and poured herself a cup of coffee. "Too many womenfolk. It's hard on a boy. My sons were the same way.'' She looked sad for a moment, and Becca remembered that Patty's dad had been Mrs. Ellrow's son.

''But is Bill just shy?'' she asked, partly to keep Patty and Mrs. Ellrow from thinking sad thoughts. ''The other kids won't sit next to him. Is there something wrong with his parents?''

''There's certainly nothing wrong with Ed and Mary Amiden!'' Mrs. Ellrow waved her doughnut emphatically. ''They're fine, hard-working people, and they've done good to more boys than I can think of.''

''No girls?'' asked Patty.

''Just boys. Ed needs help with the farm.''

''Do they have girls of their own?'' asked Becca.

''No. Seems they couldn't have youngsters of their own. Now, a lot of people just shut themselves up when that happens, but Ed said, if they couldn't raise their own, there were plenty of others around who needed help now and again. So they take boys nobody else'll take in.''

''Wow! And Bill is one of *those?*'' Patty's eyes were nearly as big as the doughnuts.

''I guess so, since he's there. But he seems a handsome, well-mannered boy, for all you say about him, Patty.''

Becca thought about the snowmobile. Maybe Bill really *did* have something to do with drugs. Maybe that was what was wrong with him, not just that he was an artist.

''Let's go out and brush Goner,'' said Patty.

''Sure,'' said Becca. ''Wait'll you see how I cleaned up the barn! You haven't been here for *ages* . . .''

''Well, it's hard to get somebody to drive me up here when the ring is just a skating pond,'' said Patty. ''But wait until spring! You'll have to chase me away with a longe whip!''

Becca giggled, and they ran outside, pulling on their mittens as they went. Becca looked back into the kitchen as she went by the window, and Mrs. Ellrow waved at her. It was sort of nice to have somebody here besides Rachel. Especially since it made Rachel clean the house.

After Patty and Mrs. Ellrow left, Becca decided she'd go up to the maple grove to see what was going on. There wasn't much to do in the house, and it was too early to get started on the stalls. So she stoked the stove, fastened her new boots tighter, and started up the steep hill along the horse trails. It was tough going; occasionally she fell through the crust and slowed herself down. By the time she was halfway to the top, she was puffing so hard she had to stop and catch her breath.

She turned around to see how far she'd come. There was the house below her. But from where she was, she could also see the hill sweep down into the valley, half a mile away. Beyond that, the neighbor's mowing rose steeply to his house—a tiny house, lost in the snow. In the distance, the mountains rose blue and gray into the winter sky. Becca sighed. It was hard to believe Vermont was in the same world as California. California was so bright: golden grass, dark green oaks, sandstone mountains without trees, silver beaches and dark waves, thousands of flowers blooming in different colors. Here there were no colors—only shades of gray, with a black spruce wood here and there.

Above her, she heard a shout and the clank of a chain; she shook herself and struggled up the rest of the path. Xeno and Tumnus bounded down to meet her, and in a moment she saw Rachel driving Mutt and Jeff along the ridge. The horses were bent forward, their heads down, as they pulled a huge log. Behind them, Rachel leaned back a little, taking long strides to keep up with them. For just a second, Becca thought of Molly and the slim, delicate way she moved. . . .

Rachel stopped the horses and waved. When Becca slogged up to them through the snow, she saw Mutt and Jeff were panting as hard as she was.

"You and Patty get Goner brushed?" asked Rachel.

"Yeah. Oh—and the doughnuts were terrific."

Rachel looked kind of pleased. "Hope you ate lots. It's going to be a while before dinner. Ed's going to have to leave the team here—it took us longer than we thought, and it's going to be dark soon. This is my last load. Why don't you go watch Ed? It's the kind of show most people pay money to see, only better. Most drivers holler at their horses, but Ed talks to his like a lover."

"Uh—can't I help you instead?"

"Not until I get the team down to the barn, and that's not for half an hour or so. Go along and look."

Rachel clucked, and the team plodded along the track. Becca turned the other way reluctantly. Even helping Rachel sounded good compared to watching Bill work. She wondered how far away Mr. Amiden's team was.

Not very far, it seemed. She could hear shouting after just a few yards. She rounded a corner and stopped short. The horses! They were twice the size of Mutt and Jeff, and completely black. A handful, too: they were prancing in place as the man driving them stopped and looked over his shoulder at a log that was stuck in the trail. Becca stepped closer, her eyes wide open. These were the kind of horses Apollo must have used to tow the sun around the world each day.

The man driving looked around and saw her. "Stay clear now!" he shouted. She nodded, looking around and wondering where "clear" might be.

‘‘Over there!’’ Bill pointed to a stump, and Becca climbed onto it.

‘‘Okay!’’ said Mr. Amiden. Bill picked up the chain that was attached to the horses’ harnesses and walked toward the log, while Mr. Amiden backed the team. The horses began to dance; Becca could feel the rhythm of their bucket-sized feet from where she sat.

‘‘Whoa, now,’’ crooned Mr. Amiden. The horses stopped, trembling. Bill fastened the chain and jumped aside.

‘‘Git, now,’’ called Mr. Amiden. His voice was so soft Becca could hardly hear it, but the horses jumped forward together, heads down, flanks heaving, feet sending cascades of snow out behind them. Still the log didn’t budge.

‘‘Whoa, there! Baaaack, baaaack, eeeeeasy . . .’’ crooned Mr. Amiden. Foam floated out of the horses’ mouths, and they tucked their chins to escape the bits. Suddenly one of them uncoiled his neck and reared, backing up on his hind legs.

‘‘Eeeeeeeasy, there!’’ called Mr. Amiden. The horse thundered down on its front legs, snorting. Mr. Amiden nodded at Bill, and Bill jumped on the log to undo the chain.

Freed from the log, the horses jumped forward, and it took Mr. Amiden a minute to collect them. He ran behind them as they trotted in a circle near Becca’s stump. She could see the muscles rippling under their shaggy winter coats as they pounded by, snorting.

‘‘Try it from the other side!’’ called Bill, who had been looking carefully at the log. Mr. Amiden nodded and drove them through some deep snow. Their trot turned into a bound and a plunge.

‘‘Whoa!’’ Bill caught the left horse under the bit and led the team close to the log at a walk. Mr. Amiden nodded at him, and he jumped back onto the log, ready with the chain. The horses were sweating now; clouds of steam rose from their huge bodies as Mr. Amiden backed them toward the log.

"Whoa!" crooned Mr. Amiden. They stopped. Trembled. Waited. Becca dug her fingernails into her palms. Bill linked the chain and jumped back over the log.

"Git!" Again they jumped forward, their huge bodies leaning over their forelegs, pulling, pulling. . . . The log gave a little.

"Whoa!" Mr. Amiden almost whispered. He backed up the horses ever so slightly, and Becca could see their muscles tighten.

"GIT!" The shout tore through the gray air. The horses jumped, strained, pulled, their heads bent down to their knees, hooves tearing the snow. . . . The log jiggled, creaked—and suddenly broke loose in a swish of snow and ice.

"Got it!" yelled Bill.

Becca stood up on her stump. She wanted to cheer; she wanted to cry. They got it! They got it!

"Okay, Bill," said Mr. Amiden. "Let's fix this chain so we kin git the log down to the sugar house. It's gittin' dark."

Bill galloped over to the team, and Becca walked toward them more slowly. The horses were standing still now, breathing hard.

"May I pat them?" she asked Mr. Amiden.

Mr. Amiden wiped his sweating face on the sleeve of his lumber jacket. "Sure."

Shyly, Becca raised her hand toward the neck of the horse that had reared. It swung its head around so it could see her, and she scratched its face under the bridle, where Mutt liked being rubbed. This horse liked it too: it bobbed its head up and down. Reaching into her pocket, she found some leftover sugar lumps and gave it one. The other horse looked over and nickered.

"Better give her one, too," grinned Mr. Amiden.

Her! Who would have thought a horse this strong was a mare! Becca crossed in front of the first horse and gave the mare a sugar lump and a scratch.

"Okay—all set!" said Bill. "Can I drive?"

Becca expected Mr. Amiden to say no: no kid could drive horses as big and spirited as these. But Mr. Amiden just nodded and gave Bill the reins. "Take it nice an' slow, he said. "They're bushed."

Becca watched Bill wrap the reins around his hands. "Yeah," she said suddenly. "If you mess things up, Zeus'll hit you with a thunderbolt."

Bill looked at her blankly a minute—then recognition flashed in his eyes. Becca couldn't believe it. A grin! Bill could grin!

The horses started down the hill, plodding quietly. Becca looked at Mr. Amiden as he watched them go. He was shorter and squarer than she'd thought he was when she'd watched him drive—not like Apollo at all. His sandy hair was cut short, and his eyes were such a light blue that they almost disappeared in his face. He smiled at her a little shyly.

"You Becca?"

She nodded. "Your team is beautiful."

"They work good," he said, starting down the hill. She trotted after him, thinking it would be hard to find somebody who was more different from Bill. Bill looked like Mr. Amiden's team just before they pulled the log—kind of bunched up and tense. Next to them, Mr. Amiden looked . . . well, tame.

By the time they got down to the barn, Rachel had the

lights on, and she was rubbing Jeff down. "Get it?" she asked.

Mr. Amiden nodded, and Becca bobbed her head enthusiastically.

"What a team!" said Rachel, shaking her head and smiling. "There's no other team in the county that can break out a log that size."

Mr. Amiden shuffled his feet and stuck his hands in his pockets. "They're good workers," he said.

"Sure," said Rachel, grinning. "And they have one heck of a driver."

Becca had never seen a man blush before. It was almost funny, though she didn't laugh, of course. But here Mr. Amiden could handle huge, plunging horses and boys nobody else would take on, and he blushed like a little kid when somebody paid him a compliment. She wondered, just for a second, what Dad would say about Mr. Amiden. Dad always said the only way to take on difficult people was to meet them head-on and fight them to a standstill. Mr. Amiden didn't seem to work that way.

Outside, she heard hoofbeats on the road, and in a moment Bill brought the huge team to the door. Mr. Amiden and Rachel unhitched them; then Bill swaggered into the barn. "I'm going to walk one dry. You can walk the other one—if you're not scared to."

He was just waiting for her to say no, so he could crow over her. But walk one of those horses? I mean, brushing Mutt and Jeff was okay, but these horses were much bigger, and she'd seen the way they carried on. . . .

Bill gave her his creep-from-outer-space look and stepped outside. "She's too scared," he said scornfully.

"Well," said Rachel, "she's led a pretty sheltered life. Give her some time."

Sheltered life! Becca hurried out into the twilight. "I'm not either scared! I was just putting on my mittens."

She took a deep breath and picked up the huge mare's lead rope. "C'mon, old girl," she said, doing her best to imitate the tone of voice Rachel used with Dancer. It sounded better when your voice wasn't shaking. But the mare stepped off at a gentle, plodding walk, and they followed Bill and the gelding down the road, turning where they turned, and walking back toward the barn. Becca reached up and patted the black, sweaty neck. "Good girl."

After two more turns, Bill waited at the barn and walked up and down the road next to her. Neither of them said anything, but Becca felt good. Bill couldn't very well treat her like a creep now, could he?

"You drive real well," she said, after four or five turns. "Wish I could."

"You could learn."

"Do you really think so?"

"Sure. All you have to do is not be scared. You'd do okay after you got the hang of it."

Maybe that was a compliment. Becca decided not to press her luck by talking anymore. It was too cold, anyway; they walked up and down forever, and she was half frozen by the time Mr. Amiden called them into the barn.

"Okay, gang," said Rachel when the big horses were settled in the straight stalls at the end of the barn, "into the pickup."

"We kin walk," said Mr. Amiden.

"Don't be silly! You've been working all day, and it's getting colder by the minute."

Becca saw Mr. Amiden look at Bill; she could see Bill was really hoping for a ride. "Okay. Thanks."

It was a tight squeeze with four of them in the pickup, and nobody said anything until they drove up a long driveway. The house at the top of the hill was small, but it was all lit up, and it looked cozy. Across the driveway, the huge barn loomed against the stars, straight and square, not at a dangerous angle like Rachel's barn. Rachel switched off the engine, and Becca thought she was going to say something about how great the place looked, but instead she said, "Bill, Becca tells me you've drawn some interesting pictures. Would you show them to me?"

As Mr. Amiden opened the door and the cab light went on, Becca saw how pleased Bill was. But Mr. Amiden looked embarrassed. "Go fetch them, Bill," he said.

Bill slid off the torn seat and raced inside. Mr. Amiden shuffled his feet. "He gits into a peck of trouble over his pictures," he said. "I don't like to git in the way of talent, or anything, but a man's got to do somethin' besides fiddle around with crayons and paper."

"What about Michelangelo?" said Becca.

Rachel raised her eyebrows; Mr. Amiden looked shy again. "He was one of them old painters, wasn't he? Well, maybe things were different back then, but these days, a boy with nothin' behind him has to . . ."

"Here they are!" Bill slid up to the pickup over the ice and handed Rachel a sheaf of papers. The Phaeton picture was on top, and some of the others he'd done in school were farther down. Becca looked at Bill. He hadn't torn them up, after all.

Rachel bent over the pictures, slowly looking at one after another in the feeble cab light. "These are excellent, Bill," she said, not the way grownups said kids' pictures were good, but the way they said books or concerts or plays were good. "You must have a good teacher."

Becca had been looking at Bill, thinking how different he looked when he was thinking about his pictures. But when Rachel mentioned a teacher, he threw his head up and stared at her with wide, scared eyes, like a horse that had seen something terrifying. Rachel noticed (Rachel noticed everything), but Mr. Amiden answered before she could say anything.

"He's had no lessons since he's come here. Before that, he was at Westminster. I think he's jist done it on his own."

"Westminster?" asked Becca.

Rachel nudged her hard, but Bill spoke up. "It's a home for JDs," he growled. "No drawing lessons there, you can bet."

The house door opened, and a square woman's figure stood framed in the light. "Bill!" she called. "Didn't you say you were gittin' firewood?"

"Right there!" said Bill. He shot off across the driveway as if he could hardly wait to get away from the pickup.

Mr. Amiden grinned. "Bashful," he said, just as if he weren't bashful himself.

"Talented, though," said Rachel. "What do you know about his background?"

"The usual. Dad drinks, mom's dead. Eleven foster homes, and he run away from all of 'em. So the authorities rounded him up an' slapped him into Westminster. But he busted out of there, and finally they asked us if we'd take him on."

"It's a good thing for him you did," said Becca.

Mr. Amiden looked bashful again. "It's nothin', really. You jist got to give 'em a little rein, that's all. You can't tie up the ones with git-up-an'-go for very long if you want 'em to work out right."

"Has he given you any trouble?" asked Rachel.

"Not to speak of. A little orneriness now an' then, a couple of fights. It's them pictures he fights about. I don't go for it, and Mary cried like a baby when she seen him. But if he's goin' to draw, he's goin' to have to stand up for himself. So I didn't say much, except to give him a few pointers on keeping his weight behind his fist."

"Sounds like a good boy," said Rachel. "He need money?"

Mr. Amiden grinned. "You givin' some away?"

Rachel grinned too. "Nope. I need a stable boy. Becca and I spend all afternoon cleaning stalls. He do anything special after school?"

"Nothin' much. Comes home on the bus, starts in on chores before Mary an' I git home. He'd probably be glad to earn some money in good company." Mr. Amiden threw Becca a glance that made her squirm.

"Well," said Rachel, "we'll let you go to dinner. Ask him. If he wants to work, I can pick him up at school when I get Becca. When he's done, I can bring him over here. It's not far."

"Might be jist the thing," said Mr. Amiden, pushing back his hat. "He's been a bit moody lately. Cabin fever, most likely."

"It gets to all of us," said Rachel. She started the pickup. "Thanks for the help, Ed. See you tomorrow morning."

They drove down the driveway, and Becca looked out at the valley below them and the mountains that loomed black against the moonlit sky. She was thinking about the snowmobile. It wasn't Mr. Amiden's. He thought Bill was coming straight home.

"You were sure right about those pictures, Becca," said Rachel. "What a talent!"

"No lessons, either," said Becca, trying not to feel resentful.

"I wouldn't count on that," said Rachel.

"But he *said*—!"

"Sure he said. And he looked scared when he said it. There's something he doesn't want us to know."

That was true; she knew it was true. But how had Rachel figured it out? "Taking lessons doesn't seem to be something he'd be scared about," she said.

"Depends on where he got the money to pay for them," said Rachel shortly, "or what he had to do in exchange for them."

Becca felt a little shiver zip down her spine.

"But of course, it may be all over," said Rachel. "And even if it isn't, if he works for me, he won't be able to get into trouble after school, will he?"

"You think he is?" said Becca.

"I wouldn't venture to guess," said Rachel. "But a little supervision won't hurt. Especially if it comes along with some good art paper and pastels."

"You mean, he's going to draw at our house?"

"If he wants. If we leave him alone."

"That's kind of neat."

"Merciful heavens!" said Rachel. "A compliment! You're letting your guard down, Becca."

Becca strained her eyes in the darkness, but she couldn't see Rachel's face. Well, she'd just let the whole thing pass. She wasn't quite sure what Rachel meant, anyway.

Chapter Ten

Bill did come, every day. He wasn't exactly company; he cleaned the stalls and then disappeared upstairs into the spare room with his paper and pastels. Still, just having somebody around made it easier to live with Rachel. She gave them orders in the pickup on the way home from school, so you didn't have to try to make conversation. And she wasn't around much, because somebody else did the work. Sometimes Patty came along too, and then, of course, there wasn't any problem about talking.

Things went pretty well until it began to get warmer. One day it went up to fifty degrees, which wasn't warm by California standards, but it sure was after three months of Vermont winter. And the horses seemed to think it was going to stay warm. When Becca and Patty groomed them, hair fell to the floor in huge currycombfuls and blew out the open barn door.

"Sugaring time!" sang Patty, watching the circling clouds of horse fur.

Bill nodded from the stall he was cleaning. "That's what Ed said this morning," he said.

"Oboy!" Patty's eyes gleamed as they met Becca's. "Sugaring time! That means riding season is right around the corner!"

That was good news, all right, but Becca didn't feel

quite so happy as she might have. For one thing, there was nobody to take riding lessons from but Rachel, and she wasn't sure she wanted to do that. For another, Rachel had told her that when sugaring started, Ed Amiden would help out, and she and Bill would have to take the bus to the bottom of the hill and walk up the road, instead of getting a ride all the way home from school. It had sounded fairly awful.

It *was* awful. The day after the taps were in and the buckets were hung, they took the bus home and got out at the same time. All the kids laughed and pointed at them. Bill started off at a swinging walk without even looking over his shoulder, and Becca was fifteen feet behind him before she knew it. She ran to catch up with him, but pretty soon he was pulling ahead again. She ran a few more steps and tried to match her strides to his, but the ruts made that hard to do. As for him, he didn't even notice she was having trouble. Why couldn't he just—?

"Could you walk a bit slower?" she puffed.

Bill stopped. When she caught up, he lifted first one foot, then the other, slowly out of the ruts, setting each one down *very* carefully.

"Not that slow!"

He sped back up, going even a bit faster.

"Bill!"

He sighed and slowed down to his crawl again. Okay. If that was what he wanted, she'd crawl, too. They inched along, side by side, not looking at each other. After a few minutes, he began to go just a bit faster.

"You going to draw today?" she asked. Maybe if she got him talking about his pictures, he'd quit being such a pain.

"Probably not," he growled.

Wow! He was even worse than usual. Becca looked out

over the brown and white valley as they came to the top of the hill. Black clouds were beginning to cover the mountains, and a wet breeze wafted by her face. "Looks like snow," she said.

Bill shook his forelock out of his eyes and looked. "Rain, more likely," he grunted.

They started down the hill, picking their ruts carefully. Becca found she could keep up now. Either Bill was going slower, or it was easier walking downhill. Anyway, he was only two or three strides ahead of her the rest of the way.

When they got to the house, Bill marched off to the sugar grove, and Becca went in. Tumnus was wild to see her; probably he'd been shut in all day. She let him out for a second, then whistled him back for a biscuit. He sat and begged while she held it up, and one of his ears cocked up straight. Rachel said she thought both ears would stand up, but Becca sort of hoped they wouldn't. He looked cute lopsided.

Tumnus crunched his biscuit. Becca unwound a sweet roll and licked the cinnamon off it thoughtfully while she lifted a cat off the pile of mail on the table. There was a letter in Molly's writing, addressed to her, and not opened. You mean Rachel hadn't . . . ? Of course not. Rachel left your stuff alone. Becca pushed the rest of that thought away and tore the envelope open.

Out fell three pictures—wedding pictures. Why, Molly had gotten married to Ben! The letter said they were really happy, and they were moving to Seattle. There was an address, in case she wanted to write. Becca sat down and, stroking the cat with her unsticky hand, looked at Molly. She looked like a photo out of *Bride* magazine—so pretty she hardly seemed real. Especially when you'd been in Vermont and had gotten used to seeing ordinary-looking people, wearing boots and dungarees. She stared at Ben and Molly. Had she really known them? They looked different. Well, not completely different, but . . .

The door whooshed open, and Tumnus jumped to his feet, barking.

"Hush, dog!" said Bill. Tumnus started wiggling all over. He really liked Bill; horses and dogs always seemed to. "Becca, it's raining, and Rachel says you have to come up and help get in the last buckets."

Bill was shivering as he bent over to pat Tumnus. His jacket was soaked through, and his hair was pasted down over his eyes. Becca got up, dumping the cat on the floor.

"Be right with you," she said. She pushed the plastic bag of sweet rolls in his direction and hurried up the steep stairs. What about those old clothes Mrs. Ellrow had brought last week? Some of them had been boys' clothes, too big and too stripy for her. Patty had said they'd belonged to her cousin John. There they were! She pulled on one of her own sweaters, grabbed a brown turtleneck and striped sweater from the bag, and hurried down the stairs again.

Bill was standing next to the stove, shivering and eating a sweet roll. "Here," said Becca, trying to sound like Rachel. "Put these on so you won't freeze while we're out there. I think there's an extra poncho in the closet." She zipped out of the kitchen before he could say anything and rummaged around in the hall closet. Good! Two ponchos and an extra down vest. Now, if he'd only . . .

When she stepped back into the kitchen, he was pulling the sweater over his head. She tried not to look smug as she handed him the poncho and the vest. Then she gave the stove more wood, adjusted the damper, and started pulling on her boots.

"What's wrong?" she asked as she zipped her parka. Bill was staring at her.

"Nothing," he muttered. "You better hurry."

"*I'd* better hurry! What about you?"

"I'm not going up there," Bill said. He was leaning over to tie his boots, so she couldn't see his face. "I've got to help Ed down in the sugar house, then do stalls. So it's your funeral up on the hill."

She made a face at him and started out the door. What made him so *awful?* she wondered, as she slogged up the hill through the sodden snow. It just wasn't fair. People who could draw beautifully were supposed to be *nice,* like their pictures. Well, Rachel had said that wasn't true, but it ought to be.

In the maple grove, Rachel looked wet and tired, and Mutt and Jeff looked positively forlorn; they hardly even raised their heads when Becca patted them. She reached into her pockets and found a yesterday's carrot for each of them: not much crunch left, but the horses didn't seem to care.

"Where's Bill? You lose him in a puddle?" Rachel asked.

"Why, he said he was supposed to help Ed in the sugar house, then clean stalls."

"Yeah? Well, maybe Ed told him this morning. That leaves the last collections for you and me. Look: you unhitch the bucket here, see? Then you pour the sap into this bucket with a handle, then you carry the whole works to the sledge and dump it. Got that?"

It sounded easy enough, but it wasn't. First of all, the snow was deep, and the rain had softened the crust so you went in up to your thighs every couple of steps. And then the sap buckets were hard to undo without spilling. Next you had to wade back through your tracks, carrying the bucket, but your tracks weren't always where you needed them. What a lot of work, just so you could have something to pour on your pancakes Sunday mornings!

Becca waded, dumped, and hauled for almost an hour. Rachel was doing two trees to her one, of course; you could never keep up with Rachel. When they met at the sledge after a while, Rachel took the bucket out of her aching hands and dumped it for her. "See the letter from Molly?"

"Yeah." Becca shook her arms. "And guess what? She got married to Ben, that guy she was dating."

"For heaven's sake!" Rachel looked at her the way she'd looked last time they'd talked about Molly. She seemed to want to say something, but then she changed her mind. "She a pretty bride?"

"Gorgeous—wait'll I show you." But then she remembered what had happened the last time she'd gotten a letter from Molly, and a perfectly normal conversation had turned into . . . She picked up her bucket and trudged through the snow, wondering if Rachel remembered.

Wade, dump, pour. Wade, dump, pour. It was sort of foggy, and the trees looked like giants, spreading their bare arms out over the snow. All of a sudden Becca ached for the way Santa Barbara smelled in the fog: ocean, wet fennel, eucalyptus. Oh, it was pretty here, all right, even in the rain, with all these ancient trees around. Maybe they were Ents . . . ; no, she wasn't supposed to think of the Book Fairy books any more. She put down her bucket and swung her stiff arms again. But Vermont was so *different.* Even when it was pretty, it wasn't pretty the right way.

"A penny for your thoughts, Becca," said Rachel, lifting her bucket.

"I was thinking about the way California smells in the fog."

"Yeah," said Rachel. "Wet acacia. Fennel. Spices."

Why, she had liked living there, after all! Becca looked at her and smiled. "Mr. Jarvis gives me a whole quarter for my thoughts."

"Price of thought is high in California," said Rachel. "That's because there's no sugaring to do."

"Huh?"

"Sugaring is miserable—right? So you sort of dream off when you do it. Sometimes you do your best thinking when you're sugaring. In California, that never happens—the weather's too good."

Becca slogged to the next tree. That was the problem with Rachel: she *liked* it here. California just didn't mean anything to her at all, even though she'd lived there with . . .

Becca unhitched the bucket from a tree, but there was nothing in it to speak of. The next tree was just the same.

"Rachel?"

Rachel dumped a bucket of sap in the tank. "What is it?"

"There's nothing in these."

"Great! That means we're done!" Rachel wiped the rain out her eyes. "You're a demon worker, you know that? Hop on, and I'll give you a lift back to the sugar house. Okay, Mutt. Git." The horses started down the track, and Becca grabbed the edge of the seat to steady herself.

"Do you think Bill does his best drawing when he's sugaring or cleaning stalls? Or does he just . . . well, fold in on himself?"

Rachel looked at her. "Don't miss a trick, do you?"

"But which is it, do you think?"

"Well, you don't draw pictures like Bill's unless you're working away on them somewhere in your mind . . ."

Becca nodded.

"But other times—well, something's bugging him. Ed's worried."

"What about?"

"I'm not sure. But I can see he's worried. I dare say he's seen boys go wrong before—he probably knows the symptoms. Well, maybe they'll talk it out. You said Bill was going to the sugar house, didn't you?"

"That's what *he* said."

But when they got to the sugar house, Bill wasn't there; Mr. Amiden was all by himself.

"Bill?" he said over the roar of the fire. "He was here a while ago, but then he left. Thought he was with you."

"He probably went back to clean stalls," said Becca. "That's what he said he was going to do."

"That so?" Mr. Amiden frowned, and Rachel watched him. But then she smiled and handed Becca a cup of something warm. "Drink this," she said. "It'll take the chill out of your bones." The chill was already nearly out of her bones: the sugar house was deliciously hot and steamy. But she was thirsty. She took a sip of whatever it was in the cup, but it was so hot she couldn't tell what it was. She took another sip, then a big swallow. Omigosh! Sweet! She sniffed it. Syrup! She was drinking straight maple syrup! She looked at Mr. Amiden, who was watching her out of the corner of his eye.

"Am I supposed to be able to drink *all* this?" she asked.

He grinned. "Only if you're made of steel inside."

"Here—let me try," said Rachel. She took a deep breath and swallowed. "Whooof!" she sputtered, shaking her head. "I always forget from year to year."

"Should've brought pickles an' saltines," said Mr. Amiden.

"And water," said Rachel. "Okay, Becca. Ed and I

have to finish up here. Will you drive the team back to the barn?''

Becca froze, in spite of the fire and steam. ''But . . . but I've only driven them twice before!''

Rachel frowned. ''Well, I was going to have Bill do it, but he's back at the barn. *Somebody* has to get them there, and they know the way. Just give them room to turn around, and they'll practically take themselves home. Bill will help you unhitch. Okay?''

It wasn't okay. She really didn't know what she was doing. She threw a pleading look at Mr. Amiden.

''Rachel . . .'' he began.

''Oh, come off it, you two!'' snapped Rachel. ''It's not like Mutt and Jeff are hard to handle. There's only so long you can coddle a country kid.''

That did it. Becca slipped out the door and climbed onto the wet sledge. The poor horses *did* look forlorn; they were shivering. It was high time they got back to the barn. She picked up the reins and wrapped them around her hands the way Bill did. ''Git!''

The horses started back to the barn at a fast walk. Well, so far, so good. Still, you had to wonder about Rachel. It was always the same. One minute, she was fun, drinking syrup out of a cup; the next, she got angry and said you'd been coddled. Other people were the same all the time. Why couldn't Rachel be like that?

It was nearly dark when she drove the team up to the barn, but no lights were on. She halted the horses and jumped off the sledge.

''Bill!''

Tumnus barked inside the house, but there was no other noise except the jingle of the horses' bits. ''Bill! Bill!''

Her voice echoed off the house. Jeff stamped impatiently. Where could Bill be? She called once more, but there was no answer.

Well, what should she do? It was too dark to drive back to the sugar house, and she wasn't sure she could turn the horses around in such a small space, anyway. Maybe she could unhitch them herself. She'd helped Rachel a couple of times. That was with the manure cart, though. Was this the same?

She inspected the harness as well as she could in the near-dark and decided it was more or less the same. You undid this buckle, then this one, then this one—there. That looked okay. She stepped back and picked up the reins. "Git!"

The horses moved away from the sledge . . . wait! wait! There was a little piece still attached! "Whoa!"

But the horses didn't want to whoa; they wanted their grain. Becca pulled on the reins, but she had too much slack. Before she even felt any contact, the sledge lurched forward, hitting Jeff on the hocks. He jumped forward, and Mutt jumped with him. The sledge jolted, wavered, then slid sideways. Becca felt a thud as it knocked her over. She pulled on the reins from where she lay, but the horses dragged her . . . then stopped as the sledge crashed against a telephone pole that was next to the barn.

"Whoa!" called Becca, scrambling to her feet. But when the sledge got stuck, the horses went wild. First one, then the other lunged forward, and Jeff began to rear and strike.

"Bill!" screamed Becca. Where was he? They'd hurt themselves!

But then she remembered yelling only made horses harder to handle. What would Mr. Amiden do? Oh, yeah. "Eeeeasy, eeeasy," she said, her voice shaking. "Easy, now, Mutt." The horses kept flailing, but she saw Mutt's ears shoot forward. Maybe if she got a bit closer to their heads . . . She inched forward, talking as soothingly as she could. "Don't be silly you big, stupid idiots. It's just stuck on a telephone pole . . . you can't move it . . . if you hold still, I'll unhitch that last little bit, there . . ."

She felt tears mix with the rain that ran down her face. "Eeeasy, now . . ." Was she soothing the horses or herself? Shaking, she reached up and grabbed Mutt's reins as close to his head as she dared, which wasn't very close. "Easy now . . ." Mutt stopped thrashing and pranced instead, his eyes ringed with white. On the far side, Jeff settled down a little bit, too.

"Back, now, baaack . . ." If she could just get them to back up one step, she could get that buckle loose. "Good boys. Now. WHOA."

They stopped, shaking. Would they stay that way? Because if they started up again while she was between them and the sledge . . . She did it, wiping the stupid tears out of her eyes. The buckle was wet and stubborn: she had to shove and shove to get it undone, and her hands were so cold . . . There. The tongue dropped to the ground between the horses. Jeff jumped, snorting, but Mutt held steady.

"Okay, kids!" she quavered, trying to make herself sound cheerful. "Let's go. Easy . . ." They jumped forward, but when they found nothing got in their way this time, they settled down into a trot. Becca pulled on the reins, running behind them over the slippery road, but they only slowed down a little. Fortunately, they turned right toward the barn, and the door was shut, so they had to stop.

Becca opened the door a crack and turned on the light. She was just pushing the door the rest of the way open when something slipped around the corner of the barn. A person. Bill.

"Where have you *been?*" she shouted. "The sledge got stuck over there, and the horses just went *wild*. . . ." She was crying hard, now—much harder than she had been when everything had been going wrong at once.

Bill stepped into the patch of light. "I . . . just . . ."

"Bill! What happened to your . . . !"

"Shhh!" Bill put his hand over the side of his face. It was red and terribly swollen, with a nasty gash bleeding at the top of the swelling. He took a few steps toward the team, but she could see he was dizzy.

"Just open the door," she said. Whatever it was could wait; the horses were starting to stamp and fuss. He did open it, and she drove the team in. She untacked Mutt, and Bill led Jeff into his stall. Neither of them said anything. She was crying awfully hard still, and Bill . . . well, if he hadn't been a boy, he'd have been crying, too. When she got Mutt rubbed down and went to help Bill with Jeff, he hadn't made much progress. He was sort of leaning against the wall, shaking.

Outside, she heard voices. Rachel! She looked at Bill; he'd heard them too. "P-p-please, Becca . . ." He shivered.

"Good God! What happened here?" Rachel's voice hardly sounded like Rachel at all.

"Becca!" yelled Mr. Amiden's voice. "Becca? Bill?"

Oh boy, they were in for it now. "In here!" she called squeakily.

She heard their boots run across the barn floor. "Oh my God!" said Rachel, looking at the two of them. Becca's awful tears started up again, and she looked through them at Bill. If she said he hadn't been there when the whole thing happened, they'd know something was up. Maybe Mr. Amiden would send him back to that home for JDs. She swallowed hard.

Mr. Amiden's hand fell on her shoulder and kind of stroked her. "Kin you tell us what happened, Becca?"

"Well . . ." she began, "I got the team back, and we started to unhitch. Only it was awful dark, and my fingers were cold, and . . . I missed a little buckle on my side. They bolted, and the sledge knocked Bill over and hit the pole . . . but I don't think it was going very fast . . . the harness is okay . . ." She gulped. "I'm sorry."

"Sorry!" said Rachel. "Sorry! They could have killed you!"

Mr. Amiden left Becca and gently examined Bill's swollen face. "Got a real wallop, there, didn't you, son? You're goin' to have a shiner tomorrow, that's for sure." He turned back to Becca. "How'd you git 'em loose?"

"Well . . . I kind of talked to them, like you do, you know—nice and easy—and I got as close to their heads as I dared."

Rachel buried her face in her hands.

"And after a bit, they settled down just a little. So I backed them up and undid the piece."

Rachel was shaking her head. "My God, my God," she whispered.

"That warn't too safe," said Mr. Amiden. "Supposin' they'd . . ."

"Yeah, I thought of that." Becca quavered. "But I didn't know what else to do. Bill was . . . having trouble getting up, and I couldn't just *leave* them there."

Bill threw her a look that made her feel as if the whole thing might have been worthwhile. But Mr. Amiden was bending over Rachel. "Now, now," he said in exactly the same tone he'd used when his horses were excited. "She's okay, and he'll mend fast enough, and the horses are okay, an' there's no harm done. Don't take on so."

Becca stared. Rachel was crying! Rachel, who drove a

team as well as a man, who emptied buckets into the sledge as if they weighed nothing at all—Rachel was crying! "Hey," Becca said, "I was just scared."

"I should hope so!" said Rachel, rubbing her eyes with her jacket sleeve and putting the other arm around Becca. "I should never have . . ."

It was about to get very embarrassing, but Mr. Amiden saved things. "Why don't you do some work on Bill's face while Becca and I git this hoss rubbed down?" he asked Rachel. That worked. Rachel helped Bill out of the barn, and Becca and Mr. Amiden hung up the harnesses, blanketed the horses, and fed everybody. If Mr. Amiden noticed the stalls were dirty, he didn't say anything about it.

When they were finally done, Mr. Amiden put his hand on the light switch and smiled at Becca. "You got a way with hosses," he said. "I'm lookin' forward to seein' you ride."

Becca could hardly believe it. Mr. Amiden—the guy right next to Apollo when it came to handling a team—Mr. Amiden said she had a way with . . .

"An' you got a head on yer shoulders, too," he said. "Any time you need a loggin' job, jist call on me." He snapped out the light—probably so he couldn't see how proud he'd made her—and he kept one hand on her shoulder on the way back to the house.

In the kitchen, Bill was sitting near the fire with an ice pack on his cheekbone. He tried to stand up when they came in, but he looked a bit teetery.

"You need a lift to the truck?" asked Mr. Amiden.

"Naw," said Bill. But Becca could see he really did.

Mr. Amiden could see it too. Without asking any more questions, he swung Bill up lightly in his arms. "Now you hold still,'' he said as Bill squirmed. ''You weigh almost as much as a sack of grain.''

Rachel and Becca walked to the door, and Rachel put her hand on Becca's shoulder as she opened it. ''You're good kids,'' she said. ''Guess we'll have to keep both of you.''

''Yup,'' said Mr. Amiden. ''Guess we're stuck with 'em.''

Bill's eyes met Becca's over Mr. Amiden's muscular arm. Really quick, before anybody else noticed, Becca put one finger over her lips and nodded.

Bill's swollen face relaxed. ''Seeya tomorrow,'' he said.

''Sure,'' she said. ''Seeya.''

Chapter 11

It only seemed reasonable that Bill would tell Becca where he'd been, after she'd covered up for him so well, but he didn't. In fact, he hardly paid any attention to her at all, not the next day, and not the whole next three weeks. Sugaring season finished off; they cleaned buckets and swept the sugar house, but he still didn't say much to her. He didn't say anything to anybody else, either, but that was nothing new. What was new was that he didn't draw anymore. In school, the backs of his papers were absolutely empty, and at Rachel's he just curled up by one of the stoves and read whatever happened to be lying around.

"What's wrong with Bill?" asked Patty, the first day she could come up to brush Goner after *her* sugaring buckets were clean. "He used to stick around, even though he didn't talk."

Becca looked after Bill, who had just thrown down his pitchfork with a thump and stalked off to the house. "I don't know. Something's biting him, that's for sure. Maybe it's cabin fever."

"Could be," said Patty. "It always gets to me right between sugaring season and riding season. In April, you just can't do *anything*. But cheer up. Just two more weeks or so. Hey, have you looked at the ring?"

Becca hadn't, so they went out together. The fence had appeared out of the dirty snow, but there was still lots of snow left inside it. Patty cantered around, making horse noises, and Becca watched her until something else caught her eye, way across the road. What could it . . . ?

Patty pulled up beside her and looked the way she was looking. "Hey!" she said. "That's Bill, isn't it? Where do you suppose he's going?"

"Probably just wants to get out of the house," said Becca. She made her voice sound casual, but she didn't feel casual at all. The pickup wasn't in the driveway; Rachel must've gone downtown for something, and Bill must've realized nobody was watching him.

"Let's follow him," said Patty. "That way, when he turns around, we can jump out at him and . . ."

"And get beat up?" asked Becca scornfully. "You know what Bill would *do* if you jumped out at him? Besides, you said you wanted to brush Goner *very carefully*."

"Well, that's true," said Patty.

So they went back in and brushed Goner until they couldn't get any more hair out. It took almost an hour, and at the end of it, Mrs. Ellrow came to pick Patty up.

"Bill need a ride home?" she asked.

"No, he's gone for a walk or something," Patty answered.

Mrs. Ellrow shook her head and smiled. "Cabin fever!" she said. "Well, let him stretch his legs."

She turned the Chevy around and bounced down the rutted road. Before the car was even out of sight, Becca was running across the brown and white pasture, looking for Bill's tracks. There they were, as big as life, wherever there was snow. But sometimes they were hard to find on the bare spots. She cast back and forth, wishing she'd thought to bring Tumnus with her. If she didn't find anything at the end of this big bare spot, she'd go back and get him.

She followed the bare spot to the top of a little rise, then saw more tracks. They were leading toward a kind of path, probably one of those old logging roads Rachel said made such great horse trails in summer. Becca hesitated. If she followed the road and the tracks, she might get caught out when it got dark. Besides, if Bill came back the way he'd gone, she'd meet him, and what would she say?

Ahead of her, something crackled, and then she heard the clomp of boots. She looked around, then scampered over to a friendly hemlock tree with low, full branches and hardly any snow under it. Perfect! She dove under the branches and lay absolutely still.

The boots kept clomping in the snow, and it seemed as if there were four clomps, too close together to be made by just one person. A horse? A bear? Were there bears? Becca snuggled up to the tree for protection. Maybe this hadn't been such a great idea after all.

"Better stop here; we're awful close to Rachel's place." It was Bill's voice—so near she almost jumped.

She waited for an answer, but none came. There was just a pause in the clomps, then Bill's boots went on toward the house. In a moment or two, she heard other steps going back the way they'd come. She peeked out from under the hemlock branches, but she couldn't see anybody; whoever it was, was on the other side of the rise.

Well, now what? She wished she'd just gone inside instead of being smart and following Bill. It was easier being curious than it was knowing that something bad, really bad, was happening. And what on earth should she do? Tell Mr. Amiden Bill was meeting somebody in the woods? That would be squealing. Well, she could tell Bill she'd seen him. But what would he do to her?

She crawled out from under the tree. In the fading light, she could see that Bill was almost back at the house; he must have been running. There were headlights coming up the road. Rachel, probably. She'd better run, too.

She did run: it was easier than trying to figure out what to say. As it turned out, she didn't have to say anything. Bill had gone to the barn, not the house, so he didn't know she'd followed him. Rachel was unpacking groceries, so Becca brought in a bag, pretending she'd just come from the barn. Talk about luck.

But luck didn't solve her problem. And, as usual, Rachel seemed to know she had one. After dinner, she said, "What's biting you, Becca? You're as squirmy as a dog full of fleas."

Becca put her plate on the floor; all four cats suddenly appeared from under the stove and looked on hungrily as Tumnus and Xeno licked off the spaghetti sauce. "Oh, nothing."

"Come on—out with it. Have a fight with Patty?"

"Oh, no. We never fight."

Rachel gave the cats a plate of their own. "Bill, then?"

"You'd have to be nuts to fight with Bill."

Neither of them said anything more until Becca finished drying the dishes and put the cats out. But as Rachel scrubbed the last pot, she asked, "Would reading aloud take your mind off whatever it is?"

Becca hung up her dishtowel very carefully. "Well, gee," she said, "I have a lot of math to do for tomorrow . . ."

"Better do it, then." Rachel dumped the water out of the pot, not very cheerfully.

Becca escaped to her room, and Tumnus scrambled up

the stairs behind her. When they got there, though, she didn't do her math. She sat on her bed and thought.

What would happen to Bill if Rachel or Mr. Amiden found out he was meeting people in the woods? Hard to say, but it might be pretty awful. Probably the smartest thing would be to stop Bill from meeting whoever it was; that way, nobody would get into trouble. But how did you stop Bill from meeting people? Especially since he never talked to you.

Becca looked at Tumnus, who was looking at her hopefully. "Oh, okay. Come lie on the bed. You just take up so much *room!*"

He jumped up and flopped down next to her pillow, where he'd slept when he was lots smaller. She shoved him over a little and pulled out her academic calendar. April 5. She crossed it off, then flipped back through the pages. Boy, she'd been here so long. But there were so many days left to cross off.

"You know, Tumnus," she said, slipping the calendar back under her pillow, "you wouldn't believe how much easier it is living in California."

Tumnus didn't look as if he believed it.

"No, really. There aren't any problems there. Or at least *I* don't have any problems there. Or at least . . . I didn't used to . . ." She stroked Tumnus's thick coat. "Anyway, even if I *did* have problems in California, Dad would know exactly what to do about them."

She put her arms around Tumnus and hugged him tightly. So many more days before she could go back. Day after day after day . . . Tumnus wiggled himself around so he could lick the tears off her face.

Chapter 12

The snow melted almost overnight. One day, it went up to seventy degrees, and the next day there was nothing on the ground but mud and brown grass. Rachel said since it was warm now Bill and Becca should keep on taking the bus and walk up the hill from the bus stop. So they did. It felt wonderful to wear just a shirt, no jacket. Becca jumped from rut to rut, humming. Even Bill looked sort of cheerful. He'd played baseball in recess that morning, and he'd hit a home run. Now all the boys wanted him on their team, even the sixth-graders.

"Is it like this all spring?" said Becca.

"Never been here in the spring before," said Bill.

"Well . . ." This was dangerous territory, you could tell. "I mean, you've been *near* here."

"That's so. Well, usually it gets nice like this, and then it gets cold and nothing happens for a long time."

"Aw . . ."

"But it probably won't snow again, if that's what's bothering you." He came as close to grinning as he ever did.

Boy, he was in a good mood, all right. Maybe now would be the time. She took a deep breath. "How're you going to meet whoever it is you see if he can't get around on a snowmobile anymore?"

Bill stopped dead in the middle of the road, as if all of a sudden he couldn't breathe. "Who told you I met anybody?"

"Nobody. I saw you one day after school, when Rachel was late." Becca began to edge away from him. He looked awfully mad, and after all, he *had* beaten up all those sixth-grade boys. "I didn't tell—don't worry," she said, a bit too fast. "I wouldn't squeal on you."

His eyes were just little slits when he looked at her. "Did you tell about that day the horses dumped the sledge?"

"Of course not! I even cleaned the stalls real early the next day, so Rachel wouldn't see you hadn't done them."

Bill's eyes stopped looking dangerous as he stared at her. "Oh."

Well, he might at least have said thank you! She tagged along after him as he started down the road again, suddenly wishing there were snow again. It'd be very satisfactory to hit him with a snowball—pow!—right between the shoulder blades. Not that she was that good a shot.

Rachel was in the kitchen when they came in, and she was wearing boots and breeches. Uh-oh.

"How about a riding lesson, Becca?"

"Sure." Maybe it was just the thing right now, when you thought about it. Bill was looking pretty upset, and if Rachel weren't busy, she'd be sure to notice.

So in a few minutes, Becca was up on Dimwit, posting up-down-up-down around the ring on a longe line, and Rachel was telling her to put her hands on her head, stretch them out to the side, reach for the sky, and all those things Amity had made her do when she'd just begun taking riding lessons in Santa Barbara.

Finally, Rachel made Dimwit walk. "Becca," she said,

reeling them into the center, "why didn't you *tell* me you were this good?"

Why hadn't she? Becca could hardly remember when it had all started, just that she wished it hadn't. "Well, I . . ."

"Never mind," said Rachel, putting a hand on Becca's knee. "It doesn't matter. Why don't you just work Dimwit by yourself for a few minutes? She knows a lot. See what you can get her to do."

Just do anything she wanted? Hey, that sounded as if Rachel thought she was a *real* rider. She walked around the ring once, feeling self-conscious, but pretty soon she forgot about everything but the horse. Trot, circle, halt. Back. Walk, trot, halt. Walk, sitting trot, and . . . Dimwit wouldn't canter. Becca tried again. Nothing. She shot an embarrassed glance at Rachel, who was sitting on the fence.

"You're leaning forward," said Rachel. "Sit tall and ask again."

Becca sat tall; Dimwit cantered. It was a bouncy canter, though, and she had trouble sitting on it. She pulled Dimwit up after two times around and looked at Rachel again.

"Not bad at all," said Rachel.

"But I was bouncing!"

"She has a rough canter," said Rachel. "If you want to sit on it, you really have to use your legs."

Use your legs? Amity had said that to the grownup who rode before her lesson in California, but never to her. "How do you use your legs after you've given her the signal?"

Rachel smiled. "That's what you'll learn this spring. It's a long haul, and I don't usually teach it at the beginning. Your legs have to be long enough to use before you can use them. Yours are, though."

Becca slid off. "Show me." She wanted to see Rachel ride, anyway.

Rachel lengthened the stirrups and swung on. Behind her, Becca heard the sound of Mr. Amiden's truck pulling into the driveway. She turned and waved, then looked back at Rachel and . . .

Dimwit was transformed! She wasn't plodding; she was stepping along with a springy walk like Fanfare's, and her nose was pointing straight down. Then she trotted: not the bone-jarring trot she'd been doing with Becca, but a smooth, rhythmic, collected trot. Becca could see it; why, oh why, couldn't she *do* it?

"Okay, now, I'll take my legs off," said Rachel. All of a sudden, Dimwit shifted back into the bone-jarring trot, and her nose stuck out in front of her. "See?" said Rachel.

"Yeah, I see, but I didn't see what you *did*."

Rachel pulled the old mare up. "I use my legs to make *her* push with her hind legs instead of pulling with her front ones," she said. "If she pulls from the front, she's uncomfortable, so she bounces you to pieces."

"Let me try." This was more interesting than you'd have thought.

Rachel swung off and boosted Becca up into the saddle. "Point your toes straight forward and take your legs off the saddle," she said.

Becca did. "Ooooh! OW!"

Rachel grinned. "Those are the muscles. Now, keep your toes straight ahead and push your legs in from the hips . . ."

"Yow! You mean I'm supposed to *ride* with my leg like this?"

"Pros have been doing it for centuries," said Rachel mildly. "Now ask her to walk, and keep those legs on."

It worked, sort of. Dimwit wasn't plodding, anyway.

They tried a trot, and it felt pretty good for a few minutes, but then Becca's legs gave out and she felt the boneshaking thing begin again.

But Rachel seemed pleased. "Hey! That's great for a first try! You're a natural, Becca!"

Really? A natural? Becca brought Dimwit into the middle, feeling kind of good.

Rachel patted Dimwit's neck. "I thought Dimmy might do for you to learn on," she said as Becca dismounted. "But that was because I thought you were a beginner. Maybe we should get you something Goner's size."

You mean, a pony? Just for . . . ?

"In fact, somebody told me about one, just yesterday," said Rachel, almost to herself. "A good one, too— though you never know until you've gone and tried them out. Maybe I'll give a call . . ."

A pony! Then, all of a sudden, Becca felt just sick. Rachel was giving her a pony; that meant Rachel thought she was going to stay! Well, of course she did. Mr. Jarvis was the only one who knew she wanted to go back. She thought of her calendar and its crossed-off days. A pony couldn't go back to California. Not like Tumnus.

"What's the matter?" said Rachel. "You look as if I'd thought of buying you a snake."

Becca tried to smile. "No, no . . . I . . . thank you . . . I just didn't . . . know what to say . . ."

Rachel smiled. "Then don't say anything—put Dimmy up instead. I'm going to longe Dancer."

She looked pretty cheerful as she strode toward the barn. Becca pulled on Dimwit's reins unhappily. It didn't feel so hot, keeping something secret from Rachel. It was bad enough not telling about Bill, but this was . . . well, it felt *more* wrong. I mean, what Mr. Amiden and Rachel didn't know about Bill wouldn't hurt them, right? But Rachel seemed to count on having her around all the time.

Bill helped Becca untack Dimwit, and they brushed her off together. He wasn't looking too cheerful himself. She wondered if he felt bad about running off and seeing whoever it was, the way she felt bad now about lying to Rachel. Well, not lying. Just not saying anything. But it really was just the same.

"Mr. Amiden's watching Rachel longe Dancer," she said. "Want to go see what's up?"

Bill shrugged, but he followed her down to the ring. When she climbed on the fence to watch, he climbed on, too—not right next to her, but a lot closer than she'd expected.

Dancer was feeling good, and he bucked every four or five strides. Rachel was laughing at him, but Becca noticed she never let him tighten the circle or pull on the line. He snorted when he saw Becca and Bill on the fence, but he kept right on going.

"No fear at all," said Mr. Amiden. "I like to see that in a hoss."

"That's because nothing bad's ever happened to him," said Rachel.

Becca hoped nothing bad ever would. Beautiful, energetic Dancer, with his long strides and floating mane and tail! Surely nothing bad could happen to somebody that wonderful. He was settling down, too. His back rounded, and his strides got longer and longer, with little pauses in between them. Bill leaned forward with that dreamy look he got on his face just before he drew a picture.

"Geez! He's almost flying!" he breathed. Becca thought of the Phaeton horses, with wings that looked like fire.

Mr. Amiden shot Bill a funny look. "Sure, he's good-lookin'. But that's all he is, besides bein' young and strong. He's never goin' to be useful to anybody.''

The dreamy look disappeared from Bill's face. Becca waited for him to say something, but he just looked down and made a hard line with his lips. So she said it herself. ''Dancer doesn't have to do anything but be a dressage horse, Mr. Amiden! He's not *made* for pulling logs!''

It sounded sort of rude, but Mr. Amiden just smiled. ''Well, that's so,'' he admitted. He drifted back to the barn, whistling. You could never tell just what Mr. Amiden was whistling; it never seemed to have a tune.

Bill looked back at Dancer. ''Thanks,'' he growled.

''For what?''

''Thanks for saying what you said. Ed just doesn't *see.*''

Becca was about to stick up for Mr. Amiden, but all of a sudden she understood what Bill meant. He was right. Mr. Amiden didn't *see.* He didn't look at things—pictures, horses, mountains—just because they were beautiful. And that was strange, because he was really good with horses, and you could tell he was a super-kind person.

And then she understood something else. Every time Bill ''saw'' something the way you had to see if you drew pictures, Mr. Amiden didn't really understand. In fact, that whole side of Bill sort of embarrassed Mr. Amiden. She looked at Bill, who was staring dreamily at Dancer again. Was that why he ran off? Had Rachel been right? Was he doing something awful to earn money, just so he could find somebody he could talk to about what he saw? That didn't make sense. He could just talk to Rachel. Rachel knew something about art; she had all those art books lying around her study.

Rachel halted Dancer and reeled him into the middle. Bill jumped off the fence and ran over to them. ''Can I walk him cool?''

"Sure," said Rachel. She strolled over to the fence and sat next to Becca. "He's going fine. I'll ride him soon."

"Will he buck?"

"Probably not." She looked across the ring at Bill, who was talking to Dancer as they walked around.

"Rachel, would you ask Bill to draw a picture of Dancer?"

"Why?"

"Well, he hasn't been drawing at all. And I thought if you asked him, he might . . ."

Rachel put her arm around Becca for just a second. "Okay."

Becca looked across the ring again. Bill had stopped talking; he looked as if he were thinking about something else. Gradually his shoulders drooped and he slouched along in his usual way. Rachel shook her head. "I hope I have a horsewhip in my hand if I ever get a chance to meet the person who's hurt Bill," she said mildly.

"Hurt him? You mean that time his face was cut?" Becca's mind flashed guiltily back to that day she'd unhitched Mutt and Jeff wrong. She'd lied to Rachel then; now she'd have to do it again. "That was the sledge."

"That's not the kind of hurt I mean," said Rachel. "Something is tearing him apart. Ed knows it, but he can't figure out what the matter is."

So Rachel knew—or at least she sort of knew. What was it in Rachel that was so tuned in to other people's feelings? Becca put her chin on her hand and watched Rachel jump lightly off the fence and stop Bill and Dancer. She felt Dancer's chest, then asked Bill something Becca couldn't hear.

Bill shook his head instantly. "I'll go put him in now," he growled.

He hurried up the little hill to the barn. Rachel walked back to the fence.

"I asked him if he'd draw Dancer. You saw what happened." She looked over her shoulder at Bill and Dancer, then sighed. "Well, I'll go call the woman who has that pony. If she still has it, we'll go look at it Saturday. Maybe we'll take Bill and Patty along with us."

"Sounds great!" said Becca. She hoped she sounded enthusiastic enough. Probably she did: Rachel turned and walked toward the house.

Becca looked across the ring at the red branches of the trees, the brown-green grass, and the gray mountains in the distance. Everything was the wrong color in Vermont, even when the weather was warm. Why couldn't things be nice and simple and always the same, the way they'd been in California when there was only Dad and his princess?

Chapter 13

Even though she felt sort of funny about the whole pony thing, Becca found it took a long time for Monday to turn into Saturday. She whiled away the time by really cleaning up the barn and practicing using her legs on Dimwit. It helped to watch Patty do it right; you could see the difference, so you knew what to look for when you tried it.

Patty was very encouraging. "Hey, you look *professional!*" she said Friday afternoon. "That was really great! I can hardly wait to see you on something that isn't a school horse!"

"Dimmy's okay," said Becca, patting the old mare.

"Sure she is, but she's stiff, and she's way too big for you. Wait'll you get your pony!"

They walked Dimwit and Goner back to the barn. Rachel was helping Bill with the stalls because Mr. Amiden wanted him home early. "How'd it go?" she asked.

"She looks *wonderful!*" said Patty.

Bill looked over his shoulder at Becca and raised one eyebrow. Becca blushed. "It's going a bit better," she said.

"It takes longer than five days," said Rachel. "But you're getting it. I can really see the difference. A pony will help, too. We'll leave tomorrow at nine. Can you two get here that early?"

"Sure!" said Patty. But Bill just shuffled his feet. Becca suddenly felt worried. Bill *was* going to come, wasn't he?

Mr. Amiden's truck rolled squeakily into the driveway, and Bill hurried out. Rachel strolled over and talked to Mr. Amiden a minute. When she came back, she was grinning.

"Guess who just can't resist coming along with us," she said.

"Mr. Amiden?" said Patty. "I thought he only liked draft horses!"

"I think he wants to be sure we get a pony that's good enough for Becca," said Rachel with a laugh.

Becca stared at her; Patty giggled.

"You mean you haven't noticed?" Rachel smiled. "Ever since that day you unhitched the team when they'd gone crazy, he's been one of your all-time fans."

Becca tried to think of something to say, but Patty beat her to it, as usual. "Hrumph!" she snorted. "Maybe he's beginning to think girls are some good after all!"

Becca decided not to listen. She liked Mr. Amiden. He wasn't like Dad or Mr. Jarvis, but it was sort of nice to have him around.

It turned out to be Bill who wasn't going. When they got together the next morning, he said he'd rather not. Just like that.

"Thought I'd clean the stalls, then draw that picture you asked for," he growled to Rachel when she protested.

Mr. Amiden looked at Rachel, then at Bill. "You might have told me before we left," he said. "There's plenty to do at home."

Bill shrugged. "I'll walk home and do it."

"You *sure* you don't want to come?" asked Patty. "Think what you'll be missing!"

"Sure," scoffed Bill. "A long ride with two girls who yak all the time."

Rachel and Mr. Amiden laughed. Bill was definitely not one of Patty's all-time fans.

That seemed to wrap it up. But just before they took off, Becca remembered she'd forgotten her helmet. She ran into the barn to get it. Bill wasn't cleaning stalls. He was tying his boots tighter. All of a sudden, she realized he'd be alone all day, and nobody would stop him from . . .

"Bill," she began, dangling her helmet by its strap.

"What is it *now?*"

"You're not going to . . ."

"It's none of your business!" He stood up, and she realized how much taller he was than she'd thought. Still, it was worth just one more try.

"Bill, if you get caught out, they'll ground you! Why don't you just come along with us? It'll be fun!"

Bill's face softened for just a second; then he looked away. "Who wants to look at an old pony, anyway!" he said.

Well, for Pete's sake. It'd serve him right if he *did* get grounded. Becca climbed back in the pickup, and they left.

"Well, here we are," said Rachel an hour and a half later. "Get ready for this—it's quite a spread."

It was. The barns extended for hundreds of yards around white-fenced paddocks. There were three dressage rings, a ring filled with brightly colored jumps, and a cross-country course that stretched out on the far side of the paddocks.

"*Hosses* live here?" said Mr. Amiden. Becca giggled. She'd been thinking the same thing, even though she'd seen stables like this in Santa Barbara. Not the one she rode at, of course. Dad said fancy stables charged you twenty bucks for driving in the gate, and everything else (like riding the horses) was extra.

An immaculate woman met them in the parking circle and shook hands with Rachel. Becca suddenly thought of Molly: this woman looked perfect in the same way, with her tailored breeches and shirt.

"I'm Betty Arnold," said the woman. "The pony's in Barn Two. This way." She led them across the paddocks and through a long barn. Patty nudged Becca; all the stalls had sliding doors with bars on them, and the floors were perfectly swept.

"Here he is," said Mrs. Arnold, opening a sliding door. "He's fourteen-two, perfect pony hunter size. And a real gentleman."

Becca stared into the well-bedded stall and met the solemn gaze of two dark pony eyes. "Oh, gee . . . !" He was beautiful: dapple gray with a silver mane and tail and a dish face. But what was wrong? He turned away instead of coming up to snuff her pockets. When Mrs. Arnold led him out, he stepped into the aisle politely, his ears pricked forward; but he looked way beyond everybody, as if he were thinking about something else. Rachel patted him, then ran her hands down his legs. Mr. Amiden backed up and looked at him.

"Real quality," he said.

"Oh, yes," said Mrs. Arnold. "That's why it's such a shame . . ."

"What's a shame?" asked Patty.

"Well, as I said over the phone, he belonged to Jessica Cole. She was one of the top riders on the circuit, and she trained him since he was a weanling. But then she stopped riding . . ."

"Lose interest?" asked Rachel, looking at the pony's teeth.

"No," sighed Mrs. Arnold. "She got sick. Leukemia. For a long time, she kept trying to ride. Finally, she just *couldn't,* but her parents kept the pony at home for her, and she went out to see him every day." Mrs. Arnold's voice choked up. "Toward the end, her dad had to carry her . . ."

"What happened to her?" asked Patty.

"She died," said Mrs. Arnold softly. "Just fourteen years old."

Rachel suddenly put her arm around Becca and held her a little too hard. Becca looked at the pony and thought of Jessica, hobbling out to see him every day, until she . . . Just for a second, she thought of how Dad had looked the last weeks he'd been home . . . Then she shook the thought away.

"What's his name?" she asked.

"Gandalf."

"Gandalf!" Becca and Patty grinned at each other, and the sadness sort of faded away. "Perfect!"

"He is perfect," said Mrs. Arnold (who seemed not to know who the real Gandalf was). "And Jessica's parents asked me to sell him to a good home. They couldn't bear to keep him."

"I suppose there have been a lot of bids," said Rachel.

Mrs. Arnold shook her head. "Lots of kids from the circuit came right away, but Gandalf just hasn't been the same pony since Jessica . . ."

"You mean he bucks everybody off?" said Patty.

"Oh, no. He's a gentleman. But he used to be so perky, and that's all gone."

"It'll take a little time," said Rachel, stroking the arched neck. "Maybe country life and another pony would cheer him up."

"That's what I thought," said Mrs. Arnold. "No showing for a while, just a bit of work and lots of trail riding, until he forgets.''

''We could do that for him,'' said Rachel. ''Don't you think, Becca?''

Becca nodded as hard as she could.

''There's one more thing, though,'' said Mrs. Arnold. ''He won't jump.''

''Not at all?'' Rachel's voice was sharp.

''Not at all. He'd jump anything for Jessica, but nobody else has been able to get him to step over a pole on the ground.''

''Did he fall?''

''Not that I know of. *She* fell—went off going over a little jump that last time she rode him. She never should have tried—she couldn't even get up. That's when she took him home just to look at. But he was okay.''

Rachel shook her head. ''I wish you'd told me that on the phone,'' she said. ''Well . . . have you got anything else, since we're here?''

You mean they weren't even going to *try* this beautiful pony who'd loved the girl that trained him? Becca looked at Patty, but Patty didn't seem to think anything of it. Well, she could always ask. ''Couldn't I try him, Rachel? He's so pretty.''

''Becca, you don't need a problem horse. You need something you can learn from and have fun with.''

''But we're here, and all . . .''

''Let her give him a try,'' said Mr. Amiden unexpectedly.

Rachel shrugged. ''Okay. Let's tack him up.''

Gandalf was very good about being tacked up, but he still stared off into the distance. Becca kept patting him, hoping he'd look at her. There was something that made her almost think of . . . she couldn't remember what. So she just patted him and mounted.

Out in the ring, Gandalf walked around obediently, then trotted exactly when she told him to. Becca sat tall and tried to use her legs right. It was easier on a pony than on Dimwit because he wasn't so wide. As she passed the gate, she heard Mrs. Arnold say, ''She's a good little rider.''

''He's a good little pony,'' said Rachel. ''If he'd just jump, now . . .''

Becca sat down the way Patty had shown her; Gandalf walked instantly. Boy! This was something! She sat tall and asked him to canter. He did. He was perfect: smooth, even, easy to sit on. What a wonderful, wonderful pony! They cantered three times around before she could bring herself to pull him up.

''He's terrific!'' she said to Rachel.

Rachel nodded. ''He sure is. Take him into the stadium course,'' she said, pointing to the ring with jumps in it. Becca headed for the ring. Suppose he jumped? Then would they get him? But suppose he jumped? Wouldn't she fall off? Sure she would; she'd never jumped. But that turned out not to be a problem. The minute they got to the ring, Gandalf stopped. Becca squeezed with her legs, but nothing happened. She gave him a little tap with her heels; he pinned his ears back and backed up a couple of steps.

''Oh dear,'' said Mrs. Arnold. ''And he was going so well for her!''

''Yeah, that's too bad,'' said Rachel. ''Well, put him up, Becca.''

Becca felt tears spring into her eyes. ''You mean we're going to let him go, just like that? Just because he won't jump?''

Rachel put her hand on Becca's knee. ''You look great on him, and he's a lovely pony. But at this price, there are too many ponies that *do* jump, ponies just as nice as this one."

"Oh, I'm sure the Coles would take much less than . . ." said Mrs. Arnold. Becca held her breath.

But Rachel shook her head. "You're not far enough along to reschool a problem pony," she said. "And some ponies never reschool, no matter how hard you try. That's a heartbreak you don't need."

Becca dismounted and ran her stirrups up, carefully keeping her face turned away from everybody else. Patty held Gandalf's reins sympathetically. "I know it's hard," she said. "But she's right. There's a kid who always comes to the shows with a spoiled horse she's reworking, and it's real sad. He *never* goes the way he should, and she always hopes that someday a miracle will happen, and he'll do it. It makes you want to cry."

Becca nodded. There had been a horse like that at Amity's stables, and Amity had felt bad because it never went well. But that horse had been beaten, really abused. Gandalf hadn't had that sort of stuff happen to him; he was just sad.

A hand fell on her shoulder. She looked up and saw Mr. Amiden. "You like him, huh?"

She nodded. It wasn't just Gandalf's good looks or his wonderful canter. She liked *him.* The whole pony. A pony that knew enough to be sad when his best buddy died. Mr. Amiden patted her on the shoulder and clomped ahead to catch up with the others.

Becca spent lots of time putting Gandalf up. She brushed him, did his feet, adjusted his halter three different ways, combed his forelock—but finally she had to put him back in his stall. She didn't close the door all the way, though; she leaned against it, watching him. She could hear voices arguing outside, but she didn't pay any attention. Rachel would send Patty to get her when they were ready to go.

But it was Rachel who came in. She put her arm around Becca's shoulders. "You really like him, don't you?"

Becca pulled away. "Yeah."

"Okay," sighed Rachel. "Head yields to heart. We'll take him on trial."

Really? Becca looked up. Rachel wasn't kidding. And behind her, Mr. Amiden made a "V" sign with his fingers. So he'd talked her into it! What a friend!

"Thank you," she said softly. "Thanks a lot. He's a wonderful pony."

"We'll see," said Rachel doubtfully. "I think I'm the second greatest soft-touch of the year." She smiled at Mr. Amiden.

But Becca hardly listened. She put both arms around the pony's neck and buried her face in his silver mane.

They did some shopping on the way home, and so it was almost suppertime when they got there. Becca was groggy from sleeping in the truck, but the first thing she did was to slip out to the barn to see if Bill had cleaned the stalls. He had. Everything was neat and clean, and the floor was swept. Things must be okay, then.

She strolled down to the straight stalls at the end of the barn; Mr. Amiden had said they'd knock out the partition between them to make a box stall for Gandalf. She leaned against the partition, thinking how nice it would be to have her very own pony in the stall. Something was lying on the floor in one of the straight stalls, and she stepped forward to pick it up.

It was a man's denim jacket, dirty and very big. As she lifted it, some things fell out of its inside pockets; she stooped and looked at them. Cigarettes, a lighter, and some keys—nothing very interesting. But all of a sudden, she was scared. Whoever had left the jacket in the barn would be back to get his keys soon, and here she was, all by herself. She'd seen what that person had done to Bill's face. What would he do to her if he found out she knew he'd been visiting Bill?

She dropped the jacket and looked around the barn. It didn't look safe and cozy anymore; it was full of shadows and hiding places. She tiptoed across it, slipped out the door, and ran to the house as fast as she could.

The next morning, she hurried out to the barn early, pretending she wanted to look at the place where the pony's stall was going to be. Tumnus bounced along beside her cheerfully, and he trotted right into the barn when she shoved the door open. Well, he was braver than she was—either that, or he knew nobody was there.

Nobody was there, and the jacket was gone. That should have made her feel better, but it didn't. It was a bit creepy knowing somebody had come over the hill, walked into the barn, taken the jacket, and disappeared again while she and Rachel were asleep.

Chapter 14

Becca had planned to say something about the jacket to Bill on Monday, either in school or on the way home, but Bill wasn't in school. Mr. Amiden had called to say he wasn't coming to clean stalls Sunday; maybe he was sick. Yeah, that was probably it. Still, Bill was on her mind most of the day, and the walk up the hill from the bus stop was pretty bleak without him.

Rachel was in the barn, prying boards out of the partition between the two straight stalls. ''Hi, there!'' she called. ''Give me a hand, will you?''

Becca hustled Tumnus and Xeno out of the way and pulled on the board Rachel pointed to. It came out with a very satisfactory ripping sound.

''Ed and Bill should be here soon to help us get this done,'' said Rachel, forcing the wrecking board behind another board.

''Bill wasn't in school today. I thought he was sick.''

''Nope. He had an appointment with a counselor in Brattleboro,'' said Rachel. ''Pull right there, will you?''

Becca pulled. ''How come he had to see a counselor?''

Rachel started in on another board. ''Guess he's in trouble. Ed didn't say much, but he sounded awful when he called.''

Becca leaned the board against the wall. You mean Mr.

Amiden had been upset when he called Rachel yesterday, and Rachel hadn't even *told* her? Boy, grownups were really . . .

Outside the barn, Mr. Amiden's truck sputtered up the drive, and a minute later he and Bill walked in the door. They'd been arguing, or something. Mr. Amiden didn't smile his usual smile, and Bill's eyes were red and sulky. Neither of them said much as they pulled the partition out and made a front for the new stall. That was sort of sad. Becca had hoped everybody would enjoy getting ready for Gandalf.

"Well, I guess that does it," said Mr. Amiden when he and Bill had hung the door. "Don't look bad at all."

Becca leaned on the stall door to try it out. "It looks great!" she said, trying to be cheerful.

Bill slouched out of the barn and began throwing sticks for Tumnus. Rachel and Mr. Amiden went out to watch him. They were talking, but Rachel couldn't hear what they said. What ever was going on? She got a wheelbarrow full of sawdust and dumped it into the stall. Boy, you could almost *feel* the air crack and snap around you when people were like this.

Mr. Amiden was leaning on the stall door when Becca came back with a second wheelbarrow load. He dumped it for her, and she kicked the sawdust around.

"You know what's wrong with that pony?" said Mr. Amiden.

"He won't jump."

"That's not what's wrong. That's what he won't do."

"What's wrong with him, then?"

"I think he's waitin' for that Jessica girl to come back an' ride him."

"But she's not *coming* back. She's . . . !"

"You think a hoss understands that? *People* have a terrible time understandin' somebody they love isn't comin, back. And people can think. Reason with themselves. Hosses don't think; they jist remember.''

Becca nodded. That made sense.

''So what you got to do,'' said Mr. Amiden, ''is not rush him. Let him know you like him, but leave him to hisself. That's hard to do with a new hoss, especially if it's your first one.''

''But if I just let him be, won't he think I don't love him? And won't he just remember Jessica more?''

''That's the hard part. You got to walk a thin line, see, right between makin' him think you don't care beans for him and fussin' over him. That's tough to do. Fact is, I don't know *anybody* who kin do it correctly all the time. Seems you always slide off one side or the other.'' Mr. Amiden rubbed his hand through his sandy hair and looked across the barn, almost as if he was talking about something besides horses.

Becca looked at the empty stall. ''Gee,'' she said finally, ''I didn't know it was going to be so *hard*.''

Mr. Amiden looked at her. ''It *is* hard. And aggravatin'. You never know if you're angry at yourself for not managin' things right, or angry at the hoss for not seeing how hard you're workin' for him. But don't take on about it. You kin do it. You got a way with you.''

''Thanks.'' Becca smiled at him and picked up the wheelbarrow handles. Mr. Amiden stepped out of her way, shoved his hands in his pockets, and clomped slowly across the barn. There was something wrong about the way his shoulders looked—sort of saggy. Dad's shoulders had looked like that when he lost a case. Becca put down the wheelbarrow and followed him.

''Mr. Amiden?''

He stopped, but he didn't turn around. That meant he was really sad. She touched his arm. "Mr. Amiden . . ."

He half turned, and when he did, she gave a hug—just a quick one, without looking at his face or anything. You wouldn't want to embarrass a man by telling him you knew he'd be crying if men cried. "Don't worry," she said. "It'll come out okay in the end."

He must have been really embarrassed, because he didn't say anything. He just held her very hard for a second, then hurried out of the barn.

Rachel wasn't looking any too happy herself after Mr. Amiden and Bill left. She snapped at Tumnus when he begged for a piece of hamburger, and she snarled at Xeno because he was lying in front of the refrigerator. Becca began to think maybe all three of them should go up to her room until Rachel's storm cleared.

But just as she was herding them toward the door, Rachel said, "Mrs. Arnold just called. She's bringing Gandalf tomorrow."

"Great!" Becca grinned. "Poor Bill! One more stall to clean."

"Well, I don't know about that," said Rachel. She got the cutting board and started to chop carrots. "I guess Bill's going to be leaving."

Chop, chop, chop. Becca watched the knife move up and down as if it were the only thing in the room. "How come?" she asked finally.

"It seems the police have found some stolen stuff at an abandoned sawmill not far from here," said Rachel. "Quite a pile of it. And they think Bill has something to do with it. Seems there's a path to it from the Amidens'." She turned and looked at Becca, her eyes looking so scary they made you want to crawl into a hole and pull it in behind you. "There's a path from here, too."

Becca stared past Rachel. From here! She thought of the day Bill hadn't been there to help her untack the team. The day she'd followed him. The jacket in the barn. Of course, a path from here.

"What kind of stuff did they find?"

"Big stuff. Stereos. A couple of VCRs. A snowmobile that was reported stolen last February."

A snowmobile! Last February! But Bill hadn't driven it. It'd been that other guy—the one with the jacket, maybe. Becca looked up and met Rachel's eyes. They weren't scary now, but they were very, very serious.

"Becca, please tell me what you know."

Becca looked down at Tumnus, who was scratching a flea as if nothing were going on. She poked him with her toe, and he stopped. "How do you know I know anything?" she said.

"I don't know. I just suspect. Bill's your friend . . ."

"He is *not!* He hardly even talks to me!"

"There are friends and friends," said Rachel. "And you stick up for people you care for. No matter what they do. So it seems reasonable to suspect that you know Bill's been running off to this place and not telling anybody. Now I know you're not a squealer, and I'd never dream of asking you to say anything if it weren't really, really important. But it is. If Bill stole this stuff, he'll be in a juvenile correction center for years and years. Do you think he'd like that?"

Becca shook her head.

"So if you know *anything* that might help the police find out what's been going on, you should say so."

She should tell. She knew that. But tell Rachel? You couldn't be sure about Rachel. She never saw . . . well, the good side of people. Like Gandalf: she hadn't wanted him because he couldn't jump, even though he was a wonderful pony otherwise. And Bill: she saw what the police wanted her to see, but she didn't see that Bill just *wouldn't* steal things. And then there was Dad. All those lovely things she and Dad had done together were just a fairy tale, a lie, as far as Rachel was concerned. She didn't see what a wonderful dad he'd been, even if he had been, well, really fixed on keeping his princess to himself. How could you tell Bill's secret to somebody like that?

She shook her head. "I can't tell you."

"Oh, Becca!" Rachel didn't look angry; she looked hurt. Well, she'd just have to hurt. After all, Dad had hurt for years and years because of Rachel. Even if it hadn't been *all* Rachel's fault.

On the other hand, somebody had to tell the police Bill hadn't stolen the stuff. Of course, she wasn't really *positive* the guy with the jacket had stolen it, but maybe she knew enough to keep Bill from being sent to that dreadful place where there weren't any art lessons.

"I'd tell Mr. Amiden, though," she said, shifting uneasily back and forth. "At least, I think I would. I'd have to talk to Bill first."

Rachel put the knife down very, very carefully. "Okay," she said slowly. "I'll give Ed a call, and we'll go up there right after supper."

She started down the hall toward the phone, and her shoulders sagged just the way Mr. Amiden's had when he walked out of the barn. But Becca didn't give her a hug.

Chapter 15

The Amidens' kitchen looked as though Mr. Amiden had started work on it quite a while back and sort of never gotten around to finishing things. There was a curtain across the bottom of the sink instead of a door, though the cabinet was all built and only needed a door to be all done. Two of the ceiling lights had nice fixtures over them, but the one at the far end of the room was just a plain bulb with a string. Three walls were painted white, but the back wall was just bare sheet rock. Everything was clean, though; the plywood floor was spotless, and the windows looked as if they got polished once a week.

Mr. Amiden was sitting in the middle of the kitchen, hunched over the red-checked plastic tablecloth with a heavy mug between his hands. Mrs. Amiden was doing dishes. But where was Bill? Becca looked through the doorless doorframe into the next room, but she didn't see any sign of him. She was going to ask Mr. Amiden where he was, but when she met his eyes, she saw something in them that wasn't usually there. She decided not to ask anything at all. Suddenly she understood why big horses and tough boys did what he said.

''Rachel says you got somethin' to tell me.'' His voice had something in it that wasn't usually there, too, though it was as soft as usual. Mrs. Amiden set a dish in the dishrack and half turned around. Her square, red face begged Becca to tell everything she knew, but she didn't say a word. She probably knew better than to speak up when Mr. Amiden looked like this.

Becca took a deep breath; not being a squealer was harder than you'd think. "I can't tell you anything until I've talked with Bill. Where is he?"

"In his room, mopin'. But you'd best say yer piece without you talk to him first. We need the truth, not what you kids decide you're goin' to tell us."

"We're not going to make up a story!" said Becca, clenching and unclenching her hands. "I just don't want to squeal on Bill until he knows I'm going to do it! Let me talk to him, and then I'll come right back. Promise."

The grownups looked at each other, and Becca didn't like what she saw in their faces. How could you convince people you weren't going to lie to them when they were all set not to believe you?

"Please . . ." she said.

Finally it was Mrs. Amiden who spoke up. "Y' know, Ed—you said Becca had a way about her. Maybe if she talks with him, she'll get him to . . ."

Mr. Amiden waved a hand at her, and she went back to the dishes. But he nodded at Becca. "Okay, talk to him. But jist for five minutes, you hear?"

Becca nodded and walked through the doorless doorframe, across the linoleum floor of the living room, and up the unpainted steps. One room upstairs had its door closed; the others were empty. She knocked at the door. "Bill? It's Becca. Can I come in?"

The door opened, and Bill looked out of it. His eyes were red and his nose was swollen. "If you got to."

For pity's sake—here she was risking her life for him! Becca stepped past Bill into the room, then stopped and stared. You could see this had been like the other rooms upstairs when Bill moved in: bare floors, unpainted sheet rock walls, a bed, and a dresser. But the sheet rock in Bill's room was covered with chalk drawings. They weren't done; like the kitchen downstairs, they looked as if he meant to come back to them someday. But they were really good, just the same. Between the windows there was a whole herd of draft horses, some leaning forward to pull imaginary logs, some rearing, some prancing, some grazing. The wall next to the door was covered with faces without bodies and people without faces. Some of the ones without faces were Mr. Amiden, doing things like sitting, walking, grooming horses. Funny how you could tell it was him. But it was the wall next to the bed that was really wonderful. It was filled with sketches of Dancer: Dancer bucking, Dancer trotting, Dancer rubbing his head against a faceless person who looked like Rachel. Everything you loved about Dancer was in those pictures—the bounce, the friendliness, the innocence.

"Well, what is it?" asked Bill.

Becca tore her eyes away from the pictures and tried to say something friendly, so he'd know she was on his side. "Those are beautiful," she said, pointing at the wall of Dancers. "It must be nice to be able to draw on your walls."

Bill shrugged and sat down on the rumpled bed. "Ed said it was okay, so long as I used chalk. Cheaper than paper, and it can be erased when he paints over it."

"Erase your pictures! But they're beautiful—just like Michelangelos!"

"Ed doesn't care about that," said Bill. "He doesn't know Michelangelo from Picasso."

No way was she going to admit she didn't know Michelangelo from Picasso either: after all, that was only because she didn't know who Picasso was. Anyway, she had business to do.

"Mr. Amiden wants me to tell him what I know about what you've been doing. And I thought if I told him about those guys you meet, maybe the police wouldn't think you stole whatever it is they think you stole, and you wouldn't get sent back to Westminster. But I figured I'd better ask you before I told."

Bill stared at her the way he'd stared when she found the dry clothes for him that day they'd begun sugaring. It was the kind of stare people did when they couldn't believe something was real. She'd probably stared at Gandalf that way. But there was no reason for Bill to stare like that. "Well?" she said. "You got to hurry. Mr. Amiden thinks we're going to make up a story and agree on it, so he wants me back in five minutes."

Bill curled up on his bed and put his chin on his knees. "It doesn't matter what you tell them." His voice sounded kind of lost.

"Sure it does! Don't you want to stay here?"

Bill shook his forelock out of his eyes as he looked up. "Why'd I want to stay with a Vermont redneck, anyway?" he growled.

"Bill Lavoie! That's an awful thing to say! Who do you think you are, anyway? A prince in disguise?"

Bill looked a bit ashamed of himself. "It's true, though," he said. "Ed's good with horses, but that's it, right? Listen—he didn't even graduate from high school! I know, because I asked him once. *My* dad has an M.F.A."

Becca stepped a bit closer to the bed. "So your dad has a dumb old M.F.A.! He doesn't take care of you the way Mr. Amiden does, does he? Because if he did, you wouldn't be here, and you'd never have lived in Westminster and all those different places you ran away from."

"It's not his fault!" shouted Bill. He shot a look toward the door, then added in a quieter voice, "Things just didn't work out for my dad, that's all. And it doesn't really matter where I go, because pretty soon he's going to be okay, and he'll get the money together and come and get me."

"Yeah?" said Becca. "And how many times has he told you *that?*"

All of a sudden, she was terribly, terribly sorry she'd said it; he looked the way she'd felt when Rachel had made her say who the Book Fairy really was. He even gulped a whole bunch of times.

"Becca?" called Mr. Amiden's voice from the bottom of the stairs. "Time's up!"

"Just a sec!" she called back.

Bill was still gulping, but she *had* to ask him. "Shall I tell them?"

He shook his head.

"You didn't . . . help those guys steal the stuff, did you?"

"None of your business."

"No, look," she whispered. "It is, too. Rachel said, a long time ago, that maybe you'd done bad things to earn money for art lessons. Is that what you've been doing?"

He shook his head, but he didn't look at her.

"Becca!" She had to go. Mr. Amiden sounded mad. She looked at Bill, but he hunched over instead of looking back. Gee, how *could* she have said that to him? Supposing Dad had been a drunk, and she'd had to bounce from one foster home to another. Wouldn't she have *had* to believe he was going to come get her? Sure she would. Rachel was wrong. People didn't have to think about the truth; they *needed* their fairy-tale worlds.

"Bill," she whispered. "I'm real sorry I said that about your dad. I bet he's a real neat guy."

Bill didn't move or look up, so she tiptoed out of his room and walked slowly down the steps. Mr. Amiden was waiting for her; he turned around and walked straight toward the kitchen. His shoulders didn't sag now.

Mrs. Amiden had finished the dishes. She and Rachel were sitting at the table, drinking coffee. Mr. Amiden sat down with them. There were only three chairs, unless you went way across the room and got the fourth one that was next to the unpainted wall. Becca decided not to go get it. Standing up made her think of those heroes who had defied their captors in front of the firing squad.

"Okay," said Mr. Amiden.

Becca shook her head. "He doesn't want me to tell."

"That's not unlikely, if he's coverin' somethin' up, is it?"

"Course not. But he isn't covering up what you think he's covering. He didn't steal the stuff."

"How do you know?"

"I asked him. He said he didn't. And he said he wasn't helping other people steal stuff, either."

"What other people?"

She wished Dad were there to help her; he knew all the tricks of getting around cross-examination. "Well . . ." She hesitated. "If he'd stolen a TV, he'd have a lot of trouble getting it to the sawmill or wherever without help."

"That's so," admitted Mr. Amiden.

"Becca," said Rachel, "do you have any reason to think Bill was meeting somebody?"

Uh-oh. "Well . . . I followed him one day, just to see where he went. And I didn't see him meet anybody." That was true. She hadn't been able to see anybody but Bill.

"But he slipped off enough that you decided to follow him, huh?"

Oops. Well, she'd said it; she couldn't go back on it.

Mr. Amiden looked at her with that terrible hard look that made people do what he said. "Why didn't you tell us he was sneakin' off, Becca?"

Becca stepped a little closer to Rachel for protection—though Rachel didn't look exactly friendly, either. "Well . . . because Bill never told *me* about it. So I guessed he wanted to keep it a secret."

Rachel shot a glance at Mr. Amiden. "I told you she was loyal, didn't I?" she said. She turned back to Becca. "Look—in general, it's a good thing to keep your friends' secrets. But this particular secret may involve theft, and it certainly involves people besides Bill. Let me fill you in on some background, okay?"

Becca nodded.

"Bill's eleven, almost twelve. Since he was seven, he has lived in eleven foster homes, not counting this one, and at Westminster. He has run away from all of them. Sometimes, authorities have found him fifty miles away from the place he's left, the very next day. Every place he's been, too, there's been a rash of thefts *before* he ran away. Now, doesn't it sound as if he's working for some gang that helps him break out of these places and steal?"

It did look bad, when you thought of it that way, but . . . "Bill's too *smart* to get mixed up with bad guys," she objected.

"That depends on what he gets in return," said Rachel.

"Bill doesn't care about money."

"Not money. Approval, friends. You say he doesn't have any friends at school. Even loners get lonely, Becca."

She shook her head. Bill wouldn't sell out for that. They didn't really *know* Bill if they thought that. "It's not true!"

She looked from Rachel to Mr. Amiden, feeling her eyes fill with tears.

They looked sympathetic, but you could see nothing she said was going to convince them. "So you're going to just let the police cart him away?" she choked. "Just like that? You're not even going to investigate?"

"Whoa there!" said Mr. Amiden. "I'm goin' to hold the cops off as long as I kin. After all, there's lots of possibilities. If Bill won't say who's helpin' him—and durned if I think he will—we got other ways to track 'em down. We were jist hopin' you'd know somethin' that'd help us out. That's all."

"Okay." That was better.

"Now," said Rachel, "are you sure you told us all you know?"

Becca looked at the grownups suspiciously. They sounded as though they really wanted to help Bill—but didn't they really think Bill had worked for a gang? Didn't they really think he was a thief? Part of her wanted to tell them about the snowmobile and the man with the jacket, but the other part wanted not to. That part knew Bill wouldn't, just wouldn't, steal stuff for other people.

"Yeah. That's all I know."

"Okay then," said Mr. Amiden.

Rachel pushed her chair back; it looked as if they were going to leave. "Mr. Amiden . . . ?"

He stopped getting up. "Yeah?"

"You know who could help?"

"Nope. Tell me."

"Bill's dad. Bill really misses him, you can tell. Maybe if you let him come for a visit or something, Bill would tell *him* what he's up to, and then you could help him out."

Mr. Amiden shook his head. "You're right, Becca. And

I know Bill misses his dad. Fact is, I never had a kid who didn't hope to git back with his real family, even if they're no-goods. But Bill's dad dropped out of sight when he was at Westminster—probably changed his name. He may've drunk himself to death by now, for all we know."

Becca stared at him, her eyes wide open. "Does Bill know that?"

All the hard look was gone from Mr. Amiden's face now. "You want to tell him? You want to tell him his old man has jist skipped off and don't give a durn about him?" He shook his head. "I thought about tellin' him—it'd be the kindest thing to do, most likely. But I can't bring myself to do it."

"Don't tell him now," said Rachel. "Let's get this other thing figured out first." She got up. "It's late," she said. "Becca and I'd better get going. Call me after you've talked to Sergeant Dave in the morning, Ed. I'll do whatever I can."

"Thanks," said Mr. Amiden, opening the door for them.

When they drove past the house, Becca saw Bill's light on upstairs. She wondered if he was still curled up on his bed, waiting for his dad.

"Rachel," she asked after a minute, "what's an M.F.A.?"

"Master of Fine Arts," said Rachel. "A degree for people who've gone through college and want to study art, music, writing, or dance professionally."

"Oh, I see. Who's Picasso?"

"A Spanish painter who died a few years ago. I have a book of his paintings if you'd like to look at it." She guided the pickup over the last bunch of spring ruts in the road. "Why all the questions?"

"Oh, Bill said his dad had an M.F.A. And he said Mr. Amiden doesn't know Michelangelo from Picasso."

"Ed Amiden is a lot decenter person than a lot of people I've met who *do* know Michelangelo from Picasso," said Rachel.

"That's what I told Bill, sort of."

"Good for you." Rachel turned in the driveway. "An M.F.A., huh? Sounds like he's not the usual down-and-outer. I suppose that's where Bill's talent comes from." She sighed as she switched off the engine. "Poor kid."

"But he draws *beautifully!* You should see his room! There're chalk drawings all over the walls. A lot of them are of Dancer."

"Dancer? Really? Maybe he's going to do a portrait of Dancer after all. That's great. I thought he'd quit drawing."

"He did, for a little bit. But I guess he couldn't stop himself."

"Some day he may stop for good, if too many bad things happen to him."

"Oh, no! He just couldn't . . . !"

Rachel tapped her fingers on the wheel. "Remember that day I was longeing Dancer and Ed said he wasn't afraid of anything?"

"Yeah."

"Remember what I said?"

"Sure. You said he was the way he was because nothing bad had ever happened to . . . oh."

"Sure. Suppose Dancer were sold time after time. Suppose he were schooled by a succession of people who were impatient, distracted, busy—whatever. Suppose he were neglected or beaten. How long could he do beautiful dressage, even though he's talented?"

Becca shivered. You didn't even want to *think* about stuff like that happening to Dancer. "Not very long," she said.

She slipped out of the truck and walked slowly inside, listening to the peepers and the warm breeze blowing through the maple trees up on the hill. ''Rachel?''

''Yeah?''

''Would Bill be like Dancer if nothing bad had happened to him?''

''Probably.''

Becca suddenly remembered how Bill had jumped off the fence and run across the ring to ask if he could walk Dancer cool. And how he'd looked when he was talking to Dancer, before he turned back into the Bill you usually saw. She looked up at Rachel. ''That's . . . sad.''

''Yes,'' said Rachel. ''It is.''

She gave Becca a hug before she opened the door. And Becca was feeling so sad and miserable about Bill, she almost hugged her back.

Chapter 16

Gandalf came, all right. When Becca got home from school there he was, standing in the new stall, looking beautiful—and miserable.

"Give him time," said Rachel as Becca hovered around the door of his stall, watching him mouth his grain listlessly. "It takes time for a horse to settle in."

So Becca gave him time. She waited a whole day before she brushed him. For a whole week, she took him out to the apple orchard and held his lead rope while he grazed under the white blossoms. Patty thought she was crazy, but Rachel and Mr. Amiden said she was doing the right thing. In fact, at the end of that long, long week, Mr. Amiden suggested she should wait *another* week before she rode him.

"Another week? A whole week?"

"I know it seems long," he said, putting his hand on her shoulder. "But every day you wait now'll pay off in the long run."

"In the meantime," said Rachel, "you can start jumping on Dimwit."

Well, that made things a little better. Jumping was fun, once you got over being scared, and Dimwit liked it.

Still, it was very frustrating. And to make things worse, Bill was being absolutely impossible. Not that it was really his fault; all the grownups had suddenly ganged up on him. Mrs. Standish watched him get on the bus every day. Rachel came and picked them up, and either she or Mr. Amiden watched him every second when he was cleaning stalls. You could see it really bugged him. He stopped talking altogether, and he stomped around the barn looking so dangerous you wouldn't even want to *try* being friendly.

"Aren't you afraid he'll run away?" she asked Rachel one day.

"He can't," said Rachel. "That's why we're watching so hard. It really goes against the grain to do it, but it's the only way we can clear him."

"Clear him?"

"Sure. Ed told Sergeant Dave he's meeting somebody for sure. So the police are keeping watch on the sawmill, and we're waiting to see if there are any more thefts."

"Have the police seen anybody?"

"Not yet."

Then the man with the denim jacket wasn't living at the sawmill; he was just putting stuff there. Was there another path to the sawmill? Becca didn't dare ask Bill.

Two weeks were finally up, and Rachel said she should try Gandalf now. Becca tacked him up, quivering with excitement, and led him down to the ring. He behaved perfectly; Rachel was really pleased. Even though Becca didn't quite know what to do with a horse this well schooled, he seemed to know what she wanted. Patty said he looked *gorgeous.* But he didn't feel gorgeous; he felt listless. She had to push him every minute.

"So he doesn't bounce along like Goner," said Rachel at the end of an hour. "Give him time, time, time! He's out of shape, and he's been hurt. It always takes longer with the ones that've been hurt." She sighed—Becca couldn't figure out quite why. "Anyway," she said, "he needs a trail ride. A little scenery will cheer him up. Go out tomorrow instead of working in the ring."

"Oboy!" said Patty. "Can Goner and I come?"

"You better," said Becca. "Gandalf and I don't know where the trails go."

So the next day they went out on their own. It was kind of exciting, riding your very own pony on the trails. You could see Bill *really* envied her. Too bad he couldn't come along. He could ride a bit; he rode Mr. Amiden's horses down to the water hole every day, and Becca was sure they didn't just walk. So . . . no, there wasn't any use thinking about it.

"Where shall we go?" asked Patty as they clattered off down the road with Tumnus and Xeno. "Oh, I know! Let's take that wide trail that goes toward the mountain!"

"Sure." Becca would rather have gone to the sawmill, but Rachel had told them they shouldn't go that way. So that was that. Still, it was lots of fun. The woods were beginning to green up, and the trail was so grassy that Goner and Gandalf looked longingly at it. Patty chatted about all the horse shows they'd go to this summer, and Becca half listened and half wondered if she'd be good enough to show.

"Hey, there's a great flat place coming up," said Patty. "How about a canter?"

"Sure." Becca gathered her reins. Gandalf took a couple of dancing steps—hey, he was coming alive!

The flat place cut between two pine forests. The ground was covered with pine needles, and the horses' hooves made hardly any noise. Goner began to speed up, and Gandalf followed suit, snorting a little at each stride. Wow! This was much more fun than riding around in a circle! Ahead of them, the trail curved to the left, and

Patty disappeared around it. Gandalf sped up, and they whizzed after her just in time to see Goner pop over a fallen log. Becca grinned and leaned forward, giving Gandalf lots of rein so she wouldn't bump his mouth.

The next thing she knew, she was flying over Gandalf's head. She saw the log shoot under her; then she landed with a crash in the pine needles. "Patty!"

Patty was pretty far ahead, but she looked over her shoulder. In a minute she'd pulled Goner up and was trotting back. "Geez! You okay?"

Becca was shaking all over. She felt her arms and legs: everything seemed to be in order, so she got up. "I guess so."

"What happened?"

"He just—hey, where is he?" She'd been so busy getting up, she hadn't even thought of him.

Patty grinned. "He was trotting back to the barn when I turned around and saw you. That's what they do when you go off, if you don't hold on to the reins. Like Rachel says, you only forget that once."

"But I didn't . . . I thought . . ."

Patty dismounted. "Hey, I'm sorry. I wasn't really laughing at you. It happened to me last summer, and now I hang on to those reins no matter what! No . . . don't cry, c'mon. I'll walk back with you. Goner bucks if you ride him double."

It was a much longer walk than you'd have thought, and being sore all over didn't help matters. But after they'd stumped along for twenty minutes or so, Tumnus barked, and a moment later Rachel cantered around the bend ahead of them on Gandalf. She was white as a sheet.

"Are you all right?" she asked, vaulting off. "Did he shy? Buck?"

"She's fine," said Patty. "There was a log, and he stopped instead of jumping."

Rachel felt Becca's arms, which really wasn't necessary. But Becca was grateful for a leg up on Gandalf. Walking was awful in riding boots.

"So he refused, huh?" said Rachel, walking along next to her. "How big was the log?"

Becca held her hands about a foot apart. "It wasn't even a log, really—just a piece of tree."

"And Goner was in the lead?"

Becca nodded.

Rachel shook her head. "Wow. Almost any horse will jump something that size if he has a lead. I wonder if he's had a spill, or something."

Becca felt her hands get cold. Was Rachel thinking of giving Gandalf back, just when she was getting to know him? "Oh, please . . . !"

"Hey, relax!" said Rachel. "We'll work on him in the ring. Here's how you do it. Put poles all the way across. Put grain on one side and Gandalf on the other. Eventually, he steps over the poles."

"Hey! that's tricky!" said Patty.

Becca nodded. Sometimes it was good to have somebody like Rachel around, who knew all about horses.

When they got back to the house, Mr. Amiden's truck was in the driveway, and he strode out of the barn to meet them. "Bill with you?"

"Oh my God," said Rachel.

Becca and Patty froze, looking at each other. Then Becca gulped and said, "It's all my fault, Mr. Amiden! I fell off, and I didn't hang on to the reins, so Gandy came back, and Rachel thought . . ."

"Cryin' won't bring him back, Becca," said Mr. Amiden. "Well, he can't have gotten far. I'll go see if I kin get Sergeant Dave to help. I passed him on my way up.'' He hurried to his truck, and in a minute he was banging down the road.

Becca looked miserably at Rachel. ''I should've hung on to the reins.''

''I should've brought Bill with me,'' said Rachel. ''Unfortunately, *should haves* won't bring him back.''

''Do you really think he won't be back?'' asked Patty. ''Was it that bad?''

''I don't know,'' said Rachel. ''He's been awfully restless.''

''Maybe he will,'' said Becca hopefully. ''I mean, he could just be warning that guy the police were after him.''

Rachel looked at her over Gandalf's back. ''What guy?''

Patty looked from Becca to Rachel in the frozen silence. ''I guess I'll go untack,'' she muttered. She and Goner nearly tiptoed to the barn.

Rachel ran up Gandalf's stirrup with a snap. ''Becca. What guy?''

''I've . . . never seen him,'' Becca whispered. ''Not close up, anyway. But I saw Bill meet somebody on a snowmobile at school once. And that time I followed him, I heard him talking to somebody. But I was hiding, so I couldn't see who it was.'' She ran up the stirrup on her side, noticing her hands were shaking. ''Whoever it was left his jacket in our barn that day we went to see Gandalf,'' she added miserably. ''But it was gone the next morning.''

''He was *here?* In our barn? And you didn't tell me?''

Becca nodded.

''My God, Becca! Don't you see! Can't you . . . !'' She took Gandalf's reins out of Becca's hands, not very gently. ''Go inside,'' she said shortly.

''But don't you want me to untack . . . ?''

"I said, go inside!" said Rachel between clenched teeth. "Can't you just do what you're told, for once, without fooling around?" She pulled Gandalf's head around and stomped into the barn.

Becca walked toward the house, pushing Tumnus away and willing not to cry. The kitchen door. The kitchen. The stairs. Her room. She plopped down on her bed, wincing when she hit the spot where she'd landed in the pine needles.

Bill had run away, and it was her fault. She should have told Rachel and Mr. Amiden about that guy with the jacket. It wasn't much of a clue, but it was something.

Bill had run away, and it was her fault. She should have hung on to the reins. Was he going to warn that guy, or was he going to *stay* run away? It didn't matter. If he came back, he'd just get sent to Westminster.

Gandalf wouldn't jump. He wouldn't even jump that little log! Rachel said almost any horse would do that. Probably Rachel would send him back. They only had him until June tenth. So he'd be gone soon.

June tenth! What was today, anyway? She fished under her pillow, but her calendar wasn't there. She hunted around and found it under the bed. It was dusty. Things had been so busy lately, she'd forgotten to check off the days. Well, she could do it now.

She checked and checked—goodness, it had been almost a month since she'd done it. There was the day Rachel had asked her if she wanted a pony. There was the day they went to see Gandalf. There was the day Tumnus had "stayed" for five whole minutes. There was the day Gandalf had come. May twenty-fifth: there was today. She wrote in the square, "G. won't jump. B. ran away." Then she crossed it off as hard as she could.

Boy, life sure was miserable. But there was something

she could do about it, right? What were all those checks for, anyway? Counting the days until she could write Mr. Jarvis and tell him she wanted to go back home, right? Well, it was a week early, but it took letters almost a week to get to California from here. She could write this very minute.

She took out the letter paper Molly had given her, sharpened her pencil on the cute pencil sharpener Dad had given her, and began.

Dear Mr. Jarvis,
It's almost June now, and you said you'd take me back to Calif. if I didn't like living in Vt. Well, I don't like it. Everything goes wrong here, and Rachel gets mad all the time.

I'd like to bring my puppy, Tumnus, with me. He weighs almost 80 lbs. now, but he's very well trained and no trouble.

You can write to me. Rachel lets me open my own mail. Just be sure you can get me back.

Your true friend,
Rebecca Davidson

It looked kind of funny when she wrote it out. After all, Rachel wasn't always mad. But things were too complicated here, anyway. There was no point staying if Bill was gone and Gandalf went back to that farm and Rachel . . .

She looked out the window. Rachel was fixing the ring fence. You could hear the sledgehammer from here. Wham! Wham! It'd be nice to have those posts standing up straight. And Rachel wouldn't come into the house for a while.

Becca tiptoed down the stairs and looked around Rachel's desk for the address book. There it was! She copied Mr. Jarvis's address carefully onto her envelope, stuck a stamp on it, and was just sliding the letter into it when she heard the back door slam. She stuffed the envelope into her back pocket and strolled into the kitchen as if nothing was up.

It was Patty. "Rachel's cooled off now," she said. "You can probably come back out."

Becca shook her head. "I'd better wait a bit."

"Boy! What'd you do?" asked Patty. "I've never seen Rachel that mad before."

Well, Becca had. That day about the Book Fairy, for instance. "Oh, I knew some stuff about Bill I didn't tell her before when she asked."

"You did? Gee, no wonder she was mad! Bill's in big trouble—I guess that's why he ran off. Grandpa said he stole—"

"He didn't!" shouted Becca. "He didn't do it!"

"But Becca! The cops . . ." Patty stopped. "Was that what you told Rachel? That you *knew* he didn't do it?"

"Nope. I don't know he didn't do it. I just . . ."

"I know what you mean." Patty nodded. "If anybody but Grandpa had told me Bill stole stuff, I'd have given them what-for. He's not like the kids at school who go to those big discount houses and . . . you know . . ." She looked out the window. "Hey! There's Grandma. I gotta go now. Cheer up. Rachel'll make peace soon."

Becca suddenly had a thought. "I bet she won't let me go get the mail with her, though. Would you mail this for me?" She handed Patty the letter.

"Sure thing." Patty looked at the address. "You got a secret boyfriend in California?"

"Not a boyfriend. Just a friend."

"Oh, sure." Patty grinned. "I'll be sure to mail it, Juliet." She ran out the door and hopped into the Chevy. As they drove out the driveway, she waved the letter at Becca and blew her a Romeo-like kiss.

Chapter 17

Bill didn't come back that night, and he didn't come back any of the next few nights. It got around school, of course, and all the kids asked Becca if she knew where he was. You could see they didn't really care about him, though. It was just exciting for everybody to think about a kid who really ran away instead of just threatening to. After a week, nobody bugged Becca about it anymore.

That was a good thing, because Becca was feeling pretty low. Every time she talked to Rachel, it seemed, Rachel would say something about what they were going to do after school let out, or next year. And every time Rachel did that, Becca felt bad. Pretty soon, Mr. Jarvis would send for her, and she'd get on a plane and leave. It wasn't really lying, not telling Rachel that, but it made you feel crummy, just the same.

And then there was Gandalf. They'd done what Rachel suggested, putting him on one side of some poles and his grain on the other. And he'd trotted right over the poles—no problem. Rachel raised the poles higher and higher, right up to three feet, and he always jumped, provided there was grain to gobble on the other side. But when they decided he was cured and Becca trotted him at a caveletti, he shot sideways, and she fell off again. And again, and again. Rachel was baffled; Becca was sore. So

Gandalf was definitely going back to Mrs. Arnold on the tenth of June. Becca couldn't figure out why she felt bad about that; after all, if she was going, Gandalf would naturally go, too. But she did feel bad.

Feeling bad about all those things made her grouchy. Finally, on Memorial Day, Rachel couldn't stand it anymore. "Take that pony out for a ride, will you? I can't bear to see you skulking around like that."

"Patty's away for the weekend."

"So take a ride by yourself! Or take Tumnus if you want company."

An order was an order. Becca meandered over to the barn, scuffing the toes of her riding boots. She didn't *want* to go riding. It was hot and Patty was gone and . . . somebody nickered as she walked into the barn. She looked down the aisle of dozing horses. Who had it been? At the end of the barn, Gandalf's pert little head stuck out over his stall door. He was looking straight at her.

"Was that *you?*"

He bobbed his head up and down—not saying yes, just saying he'd like a carrot. Well, she'd brought one. She gave it to him, waiting for him to stare dreamily over her head when he'd finished it. But he lowered his nose and poked at her pocket instead.

"Oh, Gandy!" She gave him a hug. "It's about time . . . !" But then she remembered—he was going; she was going. He'd finally gotten to like her, and she was leaving him. What would happen to him when he went back to Mrs. Arnold's? She led him out to the crossties, feeling even worse than she had before.

When she got him tacked up, she rode along the trail to the sawmill. Nobody'd be there; the police had better things to do on Memorial Day. She sort of knew the way, too. Patty had pointed it out on Thursday. It was a lovely trail, nice and wide. And *green.* Everything was green, in fact. The light green of early spring had turned into dark, shady green, splashed with sunlight and a few beginning buttercups. Summer. School would be out soon. If she were staying in Vermont, she could ride all day. . . . But there was no point thinking about that.

After she'd ridden for ten minutes or so, the wide trail went off to the left, and a very narrow path broke off to the right. Tumnus sniffed at it and started down it, but Becca called him back. "Look, silly—can't you see the real trail goes this way?"

Tumnus wagged his tail and trotted along behind her. The trail went downhill now, through some huge trees and then into a patch of little maples, poplar, and blackberries. That was where everything had been logged off, probably. It looked pretty scruffy, and Becca felt sorry for the big trees that had been cut down for the sawmill. Maybe their ghosts were floating around this brush, mourning.

She was still thinking about the trees when she came to the sawmill. It was all caved in, except in one spot where you could see the logs had gone in and the boards had come out. Becca dismounted and led Gandalf toward the place where the saws had been. He didn't really like it; there were blackberries all around it, and they caught at his flanks and tail. But she made him come. No way was she going to tie him to a tree. If he broke away, she'd have to walk home.

There was one little patch of roof left, slanting precariously to one side. It was cool under there, and very quiet. A perfect hiding place. You could see why Bill—or not Bill, whoever it was—had hidden his stuff there. But there was nothing there now. That was sort of disappointing. But then, *life* was sort of disappointing, right now. Becca turned Gandalf around, walked him back down the path, and mounted.

On the other side of the sawmill there was another narrow path. Was it a shortcut? It'd be kind of fun to follow it and see. She urged Gandalf up it and he went willingly, so it probably went in the right direction. Horses had a better sense of direction than people, Patty said. The trail was really narrow, though, and Becca had to duck from side to side to keep from being hit by branches. After a while, they came to what had once been a stone wall, though the path seemed to go right over it. Gandalf stopped. Becca sighed, dismounted, and led him over it. "Why can't you just step over it when I'm on your back, you nerd?"

She mounted again and they went on. All of a sudden she thought of something. Mrs. Arnold had said Jessica had fallen off Gandalf the very last time she rode him. Fallen off going over a little jump. Did Gandalf think . . . ? No. Impossible. Horses didn't know how to think. But, well, maybe he really thought it was his fault she'd fallen off, and that's why she hadn't ridden him anymore.

She thought about it again and again as they rode along—so hard that she didn't think about where she was going until Gandalf stopped. She came out of her daze and looked around. Oh, a fork. Gandalf seemed to want to go straight up the hill on that narrow, stony path, but there was a clearer trail to the left. She turned him that way. Tumnus bounded down the little path and followed her. Uh-oh. Maybe this was the wrong way. Well, she could always ride back if the nice clear path didn't go anywhere.

The woods changed as she trotted along. The scrub turned into a maple grove, all covered with ferns, and the trail turned into a two-track road. Suddenly Gandalf stopped and threw his head up. Tumnus pricked up his ears, too. What was it? Then Becca heard it, too. A voice—an angry voice. It seemed to come from in front of her, but from pretty far away. Then she heard another voice, a scared one this time.

Hey, what was going on here? Was somebody lost? She pushed Gandalf forward and he went reluctantly. He was jumpy; she could feel his heart beat under her legs. A few hundred yards down the trail, Becca saw a snow fence. Beyond it huddled a house, or at least most of a house. The back ell was fallen down, but the part around the chimney looked okay. It was on the very edge of the maple grove; on the other side there was lots of new growth. Probably all the new growth had been the house's front yard once. Rachel said it didn't take the woods long to move in once people moved out. But there *were* people! She'd heard them.

Then she saw one of them—a big man, carrying something. He was walking kind of funny, muttering to himself. Gandalf stepped backward; Tumnus began to growl.

Well, this was definitely not the right way home. No way was she going to ride any closer to whoever it was. Patty said there were tramps around and you wanted to stay clear of them. Becca turned Gandalf around, and he trotted back to the place the little trail went off. Tumnus scurried right up it, and Gandalf seemed to want to go, too. Should she risk it? It didn't look like more than a streambed.

Gandalf said she should risk it. He scrambled up the hill, his feet sending pebbles and little sticks flying every which way. Becca leaned forward over his neck and hung on to his mane, trying not to get brushed off by the branches that slashed by them. With a final scramble, Gandalf jumped out onto a wide path. Becca sat up and looked around. Why, they were on the logging road, right where Tumnus had sniffed at that little trail. So it was a loop! That was great. She wouldn't have to ride down that hill. She looked behind her. Wow. It was almost straight up and down.

"You're a good fellah, you know that?" she said to Gandalf. "Most ponies wouldn't go up a trail that steep."

Gandalf said it was nothing. She walked him back, rubbed him down, and gave him a couple of extra carrots when she put him in his stall. He really *was* a good pony. She should go tell Rachel that idea about his jumping. While she was at it, she could ask Rachel about that house. You had to wonder who it belonged to and what those people were doing there.

But Rachel wasn't in her study. That was funny. She hadn't been in the barn, and the pickup was in the driveway. Where else could she be? Becca looked out the window. Oh, there she was, sitting on the big rock across the road from the house. Becca trotted through the kitchen, out the door, and through the buttercups to join her.

Rachel hardly looked up when she came, which seemed strange. Maybe she was stuck on whatever she was writing; that happened sometimes, and when it did, she went for walks. And then you had to Handle with Care.

"Hi," said Becca cautiously, sitting a few feet down the rock from where Rachel was.

Rachel finally looked at her, but her green eyes were absolutely expressionless. "Bob Jarvis called about a half hour ago," she said in a whispery sort of voice. "He said you'd written to him."

Becca's ears began to sing. She knew she should probably say something, but she didn't seem to be able to find any words. She looked out at the mountains.

Finally it was Rachel who said something. "Why didn't

you tell me, Becca? We could have done things differently if I'd known you were really unhappy.''

Becca kept staring toward the mountains. Two crows flew over the valley in front of her, cawing to each other. Down in the field, a bobolink perched on a blackberry bush and whistled as it swung in the light breeze. ''I . . . it's not . . .''

Rachel was waiting for her to finish, but she couldn't finish because she didn't know what she wanted to say. She'd expected Rachel to be mad when she found out about that letter. She glanced at Rachel's face, then looked away. No, she wasn't mad. She looked . . . like Gandalf had looked when he first came. Or like Bill, when she'd asked him how many times his dad had told him he'd come fetch him. Or like her own face in the mirror after Dad had died. There really wasn't much you could say when people's faces looked like that. She got up to go, but Rachel held out one hand.

''Bob has some business in Boston this week. He said he's going to come here and talk to you and me.''

''When?''

''Day after tomorrow.''

Day after tomorrow! But that was just the second of June! She had Gandalf until the tenth! He couldn't take her back before that, could he? And how would she find out what had happened to Bill if he came and took her day after tomorrow? What about school? It wasn't out until the fifteenth! She looked out over the peaceful valley again. The bobolink was gone now.

''Okay,'' she said.

Rachel didn't say anything else, so Becca left. She wandered over to the barn and leaned on Gandalf's stall door. He nickered when she came in, but that only made her feel worse. Tumnus was flopped down on the barn floor next to the saddles. He jumped up as she went by and followed her out into the sunlight. She patted him. Would Mr. Jarvis let her take him? He'd like it in Santa Barbara. But could he come?

She poked around the yard, throwing a few sticks for Tumnus to chase, then went upstairs to her room. Day after tomorrow. She looked at the calendar and all the days she'd checked off. It had seemed so long until June, all those days ago. Now suddenly June seemed to have come faster than she'd expected.

Chapter 18

As it turned out, it took forever to be day after tomorrow. You could see Rachel was trying to be cheerful, but you could see it was all an act, too. All the things they usually talked about—like how they were going to get Gandalf to jump and how Dancer was doing now that Rachel was riding him—all that kind of thing became impossible to say. Neither of them wanted to talk about Mr. Jarvis; but Becca couldn't think about much else, and she suspected Rachel couldn't, either.

So it was a wonderful relief when Patty came over Tuesday after school and Becca could tell her what she'd thought about Gandalf and Jessica. Patty thought it was a great idea. "You might really be onto something!" she said. "Look, let's try something. First, we'll lead him over a pole and give him some grain. Then you hop on, and I'll lead him over the pole while you're on him. That way he'll see people don't fall off when he steps over things."

They tacked Gandalf up, chattering to each other as if nothing were wrong. "What bothers me," said Becca, "is that he doesn't care if *I* fall off. When he goes sideways, I just can't seem to stick, and he just looks around, waiting for me to get up."

"The nerd!" Patty giggled. "Goner does that when I go off. He always looks so innocent and surprised!" Then she looked up. "Hey, but we get right up, don't we? Jessica didn't get up. Remember? They had to carry her. Maybe he thought he'd really hurt her."

"It still doesn't make much sense," said Becca.

Patty shrugged. "You know what Rachel says," she said. "Horses only make their own kind of sense, not ours." She pushed her hair out of her eyes. "But you know," she said, "sometimes people don't make sense either. Like after my parents died. I knew they were dead, right? I went to the funeral. I went to the cemetery."

Becca nodded. Boy, she wouldn't forget *that* in a hurry.

"But then, when I got home, what I really wanted to do was call up my mom and tell her all about it. Isn't that crazy? And for the longest time after that, I kept thinking that pretty soon I'd go back to live with my dad and mom. It was really nutty." She looked out the door for a moment. Becca waited for her to say something. You forgot about Patty's parents, sometimes. She always seemed so cheerful.

"Anyway," said Patty, giving Gandalf a little pat, "if I can get mixed up like that, why can't Gandalf? Let's go see if we can unmix him up."

Out in the ring, they led Gandalf over a couple of caveletti, and he followed them, obviously wondering what on earth they were up to. Then Becca mounted, and Patty led Gandalf toward the same caveletti, holding his reins under the bit. He walked up the poles willingly enough, but then he stopped.

"Darn," said Patty. She stepped over the caveletti herself, then turned around and jiggled the little pan of grain. "C'mon, Gandy! Come get the good stuff!" she wheedled. "Thump him with your legs, Becca."

Becca thumped. Gandalf started to go sideways. When Patty reached out to grab his reins, he backed up.

"Shoot!" said Patty. "And it was such a good idea!"

"Wait a minute—try something!" said Becca. "Take the reins over his head. That's how I lead him."

"I don't see what difference it can make," said Patty. But she did it. "C'mon Gandy! Step over the nice pole!"

Gandalf stepped forward, sniffed at the pole, and hesitated. Patty pulled gently. "Hit him on the rump, Becca—not very hard."

Becca gave him a little cuff. He started, snorted, and stepped over the pole.

"Wow!"

"Whoop!"

"You *did it*, Gandy!"

Becca and Patty hugged Gandalf so hard he began to prance around. Patty gave him a bit of grain, which was what he really wanted, anyway.

"Let's try it again!" said Becca.

They worked on it for almost an hour, and by the end of the session, Gandalf was trotting over caveletti behind Patty just as if he'd never refused a jump in his life.

"This is wonderful!" said Patty. "Now all you have to worry about is explaining to judges why you jump your pony with the reins over his head!"

Becca giggled. "Maybe tomorrow he'll decide he can do it with the reins in the right place!" Then she stopped giggling. Tomorrow Mr. Jarvis was coming. The next day, for all she knew, she was leaving.

"What's the matter?" said Patty. "You look like you swallowed a bug."

"I . . . just remembered I had to do some homework."

"Well, that can wait," said Patty comfortingly. "Will you crew for Goner and me?"

"Sure. Go tack him up while I cool Gandy out."

She walked Gandalf round and round, feeling awful. He

was jumping! Well, at least he was going over caveletti. And she wasn't going to keep him. She was sort of working him for some other kid to ride.

When she led him up to the barn, Patty was leading Goner out, talking excitedly to Rachel and Mr. Amiden, who had just driven up. "Yeah! He really did it! Tomorrow you'll have to come out and see! It was all Becca's idea—honest. I just helped because somebody had to lead him!"

Were there kids in California as nice as Patty? It was sort of hard to guess, since Becca had only known kids in school in California, and kids were different out of school than in. Well, there must be, if you looked around. Still . . .

"Hurry up, slowpoke!" Patty said to her. "I'll have him warmed up in no time."

Becca hurried: it was better to hurry than to stay in the barn with Rachel and Mr. Amiden. She had a funny feeling they were going to talk about her as soon as she left. So she spent as long as she could out in the ring when she got there, adjusting oxers, poles, triple bars—anything Patty wanted. By the time they were done, Mrs. Ellrow was there and waiting.

Becca helped Patty rub down Goner, and then she went out to the car with her to say hello to Mrs. Ellrow. There was something very comforting about Mrs. Ellrow; she'd really miss . . .

"Becca, dear." Mrs. Ellrow took hold of Becca's hand through the open car window. "Rachel says you're going to leave us."

"What!" Patty stared. "Where are you going?"

"Back . . . to Santa Barbara," said Becca, looking down at the road.

"But Becca! What about Gandalf? What about Tumnus? What about . . . ?"

"What about Rachel?" said Mrs. Ellrow gently.

Of course they were surprised. They didn't know anything about Santa Barbara, and it was difficult to explain to them. . . .

"Well . . ." Becca said after a little pause, "Rachel's lawyer is coming out tomorrow. He's going to talk to us about it."

"You've got to be nuts to leave!" said Patty stubbornly. A tear slid out of one of her blue eyes.

"Patty!" said Mrs. Ellrow quietly. She smiled at Becca. "Well, I'm glad you'll talk it over before you decide," she said. "It's always a good thing to think things through carefully." She let go of Becca's hand. "Anyway, dear, I hope things will work out the way you really want them to."

Patty climbed slowly into the Chevy, and Mrs. Ellrow turned it around and drove away. Through the puff of dust the car left behind, Becca could see Patty staring at her out the back window.

She scuffed her feet as she walked into the barn. Nobody should be there now; she could just go up to the loft and think . . .

"Hullo there, Becca."

It was Mr. Amiden. Had he been waiting for her? How had he gotten there?

"Hi," she said, trying to look cheerful. "Heard anything about Bill?"

"Not a durn thing," he said. "And that makes me wonder, you know. All the other times he's cleared out, they've found him on the road or in restaurants—something like that. But there's no sign of him now. So I got to thinkin'—maybe he's hidin' somewhere around these parts."

"Right around here? But the police . . . ?"

"There's lots of places a kid kin get where the police can't," said Mr. Amiden. "So I came out here to ask if you kids would keep an eye out for him when you're out on the trails. I've been doin' a bit of ridin' myself, not that Hank and Sue are really made for it. But it beats settin' around, wonderin' when they'll find him."

She nodded, but she wasn't really thinking about what he was saying. Had Rachel told him she was leaving? Why would she have told Mrs. Ellrow and not Mr. Amiden? Well, maybe she hadn't. After all, Mr. Amiden was one of her all-time fans, Rachel had said. Maybe Rachel hadn't wanted to break the news to him.

"Uh, Mr. Amiden . . ."

"Somethin' on yer mind? You don't look too peppy."

She looked up into his light blue-gray eyes, and he smiled back at her. He didn't know. He'd never smile like that if he knew. But she couldn't tell him. "Oh, I'm just worried about Bill. I'll take a ride out tomorrow to look for him, okay?"

" 'Atta girl," he said. "Hey! Where you off to?"

"I have to do some stuff in the house for Rachel," she said, starting to back up. "She really wanted me to hurry."

"Okay, then, I got to git goin' myself," he said.

He walked back as far as the truck with her, his big hand on her shoulder. Normally, that would have been really great, but now—now she edged away from him when they got to the truck.

"G'bye," she gulped. And she ran into the house as fast as she could so he couldn't see she was crying.

Chapter 19

Rachel wasn't sure exactly when Mr. Jarvis was coming. He had a meeting in Boston in the morning; when it was over, he was going to rent a car and drive to Vermont. There certainly wasn't any point in staying home and waiting for him, Rachel said. So Becca went to school. It was a complete waste of time; all she could think about was when Mr. Jarvis was going to take her back.

She was still thinking about it as she started to walk home from the bus stop, but by the time she got to the top of the first hill, she was thinking about Bill instead. She stopped and looked out over the mountains. This is where they'd stood that day they'd first walked home together. The day she'd unhitched the team wrong. The day he'd hurt his face. She shivered, then stepped off the road as she heard a car coming up behind her.

The car didn't go by. It stopped, and the driver rolled down a window. "Excuse me," said a man's voice. "Do you know if this road goes to Rachel Herrick's house?"

Becca turned around and stared at the driver. "Mr. Jarvis!"

He looked surprised. "Yes . . . ?" Then he smiled all over. "Rebecca! What are you doing out here in the wilds of Vermont all by yourself?"

"Walking home from the bus, of course," she said.

"Well, walk no farther, fair maid!" He pushed open the door on her side of the car. "I'll convey you home in style."

She grinned and hopped in, but he was looking at her so hard she began to feel squirmy. "What's wrong?" she asked.

"Nothing," he said, starting down the road. "I'm just looking for the little girl I put on the plane in January. If it weren't for the hair, I don't think I'd have recognized you. You look great."

Did she really look so different? There weren't very many mirrors at Rachel's, and she never looked into them anyway, except to see that her hair was parted straight. She'd have to check this out when she got home.

"Hey, wait a minute!" she said as Mr. Jarvis shot past the house. "This is it!"

He stopped, backed up, and then jounced up the driveway. "So you live here, do you?" he said, gazing at the view. "Say, this is really something!"

Behind them, the door slammed, and Rachel strode out into the yard. Mr. Jarvis opened his arms and—gee, it was sort of embarrassing to see somebody hug Rachel like that. But then, they were old friends.

"Another transformation!" said Mr. Jarvis, stepping back to look at Rachel. "I don't think I'd have recognized you, either."

Did Rachel really look different? Well, maybe, when you thought about it. Better kept up, like the house. And there was something a little different about her face.

Rachel and Mr. Jarvis talked a while about the usual boring grownup sort of stuff—the trip, Mr. Jarvis's business, the view. Becca was just about to sneak into the house when Mr. Jarvis said, "Say, I hear you have a pony, Rebecca. May I see him?"

"Oh, sure!" she said. "And Tumnus! Where's Tumnus?"

"In the house," said Rachel dryly. "I thought I'd spare Bob his enthusiasm."

"Oh, let him out, if you mean the dog," said Mr. Jarvis.

"You asked for it." Rachel smiled. "I'll stay inside myself. I have bread in the oven." She went in, and in a second Tumnus and Xeno came bounding out. Xeno waved his tail politely, but Tumnus hurled himself at Becca, barking his "welcome home" bark.

"Sit, you nerd!" yelled Becca. He sat, trembling all over. Xeno sat, too. "Now, fellahs, say hello politely to Mr. Jarvis."

Both dogs held up their right front paws, and Mr. Jarvis shook hands all around. "Glad to meet you, dogs," he said gravely.

"I taught them how to do that," said Becca. "Aren't they polite?"

"They certainly are. *And* big. The pair of them must weigh over two hundred pounds!" Mr. Jarvis patted the two huge black heads, then found a stick to throw. Tumnus shot after it, yelping, and Xeno chased him round and round the yard.

"So much for perfect manners," Mr. Jarvis said with a grin. "Never met a dog I couldn't corrupt. Now, about this pony . . ."

Becca led the way to the barn. "I didn't know you liked horses."

"I'm not wild about them, but I'd like to see *your* pony. And I imagine Rachel's horses are all worth looking at."

"Oh, they are! Nobody's horses look as good as ours, except Mr. Amiden's team. Rachel spends *hours* out here, grooming them, and they get special supplements and . . ."

She tugged the barn door open, wondering why Mr. Jarvis was giving her a funny look.

He strolled down the aisle, looking over the stall doors. Dancer's stall was second, and Dancer, of course, stretched his nose way out, hoping for a carrot. Mr. Jarvis stroked the chestnut face. "What an exquisite creature! I didn't know horses *came* this beautiful!"

"He's Rachel's," said Becca proudly. "She's just started riding him, and he's so good you wouldn't *believe* it. Rachel says Patty and I can ride him in the ring soon. He's gentle like that because nothing bad has ever happened to him. See, Rachel says . . ." and she told Mr. Jarvis all about training young horses the right way.

"I see," he said when she'd finished. "Well, it's good you're learning all this. Rachel's an authority, after all. Did you know she studied with an Olympic trainer when she was a teenager? I tell you, those guys don't just take *anybody* for students."

"*Rachel* did that?! Rachel? She never told *me* that!"

"Maybe you never asked her," he said, giving her another funny look. "Where's your pony?"

"Down here," Becca closed her mouth and walked to Gandalf's stall. He put his head out and nickered.

"Seems like you two get along," said Mr. Jarvis. "Say! He's a really classy little guy! I was expecting something furrier, you know, like the ones in pony rides."

Becca wrinkled up her nose. "Oh no! He's an eventing pony—or at least he will be once we get him jumping again. But Patty and I made real progress yesterday, y'know that? She led, see, and he followed her over all kinds of poles."

"You'd better explain this to me," he said, patting Gandalf. "I didn't think it was a big deal for a pony to step over a pole."

Becca closed Gandalf's door, and they started back to the house. On the way, she told him about all the problems they'd had with Gandalf, and how she'd had to wait and wait, and work him. It was great to talk to Mr. Jarvis again. You forgot how carefully he listened to you, and how he treated you like a grownup.

"Well," he said as they stepped into the kitchen and the smell of fresh-baked bread, "it sounds as if you've learned a fair amount about horses yourself."

"She's doing very well," said Rachel. She leaned over to take the bread out of the oven, and all of a sudden there was a kind of awkward little silence. Mr. Jarvis scooped a cat off a chair and sat down. Rachel shook the bread out of the pans. Becca wished she could leave.

"Well," said Mr. Jarvis after a minute, "I bet you could use a hand with the chores."

"Ask Becca," said Rachel. "She said she'd do them if she didn't have to help me clean the house."

"Well, stable boy, what do you say?" He smiled at her.

Becca stared at his suit, tie, and shiny shoes. You forgot about those kinds of clothes in Vermont. "You're going to help me muck stalls? Like *that?*"

Rachel and Mr. Jarvis laughed, and things began to feel a little better. "Nope," said Mr. Jarvis, "I'm going to change into real clothes. Why don't you help me bring them in?"

She did help him, and it was worth it. He did lots more than muck stalls. He split wood and brought it in for Rachel while Becca told him how you cook on a wood stove. He let Becca teach him how to hitch up the team, and he watched her drive them to the manure pile while she told him about that time she'd unhitched them wrong. He fixed the loose hinge Rachel had been meaning to get to while Becca told him about Bill and Mr. Amiden. He carried the water buckets while she told him about how nice Patty was. The chores got done in no time at all, and when they went in, dinner was ready. Stew, fresh bread, double chocolate cake. Things were just about as perfect as they ever got in Vermont—and to top it all off, when she finally started up to bed, he asked her if she'd like to play hooky in the morning.

"Really?" she asked, looking at Rachel.

Rachel nodded, and Mr. Jarvis said, "Sure. I flew three thousand miles just to talk to you. I talked to some people in Boston, too, but let's forget about them—they were very dull. What's more, I have to leave Friday morning, or I'll miss my plane, which means I'll miss the boys' championship game." He smiled that smile you always liked about Mr. Jarvis. "But, of course, if you're really dying to spend a beautiful day inside the schoolroom . . ."

"Oh, that's okay!"

"Fine, then. We'll go for a walk right after breakfast."

Well, Mr. Jarvis didn't seem to realize how early you ate breakfast in Vermont. By the time he'd eaten, Becca had cleaned all her tack, brushed Gandalf, Mutt, and Jeff, and was starting in on Dimwit.

"Good afternoon!" she grinned as he walked into the barn with the dogs.

"Afternoon! It's only eight-thirty!" He patted Dimwit as Becca put her back into her stall. "You make me feel old and gray, country kid."

They walked to the top of the hill behind the house, to a place where three huge boulders stood in the middle of a field, looking out over the valley. Mr. Jarvis climbed up the biggest boulder, and Becca scrambled up after him. Together they looked out over the green mowings, the scrub-dotted pastures, white houses, woods, and bluegreen mountains. Then Mr. Jarvis lay down on his back in the sun and shut his eyes.

"Now," he said. "Tell me why you want to leave this place."

Oh dear! This was going to be harder than she'd thought. She'd forgotten he was a lawyer; and she'd forgotten how lawyers had a way of making what you had to say seem wrong, even when they were perfectly willing to listen. Dad said they couldn't help it: it was the way they were trained.

"Well," she said, hunting around in her mind for all the things she'd gotten lined up to say, "it's just not . . . *right* here."

"What's wrong with it?"

"Well, you know how in Santa Barbara the hills are gold and the trees are green? And there are all those flowers, all year round? And the beach? Well, here it's not like that. You wouldn't believe how cold it gets in the winter, and how it's gray all the time. And in spring it's brown, and then in summer everything turns green . . ." This was embarrassing; she wasn't saying what she meant at all.

He waited a minute, but when she didn't go on, he turned his head and opened his eyes so he could look out over the valley. "You have to admit, though, this isn't bad as scenery goes," he said.

"That's not what I meant," she said. "What I mean is, well, at home, things were always the same, see? And here, they're so *complicated!*"

"Mmm. How, complicated?"

"Well, like Bill. He was in all this trouble, and I knew he was. He was running off, see. But I didn't know whether I should tell on him or whether it was his business. That never would've happened at home."

"Why not?"

"Because I would . . . well, because Dad would have known what to do."

Mr. Jarvis sat up. "And Rachel didn't?"

"I never asked her. I didn't even tell her all I knew until that day I wrote to you. She was mad."

"Because you wrote?"

"Nope. Because I hadn't told her Bill was meeting somebody when he ran off."

"You don't think your dad would have been mad if you'd lied to him?" Mr. Jarvis's eyebrows went up very high on his forehead.

"Well, he might have . . ." Sure he would have. Boy, would he have been mad! Only . . . "But it wouldn't have happened."

"Why not?"

"I didn't know anybody in California the way I know Bill. And I didn't go places on my own, without Dad or Molly. So that question doesn't apply."

"A true lawyer's daughter," he muttered. "But why didn't you tell Rachel what was going on?"

"Because Rachel doesn't see . . . well, how good people are."

Mr. Jarvis looked surprised. "Really? That doesn't fit in with what you were telling me yesterday about her training that horse—Donder, Blitzen . . ."

"Dancer!" She giggled.

"Right—Dancer. How could she train him if she didn't see the good things in him?"

"Oh, but she brought him up, see. It's not people like that she can't see the good in. It's people who're messed up. Like Bill. She thinks they live in fairy-tale worlds. She *said* so."

Mr. Jarvis took off his glasses and cleaned them with

his handkerchief. "I thought *you* were the one who told me people weren't supposed to believe in fairy tales," he said.

"Huh?"

"What Rachel means," he said, "is that some people make up stories in order to make their lives easier to live."

"Right! And she says that's wrong!"

"Well, hold it. Suppose she doesn't mean what you think. Suppose she means it's okay to make up fairy tales, but you have to see the difference between what you make up and what's really happening. If that's what she means, would that be okay?"

Becca frowned. "I don't get it."

"Okay. Take your friend Bill. Yesterday you told me he spent a lot of time dreaming about the day his dad would come to rescue him. Right? But there's a difference between sitting in your room, dreaming about how nice it would be, and running away, looking for your dad."

Becca stared at him. "You think that's what he's been doing?"

"I'd say it was a reasonable conjecture. He runs off. He gets found again. He's obviously looking for *something*. Why not his dad, if that's who he really cares about?"

Becca felt her jaw dropping. Boy, Mr. Jarvis sure was smart. Why, *nobody* had . . .

"Let's take another example," Mr. Jarvis went on. "Your pony. Now, granted, you can't explain to a pony that his person has died. But has it been good for Gandalf to stand in his stall, waiting for Jessica to come and rescue him?"

"No *way!*"

"And haven't you been trying to tell him, 'Hey, Gandalf! You've got to stop dreaming off all the time and come live in the real world with me, Becca? You've got to learn to jump again and get on with your life?' Isn't that what you've been trying to teach him?"

Becca stared at him again. "How did you know that?"

"You told me yesterday. Not in so many words, but you told me."

"Oh."

"So," he went on in the tone of voice Dad used when he was summing up a case, "you admit that dreaming of finding Jessica hasn't been altogether good for Gandalf? And that dreaming of finding his dad—if that's what he's been doing—hasn't been altogether good for Bill?"

"I guess so." He really was leading up to something—you could tell.

"Then tell me something. Isn't your living here in this beautiful place, with a pony and a puppy and the first real friends you've ever had—isn't living like that and *still* dreaming about going back to Santa Barbara, where things are simpler, or the right color, or whatever—isn't that the same kind of thing Bill and Gandalf were doing?"

"No! No!" She'd let him trap her, and it just wasn't *fair!* "They're just dreaming! I really want to go back!"

"Why?"

"Because . . . because . . ." It was so *frustrating* explaining things to somebody who just refused to hear what you wanted to say! "Because . . ."

"Rebecca," he said gently, "what do you want to go back *to?*"

"Why . . . !" She stopped. What *did* she want to go back to? Whenever she thought of Santa Barbara, she thought of her house, her room, Dad's study, and . . . well, Dad. But . . . but that was crazy! The house had been sold! Dad was dead. Dead, dead, dead! She knew that! What was wrong with her, then? Was she some kind of retard, or something? She looked up at Mr. Jarvis helplessly.

"Don't you see, Becca?" he said, very very kindly. "Don't you see there's nothing for you in Santa Barbara except what you remember and what you dream?"

Becca stared out across the valley. In the distance, a little light flashed on the road where a car reflected the sun. She watched the tiny car as it crept along the road and blurred.

"I guess . . . I must've . . . I didn't . . ." She felt dizzy, and she put out one hand to steady herself. The hand accidentally bumped Mr. Jarvis; he took it and pulled her over until she was in his arms. Nobody had held her like that for a long, long time, and she was much too old for it now. But when he did it, a sort of knot that had been all tied up inside her unwound, and she cried and cried, while he rocked her quietly and stroked her rumpled hair.

When she finally stopped, he fished in his pocket and pulled out his handkerchief for her. She wiped her face and sat up a little, still leaning against him. "I'm sorry."

"There's nothing wrong with crying because you've lost somebody you love," he said. "In the long run, it's a lot better than making up fairy tales about finding him again."

Becca looked out over the valley, not really thinking. "But Dad really loved me," she said after a long time. "That wasn't a fairy tale."

"Oh, no. That was real."

"Rachel *said* it was a fairy tale."

"She said he didn't love you?"

"No . . . but she didn't like the way he did it, or something."

"That's understandable, if you think about it. Your dad loved you so much he wouldn't share you with anybody else."

Becca sat up straight and pulled away from him. "That's not so!"

"Becca. Did you have friends your age?"

She shook her head.

"Pets?"

She shook her head.

"Was there anybody in your life besides your dad?"

"Molly . . ."

"But did he want you to be with Molly when he was around?"

"Who'd *want* to be with Molly when Dad was around?"

"Anybody who hadn't been carefully trained *not* to see how simple and good-hearted and generous a person she is." His voice sounded a bit hard.

"Oh." She should write Molly a letter, probably. Molly had written to her twice, now, and she had never written back. "But Dad was—"

"A wonderful, witty, intelligent man. Sure he was! But look: he did just what Gandalf did and what Bill may have done. When he realized he was going to lose his wife, partly because of the way he'd acted, that really hurt him. And he thought he could stop hurting by loving you instead of her. He made up a fairy tale for himself, Becca—a whole world where he could love and love and love with no questions and no pain. You were the lucky person who got all the love he had to give."

"Was that . . . wrong?"

"At the time, I thought it was very wrong. Of course, part of the problem was that he was . . . well . . . bull-headed about it. And angry. So it was very hard to see that what he was really trying to do was hurt less. I quarreled with him. We got so angry with each other, we broke up our partnership and we never really spoke to each other again. Then I kept fighting for Rachel, because her pain really hurt to watch. But it didn't do much good: we lost and lost, and finally she just holed up here and sort of let everything go by.''

Becca remembered, all of a sudden, what Mrs. Ellrow had said the day she'd driven them up the hill: ''When you're not happy, you let a lot go by you'd look out for if things were going the way you'd like them to.'' Then that half thought she'd had way back then had been right. Rachel wasn't just a slob. The house back then had had something to do with Rachel's face: that sort of frozen look.

''I guess it *was* wrong, if it hurt . . . other people,'' she said slowly.

Mr. Jarvis nodded. ''But it's also wrong to get furious at somebody who has done the hurting—because then, you see, you never get a chance to sit down and talk things out. I keep thinking, maybe if I'd been more patient, maybe if I'd waited for your dad to get over his first pain, maybe if I'd told Rachel to hold off for a month or two . . . then maybe all this never would have happened. So if you're looking for wrong, I was wrong, too, Becca.''

''Is that why you came out here? Because you felt bad about being wrong?''

''Partly, I suppose. But mostly because you wrote and asked me to take you away. I promised I'd help you if you were unhappy, didn't I?''

Another car flashed down in the valley. High over the mountains, a hawk circled, perfectly motionless in the light breeze. At the foot of the boulder, Tumnus and Xeno panted in the shade. Mr. Jarvis put his hand on Becca's knee.

''*Are* you unhappy here, Becca? If you forget for a moment what you've been dreaming about, are you really unhappy with what's here?''

What's here. Tumnus. Gandalf, beginning to jump, now. Patty: "It was all Becca's idea, honest!" Mr. Amiden: "One of your all-time fans, haven't you noticed?" Bill, wherever he was. It'd be sort of okay not to have to leave all of them.

"No," she said finally. "I guess I'm not really unhappy with what's here. Except . . . Rachel . . ."

"What about Rachel?"

"She . . . doesn't really . . . well, care."

"Care about what?"

She looked up. Could she tell him? Rachel was his friend, after all.

"Tell me, Becca," he urged. "What doesn't Rachel care about?"

Well, maybe she could risk it. "Me."

"Oh, no." You could tell by his voice he really meant it. "Rachel cares for you more deeply than you can possibly imagine."

"She doesn't act like she does."

Mr. Jarvis put his arm around her. "Not everybody loves in the same way," he said. "You're used to love that owns you, that won't let you out of its sight, that won't let you fly on your own. Rachel doesn't love that way."

Becca thought about it. "But she never . . . well, not very often, anyway . . . says nice stuff or gives hugs."

"Maybe you don't let her," he suggested gently.

Becca looked out across the valley. The hawk was still hovering, circling, soaring. Two goldfinches flew by in a bouncy line, chattering to each other. Down the hill, the neighbor's cows filed slowly through a gap in the woods, walking heavily toward the watering pond.

She stood up and stretched. "Let's go back."

"Sure." He jumped off the boulder and threw a stick

for Tumnus. Tumnus streaked after it, barking joyfully, and caught it just as it landed.

The rest of the day was kind of strange. Mr. Jarvis and Rachel talked, and sometimes Becca listened. They did the chores together, and they ate dinner together, but Becca didn't feel . . . well, there. It seemed as though half her mind was still up on the rocks, thinking over what Mr. Jarvis had said and trying to decide what it was going to be like living here all the time. Mixing up: that's what Patty would call it. You didn't really know if you were glad or sorry. There'd be horse shows and trail rides and swimming (Rachel had promised). She could help Mr. Amiden look for Bill—that might be exciting. But on the other hand, it was so sad, somehow . . . even though you'd sort of known, somewhere inside you, that Dad really just wasn't *in* Santa Barbara anymore and that there wasn't any reason to go back there when it wasn't so bad here . . .

All in all, she was very glad when bedtime came and she could slip up to her room without being impolite. But she couldn't sleep. Every time she closed her eyes she saw . . . Rachel. Rachel, longeing Dancer. Rachel, striding behind the team up in the maple grove. Rachel, splitting wood. Rachel, making doughnuts. Rachel, hunched over her typewriter. Rachel, crying after Becca had unhitched the team wrong that day. Rachel's frozen face, looking out over the valley last Monday, after she'd gotten that call from Mr. Jarvis. The more she tried to sleep, the more times that last Rachel face showed up in front of her eyes.

Finally she sat up and turned on the light. This was ridiculous; she couldn't just lie there. What she really needed was a good book. She got up and looked at her bookshelf. There wasn't much on it: three or four library books, and she'd finished them all, anyway. None of them were worth reading again. What you really needed when you couldn't sleep was an old friend.

She opened her closet door. Somewhere back there was *The Chestry Oak.* She pushed back through her clothes and rooted around. This was silly! How did you find a book in the dark? She brought one armful out into her room, then another armful—not there, either. Two more—gee, she must have put the Kate Seredy books away very very first . . . there it was!

She picked it up and started back to bed, but then she turned around and looked at the heap of books on the floor. It wasn't very nice to leave your old friends just lying there in a pile. And she couldn't sleep, anyway. . . . Yeah, Prince Michael could wait just a few minutes. He'd understand.

She picked up the books one after another, dusting them off carefully, and put them in her bookcase. Much better! She climbed into bed and patted it so Tumnus would join her. After they'd adjusted themselves so there was room for both of them, she opened the book and flipped through the pictures, which were all together in the front.

They were wonderful pictures: Bill would like this book. Prince Michael, looking at the great Chestry Oak that the first Prince of Chestry had planted. Prince Michael, sitting on his father's lap while his father talked of the secret army that was going to drive the Nazis out of Hungary. Prince Michael, racing through the valley on Midnight, the beautiful, avenging Chestry stallion, with bombs flying all around. Michael, very thin, looking out over a valley in America, not very far from here, where he was going to live on a farm with Mom and Pop Brown; not Prince Michael anymore, just a lost little boy.

All of a sudden, it occurred to Becca that she knew

what that valley Michael had come to looked like now. She'd always had trouble imagining it before: valleys in California didn't look like the one in the picture. She turned to the passage: "He saw a deep, green valley spread out below him, he saw the long, sweeping barrier of distant mountains like an arm around it . . ." Hey, yeah! It was just like Vermont! And the farm he'd come to even had horses and a white house like Rachel's! She turned back to the book, knowing she'd cry if she went on reading. That was strange, because there were lots of sad and scary passages in the book, but this wasn't one of them. I mean, Michael had thought he'd lost everything he loved, but when he looked out at the valley, he found he really hadn't: "Thoughts were like music inside him, singing: This is my valley. . . . I found my valley . . . I am not lost anymore . . . my valley found me." She curled up closer to Tumnus, blinked away her tears, and read until her head finally dropped onto the pillow.

Much, much later, she dimly felt somebody take the book out of her hand, turn out the light, and kiss her very gently on the forehead.

Chapter 20

Mr. Jarvis drove Becca to school Friday; Rachel had been going to do it, but he said he had to leave early anyway, so he might as well spare the pickup the trip. They didn't say much as his little rented car bounced down the road. For one thing, there wasn't much to say; and for another, when you couldn't sleep at night you never really woke up the next day. Mr. Jarvis looked tired, too—he yawned as he drove into the school parking lot.

"So this is your prison, huh?" he asked with a smile. "Not bad, actually."

"No, it's okay. It was more interesting when Bill and I had lessons together, though. Say—do you think he's really gone looking for his dad?"

"I haven't seen all the evidence—it's just an idea."

"Did you tell Rachel?"

"Yes, I did. She thought there might be something to it. She sure liked it better than her idea about his joining a gang."

"I like it better, too."

"Well," he said, "keep me posted, will you?"

"Sure. Oh, darn! I forgot to ask Rachel for a note."

"Oh, one of those excuses from school? I'll write you one." He reached for his briefcase, tore out a yellow sheet, and wrote on it. "There! Now, give me a hug, Becca. You're already late."

She gave him the biggest hug she could manage in a car. "I wish you could stay."

He looked at her. "Can you keep a secret?"

"Of course!"

"Okay. You know that business I had in Boston? Well, it was an interview of sorts. Some friends of mine from law school want me to help them set up a partnership that does work involving rural kids: custody cases, child abuse, foster homes. They weren't as dull as I let on." He smiled. "In fact, they've been tempting me for almost a year."

"So you might be living in Boston?"

"Maybe even closer. Some of the towns they've thought about are within an hour from here. It's still in the planning stages—that's why I didn't tell Rachel about it. But if Jean and the boys are interested, we'll probably come in a year or so. And I think they'll approve. They really liked the idea when it turned up last October."

"Why didn't you go then?"

He looked at her, then he looked out the car window. "Oh, a friend of mine had just died. I wanted to make sure things were going to work out for his kid before I gave any thought to moving. When you get to be my age, my dear, a year or two doesn't make much difference. Hurry up, now—scoot!"

She gave him another quick hug, and scooted. She was halfway up the school sidewalk before she understood what he'd been saying about his friend who had died. Boy, was she ever dumb! She turned around, but he was already turning out on the main road. She watched his little car disappear around the corner, thinking how wonderful it would be if he *did* live only an hour or so away. Well, she'd better get . . .

"Becca!" Patty was standing in the doorway, waving wildly. Becca hurried in. "I'm supposed to be in class," whispered Patty, "but I saw you out the window. Are you okay?"

"Yeah, I'm okay. I was absent because we were talking."

"And . . . ?"

That's right. Patty still thought she was leaving. Was it only two days ago she'd thought she was leaving, too? It seemed lots longer than that.

"Well?" Patty looked at her pleadingly.

"I'm not going." She waited for Patty to whoop or jump around, but Patty didn't.

"You mean they won't let you go?"

"Nope, I mean . . . well, you know what you said about your parents? How you wanted to call your mom after the funeral?"

Patty nodded, and all of a sudden she looked lots older than she really was. "It's okay," she said. "You don't have to explain. Let's go riding tomorrow morning, okay?"

Becca nodded, feeling a little awkward. "Yeah, let's."

There was a little pause, then Patty said, "You'd better get that to the office." She pointed to the note.

"Yeah, I'd better." Becca opened it. "Oh my gosh!"

Patty looked over her shoulder as Becca read it a second time.

To whom it may concern: Rebecca Davidson was not in school yesterday (6/4) because she was considering the intellectual and spiritual complexities of mankind.
Yours truly, R. D. Jarvis, LL.D.

"Oh no!" Patty giggled. "What'll Mr. Corey say when he reads *that?*"

Becca tried to keep a straight face like Rachel's. "No

problem. I don't think he can read words that long, so he'll just file it."

They were both still laughing as she walked into the office.

Saturday morning the phone rang, and Rachel answered it. "That was Jenny Ellrow," she said. "Patty has a dentist appointment, so she can't ride this morning."

"I'll wait until this afternoon, then."

Rachel looked out the window. "Better go now, if you're going. It looks like it'll storm later on."

So Becca tacked Gandalf up and started down the trail to the sawmill. She'd decided she wanted to follow the trail past the mill and go down to the lake. There were plenty of cabins near the lake, she knew, and most of them were empty. Maybe a smart guy like Bill would stay in one of them, instead of hiding out way off in the woods.

It was farther than she'd thought. On the other side of the sawmill, the road went downhill for a couple of miles, crossed a dirt road, and then wound along for another mile or so to the lake. When it reached the lake, you could see the trail went along its edge, usually, but at this time of year it was covered with water. Shoot. Becca stopped Gandalf and let him take a drink. As he sipped, slurping the water around his bit, she noticed for the first time how heavy and thick the air felt. The water in the lake was absolutely still, reflecting the mountains and the black clouds that were gathered above them.

Well, they'd better get back. It was going to rain soon, and they couldn't get any farther unless they went the long way around. Tomorrow she and Patty could go that way and look at the cabins. Becca looked out over the lake once more. Was Bill really out there somewhere, hiding?

Or was he miles and miles away, looking for his dad? How did you *find* somebody who just disappeared?

A breeze rippled the lake, and Becca could hear it growing stronger in the pines near where they stood. ‘‘C'mon, Gandy—we'd better make tracks.’’

He made lovely tracks: he cantered springily up the grassy trail, swishing his tail and asking to go faster. Was this what Mrs. Arnold had meant about his being perky? They came to the road in no time at all, and she slowed him down. ‘‘Good boy!’’

There was a police car parked on the road, and the policeman Rachel and Mr. Amiden called Sergeant Dave was leaning over the trail on the opposite side. His real name was David Boyd; his daughter Amy was in fourth grade, and she was going to start taking riding lessons from Rachel this summer. Becca rode up to him. ‘‘Hi!’’

‘‘Hello, Becca. You been at the sawmill?’’

‘‘Just went by.’’

‘‘Anybody there?’’

‘‘Didn't see anybody. Something wrong?’’

‘‘Oh, somebody just lifted some tools from Ballantine's cottage. I was wondering if it was worth driving down the trail. It's supposed to storm, and if it does I'll never get the cruiser out of there.’’

‘‘I'll look if you want.’’

He looked up at the sky. ‘‘Think you'd best get home instead.’’

She looked up, too. ‘‘Well, it isn't too far from here, the way I go,’’ she said.

He frowned. ‘‘You seen a Vermont thunderstorm yet?’’

‘‘Nope.’’

‘‘Well, you really don't want to be out in one. If you get caught, hole up somewhere, you hear? Somewhere low, where the lightning won't strike. I don't want to collect a fried pony at the end of a hard day."

"Okay." Becca smiled, but she didn't really feel too smily. They'd better hurry.

"Tell you what," he said. "I'll stop by Rachel's and tell her you're on your way. Otherwise she'll worry."

"Thanks!" Becca tapped Gandalf with her heels and they set off at a fast canter. When they got to the sawmill, he was breathing hard, but he didn't want to stop.

"Look, silly," she said. "It'll just take a minute! He's telling Rachel where we are, so we can do him a favor!"

Gandalf said he really didn't want to do this, but she found some sugar in her pocket and bribed him to follow her down the blackberry-lined path. It was getting awfully windy: the blackberries reached over to claw at them, and the sawmill creaked and groaned as they peered into it. Gandalf threw up his head and stopped. She turned and faced him. "Look, you bundle of nerves! The sooner I check this out, the sooner we get home! See?"

He didn't see. He reared, backing up, and she had to go with him. Like Rachel said, when push came to shove, a horse was bigger than you were. What was wrong with him? Something hit her helmet—a stick, probably. She looked around, then up. The sky was an awfully funny color: black and almost yellow. Something big and white hit her hand. Gandalf snorted. Then, suddenly, big white marbles were falling everywhere. Snow? No, hail!

"Geez!" she breathed. "Let's get out of here, Gandy!"

He was so nervous she could hardly mount him, and the instant she settled in the saddle, he shot toward the shortcut. Becca grabbed a handful of mane and fished for her stirrups. Branches slashed by her face as they raced up the narrow path, and the wind roared louder and louder. The yellow woods suddenly flashed white in front of her, and then a cannon went off somewhere. No—that must be thunder. Who would have thought thunder was that *scary?* Becca buried her head in Gandalf's mane and shut her eyes tight. But it didn't help. The hail tore through the leaves, pounding them with sticks and branches, and there was another one of those terrible white flashes. This time it snapped, and the bang came right after it. Somewhere in her mind, Becca heard Sergeant Dave say, "Hole up somewhere low . . ."

She opened her eyes and looked ahead. They were on the wide trail, now, almost at the fork. It wasn't very far, now. . .

SNAP—BANG!

Gandalf stopped so suddenly she would have gone over his head if she hadn't had her arms around his neck already. A hundred yards up the trail, something was smoking. A tree! It was all black along one side, and as she watched, it creaked, leaned, and crashed down on the trees around it. "Oh, Gandy!" she whimpered. "What'll we *do?*"

She looked toward the steep path. It was hardly a path anymore. There were branches all over it. Could they make it? Should they even try? Suddenly she remembered the house that wasn't far from here. "Let's go there, Gandy. Maybe there's a shed we can wait in."

She turned him down the trail. He didn't want to go, but she insisted. "Remember?" she said above the wind, trying to sound brave, "No fried ponies. We stay down here."

It took forever to get to the house, even after she got him going. The hail stopped, but it turned to rain that was so thick you could hardly see. Becca's reins got slippery and she was wet and shivery in just a few moments. There was the house! She dismounted and led him around the snow fence, peering ahead into the rain and wind. At the end of the fallen-down ell there was a shed. Maybe they could hole up in there. That way, the tramp wouldn't even know they were there.

She led Gandalf into the shed, feeling in front of her with her feet. It was okay: the floor was dirt, and there was even a clear place on one side. As Becca's eyes got used to the dark, she saw a lot of bottles and some old paint canvas on the other side, mixed in with some old two-by-fours and other scrap lumber. She tied Gandalf up by the reins, even though you weren't supposed to, and loosened his girth. "We'll wait here until the lightning stops," she told him.

But Gandalf didn't seem to be very comfortable. He kept looking over his shoulder, and his ears were pricked up as high as they could go. Becca listened, but she couldn't hear anything except the wind and rain.

Something flashed out in the yard. Gandalf pulled back on the reins and rolled his eyes. "Shhh . . . !" whispered Becca. But he stepped sideways, his nostrils flaring.

Then she heard it, too. *Squish, squish.* Pause, while the light shone around the scrub that had once been a yard. Then again, *squish, squish, squish.* Somebody was coming. Becca shrank behind Gandalf, but he wasn't any help: he shot sideways, then started as his haunches hit the wall. Something leaning on the wall fell over.

"Who's there?" said a voice. It sounded like a voice that meant business, though it wasn't very deep. Becca held her breath.

A beam of light shot across the dark shed, and Gandalf pulled on his reins again. Becca stepped forward to untie him so he wouldn't break the reins, but as she did it, the light shone right in her eyes. She froze, blinded.

SNAAAAP! There was a little pause before the bang this

time. But the lightning went on for what seemed like forever, and the flash lit up somebody standing in the doorway—somebody not tall enough to be a grownup. Becca put her hand in front of the awful light, trying to see more.

"Becca?!" said the voice. "What the . . . !"

The person pointed the flashlight at the floor, and she could see a familiar slouch silhouetted against the dim light outside. "Bill?"

"Yeah, Bill. Think I was a murderer?"

"Geez, something like that! You scared me enough! What're you doing here? Mr. Amiden's been looking all *over* for you, and the police and everybody . . ."

"Shhhh!" He looked over his shoulder. "Listen, you can't stay here."

"Can't stay! But look what it's *doing* out there! That's why we're here! We almost got struck . . ."

He scuffed the toe of his sneaker on the floor. "Well, okay," he growled. "Come on in the house where I can watch. But you've got to leave if I say to, hear?"

Bill disappeared out the door, and she gave Gandalf a hasty pat and ran after him. He slipped between two sagging uprights in the fallen-down ell, and when she followed him, she found herself in a room that smelled like rot and dirt and something else she couldn't quite place. Like a cocktail party, she thought suddenly. Only you obviously didn't have cocktail parties out here.

"Come on in front," he said. "I've got to look out the windows."

"How come?"

"None of your business!" he said over his shoulder. But when they got to the room in front, he looked a bit more friendly. "I shouldn't say that," he said. "You've been okay."

"Thanks," she said sarcastically.

The room had been a pretty room once. The wallpaper had been white, with an old-fashioned star pattern on it. There was a big fireplace with a stove set in it, and the floors shone through the dirt with the kind of shine good floors are supposed to have. "Whose house is this?" she asked.

"I don't know. Ours, I guess."

"Ours?"

He ignored the question. "But I'm leaving. Tomorrow."

"Where are you going?"

"Canada."

"All by yourself?"

He looked at her a long time, as if he were trying to decide if he could tell her. Finally he sighed. "Okay, look. Remember how I told you my dad was going to get the money together and we were going to take off?"

She nodded, opening her eyes wider and wider.

"Well, he did it. He came last January. He always finds me—everywhere I go, he finds me." Bill's eyes looked almost friendly. "And this time, he's done some paintings and sold them. And I threw in the money Rachel paid me for cleaning stalls . . ."

"All your money!"

"Sure—I want to be with my dad," he said simply. "What else would I spend it on? Ed gave me everything I needed."

"Is your dad . . . I mean . . . did he stop . . . ?"

Bill shifted uneasily onto his other foot and looked out the window again. "He's fine."

"Was . . . was he the one who hit you, that day I unhitched the team wrong?"

"He didn't mean to," said Bill quickly. "And anyway, that's the last time he's done anything like that. I told him

I'd clear out for good if he did it again. He kind of saw the light then. That's when he started painting again.''

''He's a painter?''

''You bet he is—a good one. He used to teach painting, and he did a whole lot of shows before . . . well, before. And right now, he's getting money for the last one. He should be home by now—but I guess he holed up in the storm, like you.''

Becca looked at the old wallpaper, thinking. ''Then you didn't . . . have anything to do with that stolen stuff?''

''I told you I didn't.''

''No, I mean 'you'—you and your dad.''

''His money came from painting, I tell you!''

She frowned and studied one of the wallpaper stars, trying to decide if he was lying. It didn't sound like it.

''You been drawing yourself?'' she asked after a long pause.

That had been the right thing to say: he looked away from the stupid windows and smiled. ''Yeah. Want to see?''

He started toward a back room, and she followed him. It was cold in there—you could see a huge hole in the wall. But there was lots of sketch paper around. Most of the sketches looked like Bill's. The house. Dancer again. A tree. Then an interesting face, with dark eyebrows like Bill's.

''That your dad?''

''Yeah. There are better ones over here. We did portraits for a few days, and I got better.'' He pulled out a charcoal sketch of the same face she'd seen earlier. But it looked interested and sort of dreamy, the way Bill's did when he was drawing.

''I like that one,'' she said. ''You're really good, you know that?''

He shrugged. "Like Rachel said, I got a good teacher." He grinned. "Boy, was I scared when she said that! I thought she'd found out somehow."

Becca nodded. She remembered. "You got any of your dad's sketches around?"

"Sure." He pulled a sketchbook out from under the table and opened it. The sketches were lots like Bill's, only—well, Bill's were good, but these looked . . . professional, maybe. Every single line was in the right place. She leafed through it. "Oh!"

He looked over her shoulder. "Oh, yeah. He did that last week, when I was sleeping."

It was Bill, sound asleep, with all the usual Bill expression gone. Just a kid's face, with long lashes, a delicate-looking face (Bill's face, delicate? she shot a glance at him—well, yes). The right arm was crooked over the top of his head, and he looked peaceful and happy. Lots younger than you thought of Bill looking. "That's really wonderful," she said.

Bill looked at it, and his face looked almost like the face on the page. "Yeah. Like I say, he's really good."

Suddenly, he stood up straight and listened. Then, two rooms away, a door opened, creaked, slammed shut. A man's voice shouted, "Bill!"

Bill's face froze. "Stay here until I've gone," he whispered. "Then slip through that hole we came in and go home."

"Can't I meet your . . ."

"Bill! Where are you?" The voice was slurred and much too loud.

"No," breathed Bill. "Just *go*."

He took the flashlight with him into the front rooms, leaving her in near darkness. Somewhere in her mind, she realized the rain had stopped.

"Hi, Dad." Bill's voice sounded high and thin. "Sell the painting?"

"Th' bastard wouldn't give me enough for it," slurred the other voice.

"You told me he gave you an advance check for half of it. Isn't that enough to get us started, anyway?"

"Started?" The voice seemed to be confused. "Where you wanna start?"

"Well, you *said* . . ."

"I said, I said, I said! You always remember what I said. Look, let's just stay here a while, huh? Just you and me? We've been doing just fine . . ."

She had to get out! She had to find Rachel! Bill's dad was doing just what he'd always done—promising to get everything together, then not doing it! Becca inched toward the hole, holding her breath.

"Okay, Dad." Bill's voice sounded completely flat. "Just lie down here, and I'll . . ."

Becca tripped over something, and it crashed to the floor.

"Whazzat?" shouted Bill's dad's voice. "You got somebody back there? Like the cops? Or the Amiden fellow?"

"Dad!" Bill's voice rose higher and higher. "It's just the wind, blowing bits of the old shingles off! You've heard it thousands of times before . . . !"

"Outta my way, you little squealer!" A chair fell over, and Becca heard heavy footsteps coming toward the room. There was the hole! Now if she could just slip through before he found her . . .

"Outta my WAY, I said!"

"Dad . . . Dad . . . please . . . !"

There was a terrible soft thud, and Bill screamed. Becca slid through the hole and ran as fast as she could to the shed. Gandalf was tugging at his reins; she untied them, tightened the girth, and started to lead him out. Wait! Bill's dad might be out there! She mounted inside, so she could come out running. Was he there? She dug her heels into Gandalf's sides, and they shot out of the shed.

He was there, and he was bigger than you could possibly imagine. His black hair was long and half covered his face, and he was carrying something—a gun? No, just a stick. Gandalf jumped sideways as the man reached for the reins, and Becca almost fell off.

''Go, Gandy!'' she yelled, grabbing his mane.

''Oh no, you don't!'' the man yelled. ''No little kid's going to squeal on me . . .'' He aimed a swing at Gandalf, but Gandalf snorted, sidestepped, and ran straight for the snow fence. Becca pulled herself back into the saddle and grabbed for the reins. He was going right for it! And Bill's dad could corner them when he stopped! She pulled frantically on her right rein, trying to aim him for the gap, but Bill's dad was lots faster than he should have been—he was running toward the gap, laughing. . . . Oh, Rachel, Rachel! Help, Rachel!

Suddenly something—or nothing—or nobody—said, ''Put your legs on and *ride him at the fence*.'' But that was Patty, and Goner usually jumped. . . . Bill's dad was almost at the gap now, and Gandalf hesitated. He was going to stop! And if she went off, Bill's dad would . . .

She watched the fence come nearer. Four strides, three . . . She clamped her legs on as hard as she could and leaned forward. ''Git!'' she yelled. Two, one—and they sailed over the fence with a foot to spare, landing with a thump that made Becca lose both stirrups.

Slipping and sliding, she hauled herself back in the saddle, trying to find her stirrups, ducking as branches slashed by her. . . . Where were they going? She squinted, trying to see the way ahead. Hey, they were going the wrong way, there was something there, a blue flash—lightning? Gandalf was going slower now; somebody was there . . . She hit out—"No, no! Don't hit me! I'm Bill's friend!"

"Whoa there, now! Nobody's gonna hit you! Easy . . ." It wasn't the same voice . . .the man was much smaller . . . "Hey, easy there, you're all riled up . . ."

"Mr. Amiden!"

"Sure. Now listen, what's all this about? Storm's all over . . . Rachel's right here to take you home . . ."

Rachel! Becca slid out of the saddle as Rachel came running up. "Rachel, Rachel, oh, Rachel!"

Rachel's arms were around her in a moment, and Rachel was bending over her, asking if she was hurt, if she was all right. . .

"I'm okay—no, look, I'm not—right back there is Bill's dad, and he hurt Bill and he tried to cut Gandy and me off at the snow fence, and Gandy *jumped* it, Rachel—but you've got to get Bill because he's hurt, his dad hit him, I heard him scream . . ."

"Easy there." She looked up out of Rachel's arms. Sergeant Dave was looking at her very seriously. "You say somebody's hurt at the old Ward place?"

"Bill! Bill Lavoie! And his dad is there with him, and you'd better hurry . . ."

She heard a lot of footsteps go by. How many people were here, anyway? She looked up at Rachel. "How did you . . . ?"

"Sergeant Dave dropped by just before the storm broke and told me you were all the way down at the lake. Then the storm got worse and worse, and we knew you couldn't possibly make it." Rachel's voice sounded a little shaky. "So we called Rescue and Ed, and Ed knew what logging trail you had to be on, or near. So we all came to help you.''

Becca let go of Rachel and looked around. There was a police car sunk halfway up to its hubcaps in the muddy trail. Behind it was a rescue truck, its usually white sides all splattered.

''You came all the way down here? Just for me?''

''Just for you.'' Rachel shook her head. ''And when I think I let you go out before the worst storm I've ever *seen* up here . . . !''

''Hey, it wasn't your fault! And I'm okay . . . only Bill's dad . . .''

''He didn't hurt you, did he?'' Rachel bent over her again.

''No, no—Gandy got me away, or he would have . . .'' Becca shuddered.

Rachel put one arm around her and patted Gandalf with the other. ''He's a gutsy little pony.''

''Boy I'll say! See, we were in the shed, and Bill's dad was coming, and I just rode right out. He tried to hit us, Rachel! But Gandy just took off and jumped the fence . . .''

Rachel held her tighter. ''And you're a gutsy little kid. Good God! You rode right over him?''

''Well, sort of. I mean, I didn't know what else to do.''

Rachel breathed a long, shuddery breath. From behind them, they heard yelling, and Gandalf pricked up his ears.

''I think we should go help . . .'' started Becca.

''No way! The people who can take care of things best are already there.''

''But Bill . . . he might want to talk to me, or something. He'll think I squealed on him . . .''

''You mean you knew he was here all along?'' Rachel stared at her.

"No, no! I just found out today when I went into the shed because the tree on the shortcut trail got struck! Honest!"

Rachel believed her; you could tell. "Okay," she said. "We'll walk back there, but we're not going anywhere near the house, you hear?"

It was farther than you'd think to the house. Becca began to shake as they got nearer, and Rachel took her hand.

"There's the fence he jumped," she whispered.

"Great glorious heavens! He jumped *that?* And you stayed on?"

"I don't think I would've if I hadn't been so scared. I lost both stirrups, and I sort of slid . . ."

Gandalf began to dance around, and Rachel had to let go of Becca's hand to steady him. Two policemen were leading Bill's dad out of the house, and Mr. Amiden hurried after them. When he saw Becca and Rachel, he jogged over to them.

"Bill's in bad shape," he said. "They're bringin' him right out, and I'll go with him to Bennington."

Rachel took Becca's hand again. "How bad is it?"

"Hard to say. Couple of cracked ribs, a broken collarbone—that'll mend okay. But there might be stuff wrong we can't see . . ."

Rachel held Becca's hand so hard it hurt. "Was Lavoie . . . ?"

"Sure was." Mr. Amiden's face was set and white. "Look, I'm goin' back inside. I'm afraid of what I'll do if I get near that—" He whirled around and ran back in, lifting up a clenched fist as he passed Bill's dad and the two policemen.

But when Bill's dad passed them, he didn't look dangerous. He didn't even look so terribly big. His dark hair was covering most of his face, but you could see. . .

"Rachel," whispered Becca, "was he crying?"

Rachel nodded.

"Because they caught him?"

"Probably not."

She watched the policemen hustle Bill's dad into the squad car. "Rachel?"

Rachel was watching, too. "Yeah?"

"Remember when you said you wished you had a horsewhip with you when you met whoever hurt Bill? Well, if you had one now, would you . . . ?"

Rachel slipped an arm around Becca and looked down at her. "No. No, I wouldn't. Not now."

"That's funny," said Becca. "Neither would I. But he really hurt Bill!"

Rachel nodded. "Horsewhipping him wouldn't fix Bill's collarbone."

"No. . . . You know, Bill showed me a picture his dad drew of him. It was really . . . good. . . . Well, not just good, but . . . like he really *liked* Bill."

"Bill's dad is an artist?"

"Yeah, but that's not what I mean. I mean, how can he hit Bill so hard if he can draw pictures of him like that?"

"He draws Bill when he's sober—he hits him when he's been drinking."

"But that . . . that sounds so simple! Is that *all?*"

Rachel looked down at her again. "No, it isn't simple, and no, it isn't all. I can't even begin to explain it to you, though."

"Because I'm not old enough to understand, right?" said Becca bitterly.

"No," said Rachel. "Because I don't understand it myself."

"Oh."

Over at the house, the door squeaked open and two rescue people came out, holding a stretcher. As they came through the gap in the snow fence, Becca stepped forward to speak to Bill. But Bill's eyes were closed, and his head was turned to one side. He looked so small and so . . . helpless. Not like Bill at all. She stepped back, and the rescue people carried the stretcher by the squad car. Bill's dad looked out, then dropped his head in his hands.

Becca turned to Rachel and buried her face in Rachel's raincoat. "Can we go home now?"

"We sure can," said Rachel. "But you must be awfully tired. Why don't you go in the ambulance as far as Amidens'? I'll lead Gandalf up the hill and pick you up as soon as I can."

Becca shook her head.

"Hey, listen—you sure? It's going to be a tough trip up that hill. There are branches all over the place."

"Yeah, I'm sure. I want to be with you."

"Really?" Rachel half frowned, looking at the ambulance, which had finally finished turning around.

"Really," said Becca. All of a sudden she put both arms around Rachel and started to cry. "Really, really, really!"

Rachel held her very tightly for a long time. "Okay," she said finally. "We'll take it easy and do the best we can."

Chapter 21

"Well, he's home," said Mr. Amiden a week later. He leaned against his truck as if he were so tired he could hardly stand up. "But it's goin' to be a while before he's like he was."

Becca and Patty looked at each other. Was he going to try to give them a lecture like the one all their teachers had given them in school: "Of-course-he-won't-be-himself.-How-would-you-feel-if-your-dad-hurt-you?" As if you could hear about a kid getting beat up by his dad and *not* think about what it would do to you—and not just to your broken bones, either.

But Mr. Amiden didn't give the lecture; he just stood there, looking tired. Finally, Becca asked, "Can I go see him?"

"Yep. He said he wanted you to come. Kin you make it tonight?"

"Yes," said Rachel, coming up behind the girls, leading Dancer. "What time?"

"Oh—seven, I guess." Mr. Amiden patted Dancer; Becca wondered if seeing Dancer made *him* think about what Bill should be like. Suddenly he smiled a tired smile at Becca. "Say, I hear you're gonna keep that pony I talked your mom into tryin' out."

"Yeah," she said happily.

"Well, now—didn't I tell you?" he said to Rachel. "Didn't I tell you she was the only kid alive who could bring a hoss like that around?"

"As I recall," said Rachel, "all you said was he'd be worth the risk. But we won't quibble over words. He's a great pony."

"And he jumps now!" said Patty. "At least, mostly."

"Only mostly?" Mr. Amiden frowned.

Becca giggled. " 'Mostly' means when I get after him. If I dream off or chicken out, he knows in a split second, and he ducks out."

"Sure," said Rachel. "Jumping takes energy, after all. Why should he go over the jump when you don't really want to?"

Patty and Becca grinned at each other. How many times had they heard *that* before? Mr. Amiden grinned, too.

"Well, then, I guess he's jist a normal ornery pony," he said. "That's good." He climbed back into his truck. "Seeya later."

Patty scuffed her foot back and forth as he drove off. "I wish Bill wanted to see *me*."

"Well, I found him in the woods," said Becca, as comfortingly as she could. "He probably just wants to growl at me."

Patty looked at her. "What're you going to say to him, anyway?"

"I don't know," said Becca. And she didn't. She had no idea at all.

Bill wasn't in the Amidens' kitchen when she and Rachel walked in at seven. Becca looked around. "Where is he?"

"Upstairs," said Mr. Amiden. "It's goin' to be a bit before he's up an' around."

"Don't stay too long, dear," added Mrs. Amiden as Becca hurried toward the door. "He's feelin' poorly."

Becca hurried up the plywood steps and knocked at Bill's door. "It's me, Becca. Can I come in?"

"Yeah." The voice on the other side sounded sort of weak. Becca took a deep breath and went in.

"Hi, Bill . . . !" she began, trying to sound cheerful. But when she got all the way into the room, she stopped. Bill was lying on his bed, looking very pale and sick. But his bed had a new bedspread on it. His plain wooden dresser was painted gleaming white. The windows had curtains on them. And there was one of Mrs. Amiden's beautiful hooked rugs on the floor. That wasn't what stopped her, though. "Bill! The walls . . ."

"Oh yeah," he said, as if it were nothing at all. "They fixed up the room when I was in the hospital."

"But . . . but your pictures . . ." She looked helplessly at the gleaming white walls. They were freshly painted and bare. Absolutely bare. "Couldn't you have . . . I mean, if you'd asked, Ed surely would have . . ."

Bill shifted uncomfortably on the bed. "I asked him to paint over them," he muttered, not looking at her.

"Oh, Bill!"

"Don't take on about it," he growled. "It's none of your business."

"Okay, okay. Look, we're going to Brattleboro tomorrow. I can get you some pastels and charcoal and stuff, if you tell me what you . . ."

"Don't bother."

"It's no bother! I mean, what're you going to *do* until you can get up?"

Bill sat up a little straighter, making a face because of the pain. "Look," he said, "I'm not drawing anymore, okay? So just forget it."

"Why not?"

He gave her his creep-from-outer-space look. Boy, you forgot how that look made you feel when you hadn't made Bill mad for a while. "Do I really have to explain it to you?" he said angrily. "Geez! You were *there!*"

This was awful. She hadn't wanted to talk about that day in the woods: the sooner they both forgot about it the better. And she hadn't wanted to make him mad, either. She stood still, looking at the pattern in Mrs. Amiden's hooked rug. But he went right on.

"And I'll tell you what," he said, his voice getting louder, "I'll tell you something only the cops and I know. You know those pictures he said he was painting to make money? Well, he didn't paint them. He just started them. Then, when I left, he threw them down in the cellar of that old house, and he went right on . . . doing what he'd been doing before to get money." He coughed; she looked up just in time to see how much coughing hurt him.

"Hey, take it easy," she said. "You'll . . ."

"It's okay." But he was almost whispering.

She should go. She wasn't supposed to get him tired, and he looked exhausted. She moved toward the door.

"Don't go for a sec," he whispered.

She turned around, surprised. He was lying with his head back, breathing very carefully. If he said anything, she sure wasn't going to be able to hear it from where she was. She inched slowly toward him across the new rug, waiting for him to snap at her again. When she was almost next to his bed, she stopped. "It's . . . okay . . ." she said. "Look, you don't have to draw anymore. I was just surprised, that's all. Okay?"

"Sure." He frowned. "Nobody'll tell me what happened to Dad," he said. "Will you?"

"How come they won't tell?"

"I guess they don't want to worry me, or something. Or else it's so terrible they don't dare."

Why did he care, if he hated his dad so much? He wasn't even going to draw anymore because of his dad. So why . . . ? "I don't know very much, myself," she said cautiously.

"What's the matter with you?" he whispered scornfully. "You afraid I'm going to nip off and join him again? Or are you just lying so I'll stay all nice and quiet, like a little baby?"

"Bill . . ."

"Beat it, willya? Geez! I thought *you'd* understand, at least."

"You did? Really?"

You could see he would have shrugged if he'd dared. "You understood all the other stuff."

No, she hadn't. She hadn't understood anything at all. She hadn't even known where he was going or why.

"Just go away, willya?" He turned his head toward the wall.

She turned around—but then she changed her mind. "Look, I don't think anybody knows much about your dad yet," she said. "There's going to have to be a trial. It takes a long time to get trials going."

"How do you know?"

She glared at him. "My dad was a lawyer!" she snapped. "He dealt with this sort of stuff every single day, and I just sort of breathed it in . . . like you and drawing."

He looked interested for a moment. "Really?"

"Yeah, really! Would I lie to you?" Suddenly, she stopped being angry and grinned.

He almost smiled back. "Okay, I believe you. So what about my dad's trial?"

"Well, Rachel says before it happens, there are going

to have to be lots of tests and stuff. And probably they'll get him to some state place where they dry people out—you know, make them stop . . ."

"Yeah, I know." He gave her his creep-from-outerspace look again, but it wasn't quite so bad this time.

"And . . . I guess that's all I know."

Bill turned his head to the wall. "But he'll go to jail, won't he?"

"How should I know? That's what trials are *for*." She looked at his face. "But I suppose he will, for a while, anyway."

He didn't say anything. She began to wonder if she should go, but just as she started to, he said, "You can't paint in jail."

"Why not? There can't be much else to do."

"There's nothing to paint, that's why. Like in Westminster, I didn't draw, because all there was, was walls."

"You can't paint if you drink all the time, either," she pointed out. "Maybe if he stops drinking and has some time, he can paint stuff from memory. You know, the way some people write books in prison."

He wrinkled up his nose. "That's a fairy story."

"So what's wrong with fairy stories? All sorts of stuff goes wrong—there are dragons and terrible quests, and everything looks just *awful,* but finally things go okay, and you live happily after all."

"Happily ever after, dope! And anyway, nobody really believes that!"

"You mean people have been wrong all these years, making up stories that came out okay at the end?" she asked.

He looked at her suspiciously. "You didn't make that up all by yourself, I bet."

"Well, no. Mr. Jarvis did. He used to be my dad's partner."

"Didn't think you could have an idea like that on your own."

"Thanks."

They were still glaring at each other when Mr. Amiden's voice floated up from downstairs: "You better wrap it up now, Becca!"

Boy, talk about being rescued! She moved toward the door. "Look," she said. Bill was being just *awful,* but then, he'd had a hard time. "I have lots of books. Would you like me to bring you some when I come tomorrow?"

"Yeah," he said. "That'd be okay. Ed doesn't have much around."

"Okay, then. Seeya."

She turned around and lifted the latch.

"Becca . . ."

She looked over her shoulder. He was looking at her as if he really wanted to tell her something. But as she waited for whatever it was, he changed his mind and his face turned back into Bill's usual face. "Just don't bring me any *girls'* books," he said.

"Would I do that to you?" she asked scornfully. She went out, closing the door a little harder than she meant to.

Epilogue

"You know," said Patty as they collapsed in the front seat of the pickup at the end of the show, "I think Bill is sweet on you."

"Oh, come on!" Becca looked up from her ribbons. She was writing on the back of them. "Trail horse" on the yellow one. "Pleasure horse" on the green one. "Equitation" on the white one. She'd done pretty well, all things considered. What you learned when you went to shows was how much better some kids rode than you did. "Where's our second place?" She looked around.

"You're sitting on it," said Rachel as she got into the truck. Becca pulled it out from under her and wrote "low hunter" on it.

"Rachel, Patty thinks Bill is sweet on me."

Rachel laughed. "I'll die laughing the day Bill's sweet on anybody! What brought this up, Patty?"

"Well, when Becca was jumping, he was watching her really carefully. And then, out of nothing, he asked me when her birthday was. I said it was in a couple of weeks. Isn't that right?"

"Yeah," said Becca. "September twooth."

Patty giggled. "What does the twooth fairy give you on your birthday?" All three of them groaned.

But there was no question about it. Bill was acting very

mysterious after that. Sometimes he slipped up to the loft. Or sometimes he went into the house when they were working in the ring. Becca worried about him a little bit. But she thought things were better now that he was going to that group of kids who had alcoholic parents. He wasn't any more polite or anything, but he was around more. And if you asked him very nicely, he'd go for a trail ride with you—if you promised not to giggle.

Two days before her birthday, she saw him slip up into the loft just before Patty started working Goner. "Hold it!" she called to Patty. "I'll be there in just a sec!"

She didn't even hear Patty answer as she crept up the loft ladder. Bill was up there, all right, but there wasn't much noise. Just a little scratching sound. She poked her head up for a minute, then ducked down. She could hardly force herself to sneak down the ladder, and when she got outside, she did three cartwheels in a row, colliding with Tumnus on the fourth.

"What's up?" Rachel asked.

"Oh, nothing," Becca ran down to the ring, grinning. He was drawing! Bill was drawing again!

But of course he wouldn't tell anybody. She spent the whole next day wondering if she'd burst with the secret. That was okay. You were supposed to look happy before your birthday.

At the end of the day, Bill came in from the barn early, while she was still making dinner (it was her turn: she and Rachel each made dinner every other night during the summer because the stove got so hot neither of them could stand it every night). "I got something for you," he said.

"Yeah?"

"Only you've got to promise not to open it when I'm here."

"Well, okay." She looked around. "Where is it?"

"In the loft. You can go get it tonight."

"Couldn't you give it to me tomorrow, like everybody else?" she said.

"Nope. I'm going to visit my dad tomorrow."

"Really?"

"Yeah. Rachel worked out things so I could see him sooner than I thought."

"Gee—that's great!"

"I don't know," he said, shifting back and forth on his feet. "But I've got to go, anyway."

"It might not be as bad as you're thinking," she said.

"I didn't say it *would* be bad!"

"Have it your way."

He patted Tumnus and Xeno for a minute, then straightened up. "Well, Ed's here. I'll seeya."

"Seeya."

He ran out the door, slamming it so hard she jumped. Geez! And he hadn't even wished her a happy birthday! What kind of a friend was he, anyway?

Rachel came in a few minutes later and splashed water on her face at the sink. "Boy, is it ever hot in here—and out there!"

"Sure is. Hey, listen—Bill said he left something for me in the loft. Can I go get it?"

"Go ahead. I'll watch the biscuits."

Becca tore over to the barn and climbed up the loft ladder. It was so hot up there she could hardly breathe. Where had he left it? Oh—there, that envelope on the lowest stack of bales. She grabbed it and started back to the house. Should she open it tonight? Or should she . . . ?

"What? You haven't opened it yet?" said Rachel as she came in.

That did it. Becca undid the clasp. Inside was a pastel

drawing. She slid it out carefully so it wouldn't smear. "Oh!"

"May I see?" said Rachel. "Or is it a secret?"

Well, it was sort of a secret, but it was a secret about fairy tales, and she'd never guess. Becca put the picture down on the table; Rachel leaned over it a while, not saying anything at all.

"It's really . . . wonderful," she said finally, looking at Becca. The green eyes showed that she understood just how wonderful it really was.

"Yeah."

Becca looked back at the picture. The first thing you noticed was the cloudy sky on the page—all gray and pinks, like the sunset over the valley. Somehow, Bill had managed to make the clouds into a sort of knight on horseback, fighting a cloudy dragon. Below the clouds, there were mountains, a few trees, . . . and a girl with red hair, riding a gray pony toward a jump.